THE DRAGON

AND

THE KING

Book Two in the Scroll Saga

This book is dedicated to my children and their offspring.

Always consult the Scroll.

The Dragon and the King

Copyright © 2018

Author: Jared Dodd

Editor: A'ndrea McAdams   glorybwriting.wordpress.com

Proof readers: Cathy Andrus, Al & Val Kayser, & Christy Mowery

Cover and book design: Amy Dodd

First Edition - Printed in the U.S.A

Characters from The Castle and the Scroll:

Caleb: a captain of the Oasis; husband to Elizabeth; father to Benjamin, Isaiah, Violet, Rose, Lily; ability to sense dragons

From the Oasis

Elizabeth: adopted daughter of Captain Samuel and wife of Caleb; ability to create an invisible shield around her loved ones

Benjamin: eldest son of Caleb; ability to sense those in danger who need assistance

Captain Samuel: ability to train warriors

Captain Enoch: ability still unknown to the reader

Captain Benjamin: killed by dragons; ability to prophesy the future

Justin: friend of the Caleb and ex-Castle attender; leader in the Oasis

Stephen: ability to strike the ground and cause dragons to stumble

Jedidiah: son of Stephen; killed first dragon at thirteen years of age

Nathan: dear friend to Caleb; ability to force people out of harm's danger; father of four

Leah: wife of Nathan

Levi: eldest son of Nathan

From the Castle

Captain David: captain of the Castle in Ravenhill

Joseph: son of Captain David; dragon breeder

Eric: leader in the Castle

Simon: constable in Ravenhill

Edgar: son of Simon; dragon breeder

Caroline: devoted Castle-attender; led astray by Edgar

From the village of Greystone

William: father-figure to Caleb; killed by raiders

Joanna: widow and mother of five; saved from raiders by William and Caleb.

Chapter 1

The morning fog clung to the cold, rank swampland. I gripped my sword tightly, expecting at any moment for a dragon to emerge from the mucky water which surrounded us. Five warriors accompanied me on this hunt: my dearest friend, Nathan; his eldest son, Levi, who was twenty-seven years of age; Justin, Jedidiah, and my son, Benjamin, who was now eighteen years old.

It had been nineteen years since my marriage to Elizabeth. My old life, as I called it, seemed like a distant dream. All I now knew was love, community, the Great King, and slaying dragons.

Nathan peered through the thick brush leaves. "This doesn't make sense," he whispered. "The dragons should be here."

"I agree," said Jedidiah. "Their tracks end here."

"And also begin here," observed Justin. "Look! The tracks not only lead up to the water, but also exit from it. It's as if there is some kind of lair beneath us."

We continued to wait patiently for another hour.

Jedidiah sighed with some frustration. "I'm tired of not having answers. People are disappearing and we need to know why." He then turned to Levi, "How many people from the village have been taken?"

"Thirty-eight," Levi replied. "This last victim was a young woman, about twenty years of age. She has been missing for three days."

"This is the place," I said resolutely. "I'm sure of it now. I can sense them. They are coming closer to us, and they are many."

"Should we return to get more soldiers?" Benjamin asked.

But no one was able to answer him, for something was happening which stole away our attention. There was a commotion, not too far off, on the edge of one of the many bogs that surrounded us. Suddenly, and to our horror, a young girl emerged from the water. She was covered with gunk, sputtering and trying to catch her breath, with tears streaming down her muck-covered cheeks. She reached over and grabbed the edge of the wetland, pulled herself out of a bog not too far away, and began running towards us, her voice breaking the still silence of the cool morning.

"Help!" she shouted hysterically. "I can't get away!"

We began to make our way toward her, but three large red dragons burst suddenly from within the bog, shooting the foul water up in the air like a geyser. The dragons had their fire upon us immediately, after which they came at us with an aggression I had rarely seen. We were hard pressed but stayed together. The girl, seeing the danger, turned around and tried to escape another way. Her appearance was horrible and desperate, like something from a nightmare.

"Shield wall!" Nathan commanded, and we quickly came together.

"Wait till they take a breath!" I ordered, as we kept our shields between us and the fire. The fire soon subsided. "Now!" I shouted.

We quickly sprinted in every direction possible, causing the enemy to turn this way and that. I came upon the nearest dragon and was able to distract it long enough for Benjamin to strike its flank. The beast let out a howl and spun its tail back at my son. Benjamin leapt high in the air, while at the same time completely severing the tail from the dragon. The creature was so afflicted by this injury that it didn't see Jedidiah come from behind and was unaware of him until he sank his blade deep within its back.

I had no time to rejoice, for another dragon was upon us. It was strong and full of rage and had us pressed against the shore of a bog. A shield then flew through the air and hit the beast in the head. The armor did little more than annoy the dragon who turned to see Justin, standing alone and without a shield. The dragon inhaled deeply with the intention of vaporizing his opponent, but Justin hastily lifted his sword. As he shouted aloud, something like lightning shot from his sword and struck the dragon to the ground. Nathan was waiting and severed the beast's head from its body.

The third dragon, seeing he was now alone and overcome, began to retreat back into the marsh. His tail, which was as quick and harmful as a serpent, shot out and took hold of the woman's ankle, and picked her up high into the air. The dragon quickly dove back within the murky water and disappeared. We watched with dismay as the woman, who was screaming frantically, was violently immersed into the swamp within a second—and was seen no more.

Chapter 2

We all stood there in shock, for we had no chance of saving the girl.

I helped Jedidiah up from the ground where his final engagement with the dragon had left him.

"You fought well," I told him. "I was there, many years ago, when at the age of thirteen you killed your first dragon. I knew at that moment that you would be mighty in the kingdom of the Great King. Your father would be proud of you."

It had been nearly ten years since Jedidiah's father, Stephen, had died. It was an honorable death, for he was leading a band of warriors deep into dragon territory, and being overcome with many foes, he stood his ground, allowing his comrades to escape. It was said that he fought till his final breath.

"It is settled," Nathan said. "There is something down there, for that girl came up out of the water and had obviously been down there for some time."

"That's true," agreed Justin. "No one could have held their breath for that long."

"But how does this help us?" Jedidiah asked in frustration. "We know this is the place, but we still don't know the enemy's plan. What are they doing with these people?"

"There's no way to be certain," I answered. "But let's leave while we can, before more dragons come."

Jedidiah's brother, Daniel, was waiting for us about a mile away. He was a scout, his ability being that of swiftness and vision, and he had been guarding our flank for the four days we had been tracking the dragons. Daniel had, like his brother, been without a father for the last ten years. For my own part, I tried to spend time with him when able. He was now nineteen years old and was a man made in his father's image.

As we approached, Daniel shook the hand of his brother. "It looks like you encountered a few dragons," he said with a smile. "I'm glad to see you still in one piece."

"We could have used your sword," Jedidiah replied. "But I know we needed a rear-guard."

Daniel then turned to me with a look of respect. "Captain Caleb, what can I do to help?"

"We return to the Oasis at once," I replied. "Please scout out the trail, and tell the elders we come with grave tidings."

Daniel nodded in respect and was gone with such speed that if you blinked twice, you could no longer see him.

On the eve of the following day, we arrived in the Oasis, which had been my home for many years. My dear wife, Elizabeth, greeted me as she always did: with the warmth and serenity of a summer morning. My three daughters also fled into my arms, and I kissed them.

"They were worried about you," Elizabeth said. "There is strange talk within the village that is reaching us here. Between the disappearances in town, and the changes in the Castle, all of our people are plagued with restlessness."

"Everything will be fine," I assured her. "The Great King is with us." I then looked at my daughters who were still close to me. "How are my girls doing?" I asked as my eyes danced upon their lovely faces.

"We are well, Father," they all replied.

The Great King had blessed me with three daughters; Violet, who was sixteen; Rose, who was twelve; and Lily, who was seven. Violet, the eldest daughter was born a twin. Her brother, Isaiah, had died four years earlier. The scar that it left upon all of us was most severe, though in a way, the loss was heaviest to Violet.

"You should be so proud of your girls," Elizabeth said cheerfully. "They get their work and studies done by early afternoon, leaving them the rest of the day to tend to the needs of the people."

It was then time for dinner. The aroma of the warm bread and stew filled the small home, as the fire's crackle was a comforting melody. As my wife and four children ate, I pushed my dish aside and unrolled the Scroll, as was my usual custom, and read to my family.

"Remember," I told my children, "the Great King has called us to be people set apart, different from the rest of the world, because we hold true not to ourselves but to Him. Even if it should cost us our lives, He is worth it. We must count the cost, my children, of following Him, so that we might never falter. Death, even early in life, if it is for the Great King, is better than many years of living for self. For if you die for the Great King, you will live forever with Him. But if you live for yourself, you will die forever without Him in the place of eternal fire."

There was a knock on the door. My youngest, Lily, answered the door, for she delighted in doing such tasks as often as she could. Nathan entered the house and informed me that there would be a council meeting that evening.

"Can I go, Father?" Benjamin asked.

"Of course," I replied with a smile. "You may always go where I am."

An hour later, my son and I found ourselves around a fire with nearly twenty men. I was exhausted, but I knew that there was dialog that needed to take place. Captain Samuel, who had now grown quite aged but was still a man of skill and energy, began the council.

"Nathan has given me a full report of all that happened at the swamps," he said. "We know where the enemy is taking these captives from the village, but we don't know why they are taken. This we must explore further, but at present, we have other matters to discuss. Tomorrow, there is to be an announcement of some kind from the Castle. The bits and pieces that have reached my ears are frightful, though I must say not overly surprising. You all know about the prophecy that Captain Enoch gave us before he died. Desperate and trying times are before us. Still, we must learn from the Great King what to do. I fear that Captain Asa is about to implement something truly dreadful."

Captain Asa was the latest captain of the Castle. Captain David, who had been captain for nearly twenty years, had disappeared eight years earlier without any clue of what happened to him. Some rumors said he went far to the south, though no one seemed to know for sure. For some time, it puzzled me, and I thought about it often. What persuaded Captain David to leave? Was it a sign of his repentance from playing Castle politics? Or did he become overly depressed after the death of his wife? No one seemed to know for sure.

Captain Samuel continued. "I think that it would be best for Caleb and Nathan to go to the Castle tomorrow and hear this message. In the meantime, we will send out our scouts to seek some kind of evidence as to what the dragons are doing in the swamps."

Benjamin and I returned to our home, and I immediately addressed my family. "There are many tasks before us," I said, "and all of us have a role to play."

My wife and daughters came before me, filled with enthusiasm. I treasured seeing them so eager to help. Most of the families I had seen in the village and Castle were always separated, with independent visions and priorities. Their homes were more like an inn than a family dwelling. And yet, to be a family of united vision, to be a team that joyfully worked together, was one of my greatest experiences.

"Tomorrow Nathan and I are going to the Castle," I began.

"The Castle?" my wife said somewhat alarmed. "Are you sure, my dear? It's been years since you set foot in that place, and it isn't as friendly toward our people as it used to be. Hostility surely awaits you there."

"I agree," I said kindly. "But it is necessary. There is an announcement of some kind, and Captain Samuel is convinced that we need to hear it."

"How can I help?" Benjamin asked.

"You must go into the village tomorrow and visit with the families of the victims of those taken away by the dragons," I replied. "See if there are any patterns or reasons behind the disappearances."

"May I go with my brother?" Violet asked.

I hesitated. Violet was now sixteen—considered a grown woman—but her eyes always reminded me of Isaiah, her deceased brother.

Elizabeth seemed to be able to sense my concern. "Violet is so good with people who are grieving and in need of comfort," she said. "You have seen her work with the orphans and widows. Think of how well she would assist her dear brother."

"This is for certain," I said, smiling at my dear Violet. "You are such a woman of beauty and skill. You will accompany Benjamin."

"And I think," Elizabeth said slowly and thoughtfully, as to entreat me in the most delicate manner, "that Daniel should also go with them."

At this, I noticed Violet slightly bite her lower lip with an excitement that she tried to conceal.

"Daniel?" I repeated.

"Or course," Elizabeth said kindly. "He would be able to deliver any messages."

I nodded in agreement.

"And what of myself and the other girls?" Elizabeth asked quickly, carrying on the conversation.

I thought for a moment. "Matthew's wife, Ruth, has she had her baby yet?"

"Not yet," my wife replied. "Though she is due any day now."

"You know as well as any," I said to my dear wife, "the help needed to a family when their queen is due with child. This will be their third child, and all of their children are quite young." I then looked upon Rose and Lily. "What do you think we should do for this family?"

"I think we should take them food," Rose replied.

"Not only that," added Lily, "but we should also tidy their home and play with their children."

"What wonderful ministers you girls are!" I exclaimed with pride. "So be it. Tomorrow, as the sun rises, each of us will be about our specific task. How blessed I am to have such a wife and children to aid me in the vision of the Great King."

The following day, Nathan and I attended the Castle in which I hadn't set foot since prior to Captain David's disappearance. The Castle was a difficult and uncomfortable place for us because not only were there signs of compromise and misunderstanding, but there were also dragons everywhere. And many of them were no longer leashed but walked about in freedom or stood still as sentinels.

Being in the Castle also reminded me of Caroline and how I had witnessed her decline through her relationship with Edgar, Constable Simon's son. She was such an amazing young lady in the beginning. She loved the Great King and adored the Scroll. But she gave her heart to the wrong boy, and it was her ruin. For they eventually separated, and she committed suicide not long afterward.

Captain Asa now took his place on the stage, and there were two young, red dragons on both sides of him. I had never spoken with him, but it seemed to me that there was something hidden and dark deep within him.

"A new age is dawning," he began. "A day of freedom and unity amongst the people of this world. The Scroll says, *They shall all be one,* and that is what is happening. We and the world are joining together. Human and dragon are joining hands."

A shiver ran down my spine and my stomach churned. Captain Asa was quoting the Scroll but was completely taking it out of context, a practice that I had heard was much more common in Castles.

"We are followers of the Great King," he continued. "He who created all things and called them *good*. He led us in the beginning, and He continues to lead us today. For many centuries, up until just recently, He led us through the Scroll. And we all know that the Scroll is a wonderful story and poem; its words are useful. But we are now coming into a fuller season of His Kingdom. For the Scroll was a good tool, during its time, but now the Great King has written His words upon our hearts. We no longer need the Scroll, for the Great King has imprinted His words within our very soul. And it is one word, above all, that He has put within us. LOVE."

Everyone awed at these words and seemed to be mesmerized by them.

"Behold!" he said, putting a hand on the dragon next to him. "Dragon and human stand together. The dividing wall that for so many years brought about enmity and warfare has been abolished. We have not only tamed the dragons, but we have made them our friends and allies."

The gathering began to applaud, almost frantically. Captain Asa motioned for silence, and his countenance grew grim.

"There is only one enemy remaining!" he said. "For the only thing in the way of love is intolerance. Open-mindedness, by way of contrast, is the language of the Great King. He desires peace: a peace that requires acceptance of those who are different. Intolerance stands in opposition to this dream. Intolerance, the enemy, says that its way is the only way of seeing things. Think, my dear beloved, about all the insights and understanding that intolerance extinguishes. It stops the progressive journey of enlightenment. But not for us! We now see clearly! The ultimate and perfect revelation of the Great King has been made known. Dragon and human unite as one, to fight against the true enemy of the Great King: *intolerance!*"

Everyone arose to their feet and cheered. Nathan and I were taken back and sat there dumbfounded by how so many people could be so easily swayed. I quickly looked about me and noticed a man who also remained seated. He seemed to be different, like ourselves, and had a very troubled look on his face. I looked the other direction and noticed Simon, whom I hadn't seen in some time and hadn't spoken to in years. He was looking right at me, with an expression that wasn't welcoming.

"And so," Captain Asa concluded, "It is time for us to weed out the intolerance from among us. With our main hall's new addition—we are calling it the Hall of Devotion—you will each be given an opportunity, next King's Day, to demonstrate your allegiance to the Great King by being tolerant, open-minded, and accepting. We must remember, as it alludes to in the Scroll, that to accept others is to love others, and to love others is the will of the Great King. So, prepare your hearts, my flock, to embrace this love, and so all war and strife and differences will cease. Yet, if there be some who will not embrace this love, they will be the final enemy of the Great King."

Everyone cheered again, the musicians began their song, and the service was concluded. I quickly informed Nathan of the man I had witnessed who seemed to be set apart from the Castle, and we intentionally caught up to him. His face was like one who was terrified.

"Excuse me," I said to him. "You must not be afraid of us, for we are not of this group but are outsiders. You seem like us, not wanting to go along with this message."

The man hesitated for a moment and then spoke slowly and with some fear in his voice, "How can I go along with it when it is so opposed to the Scroll?"

I smiled. "What is your name?" I asked.

"My name is Judah," he said. "I have been attending this Castle for a few months, out of obedience to the Scroll, but this is something that I just can't seem to embrace."

"You need not embrace it," said Nathan. "We can help you."

"But I'm afraid," Judah said. "Haven't you noticed that the people disappearing in the village are not a part of the Castle? I am convinced that if I stay here, I will not disappear. But I'm also scared of all the Castle is doing. I feel trapped."

I understood the thoughts and struggles of this man. I had felt them many years earlier, back when the Castle was in more alignment with the Scroll. I couldn't imagine the amount of confusion he was dealing with.

"You don't need to be trapped any longer," I said.

"Whatever you do," Nathan said. "I wouldn't come back here, especially not next King's Day when this *opportunity* to embrace tolerance and love is offered. I'm sure it will be a trap of some kind."

"I don't know," Judah said, shaking his head. His eyes were suddenly filled with fear, and he seemed to be looking behind us. He then turned around and left abruptly. A hand was then placed on my shoulder, and turning around, I saw that it was Captain Asa.

Chapter 3

Instantly I had that same feeling from so many years before, when Captain David and I had our falling out. It is a feeling hard to describe, for Captain David believed in the Great King, and he believed in the Scroll, yet we were worlds apart in our application. Despite our differences, we were still brothers, and of this point I had to be reminded often because of the damage I saw take place at the Castle. It took many months for me to embrace in my heart the reality I saw in the Scroll: I was to fight for Captain David and not against him.

Now I was looking into the eyes of Captain Asa. Captain Samuel had often told me that the eyes were the window to the soul, and in Captain Asa's eyes, I was afraid of what I saw. I wanted to believe that he was good, and that we were brothers, but something about him frightened me.

"Gentlemen," he began, grinning ear to ear, "It is an honor to have you here with us today. Eric, our Executive Captain, speaks so highly of you."

These words left me speechless, for I knew that Eric was no friend to our cause.

"These are exciting times," he continued. "Never before in the history of the Castle have we experienced such victory over the dragons. Every year, more and more of them are tamed under our skill and power. Yet not only have we found victory over the dragons but also victory over ourselves, for though our forefathers were people of courage, they didn't possess the love that we now have attained."

I could sense the uneasiness of Nathan at such empty and worldly words. I knew the proper response to such folly, as did Nathan, but we had learned over the years that sometimes silence is a better response to the thoughts of the world. Just because you had the correct answer didn't mean that the answer should be given. Besides, I sensed that a reply was exactly what Captain Asa desired.

He waited, and then seeing that we remained silent, continued. "I don't blame you for your silence, my beloved children," he said poetically. "I know that our ways are hard for you to accept, you who have been distant from these revelations and therefore stuck in your ways. I know you mean best, but times have changed. The Great King is on the move, that is to say, the Spirit of the Great King, or better put, the idea of the Great King is progressing in the minds of these people. It is ideas that change the world, and there's no idea greater than the love of the Great King. I do hope to see you next King's Day, as we give you the opportunity to demonstrate a heart of tolerance and acceptance. Until we get to the point of embracing the culture surrounding us, we remain archaic in our thinking, and we hinder the true work of the Great King. Well, gentlemen, I'm sure you have things to do. Happy King's Day to you."

He bowed slightly and left us. I turned and looked for Judah, who we had been speaking with before, but he was nowhere to be seen.

"I think we had better be going," Nathan said to me. "I don't think I can bear anymore of this place."

"No indeed," I said with a grin. "Though, I am impressed that you held your tongue as you did."

"Miracles are possible," he replied.

We were coming out of the main exit where two dragons were perched, one on each side of the large doorway. The creatures were about fifteen feet in length and were so still I wondered if they were real. As we passed by, one of them turned toward us and glared and opened his mouth. His tongue shook, slightly but quickly, within its mouth as his eyes were fixed upon us. Nathan gripped his sword.

"Stay your blade," I said quietly.

"If that dragon opens its mouth any wider, I will cut off its head with one stroke," Nathan said with aggression in his voice.

"It would be the last thing you ever did," spoke a voice from behind us, and turning around, we saw Eric. It amazed me to think that this man, who nearly two decades before had attempted to show me my ability, now considered me an enemy and an outcast. "These dragons are our friends," he continued. "They look at you the way they do because they can sense your bigotry and narrow-mindedness."

I suddenly felt at liberty to speak. "They look at us the way they do because they know that we are the enemy and that we have been commissioned by the Great King to cut off their heads."

Eric scoffed. "The enemy?" he said. "If you are their enemy, then you are our enemy as well, for we have aligned ourselves with the dragons."

"You have indeed aligned yourselves with the dragons," Nathan said. "And in doing so, you have declared war against the Great King Himself. Haven't you read in the Scroll the words, *I hate dragons*? The Scroll also says, *To love the Great King is to hate dragons*."

"You can quote the Great Scroll all you want to," Eric said. "We have found the true interpretation. How can I show you? It's impossible, because you are so nearsighted and blind. You rebels, with your legalistic interpretations and your uncompromising ideas, are so frustrating! Listen carefully. A war is coming. And you are becoming, more and more, outnumbered. The Great King has given us a vision of a perfect world, and it is a world without you. It is a world without extremists and naysayers. You had better rethink things, and quickly. Otherwise, you will find yourselves on the losing side of this conflict. You will find yourselves amongst the minority."

Nathan smiled. "Even if it be only one man—if he be with the Great King, he is the majority."

The dragons began to hiss and extend their necks out towards us. We both placed our hands on our swords and stood boldly before each of them. They reluctantly retracted back upon their perches.

"Get out of here!" Eric said. "And don't come back until you're willing to be tolerant!"

We turned and continued towards the forest.

"Please tell me we won't be going there again," Nathan said.

"I hope not," I said. "Though, I do wish we had spoken more with Judah. He seemed sincere."

"If he was, then he won't be going back there," Nathan assured me.

Within half an hour, we were within the Oasis among our families.

Elizabeth, on seeing me, threw her arms around me and embraced me dearly. We had been married nineteen years, and every year brought with it a deeper love and appreciation for one another. We shared our hearts with each other, mainly rejoicing in our family. I knew that I was destined to lead our people, but my greatest joy was in leading my family. They were my dearest friends and my greatest allies.

As I came home, I found Rose and Lily preparing lunch for the family they were about to visit. Benjamin and Violet had left early that morning to go visit the families of victims who had disappeared.

"Did Daniel go with Violet and Benjamin?" I asked my wife.

"Yes," she said with a smile. "He was waiting for them just on the porch."

"Did you take the time to inform him that no man is worthy of my daughter?"

She looked at me with humored surprise. "My dear Caleb," she said. "Do you not find him even close to being worthy?"

"To be honest," I replied, "I find him very worthy. Daniel is an honorable man, just as his father was. I feel almost like a father to him, in fact."

"As you should," she replied. "You have always taken an interest in him and loved him. Do you not think, perhaps, that the special bond you two share was in the Great King's design for him to be your son-in-law someday?"

"I have thought that," I said solemnly, "for some time now. It is just that the idea of my Violet getting married is both wonderful and painful at the same time. Do you think she is ready?"

"She is sixteen," my wife said plainly. "And has already shown herself to be a capable and admirable woman. I think she is more than ready."

I nodded in agreement. "Or perhaps you are just ready to be a grandmother," I jested.

"Well," Elizabeth said smiling ear to ear "that too of course."

I called Lily and Rose to me and hugged them. "What a wonderful meal you've prepared!"

"Not only that," said Rose, "but I also prepared some ointments for any who might be feeling ill."

I looked at my beautiful Rose. "You are always thinking of others," I commented kindly.

"She has since she was young," added my wife, "especially with regards to their health."

"Go now, my excellent ladies," I said. "You will greatly bless your brethren."

As they departed, I went to the council meeting that I knew had already begun. Most of the men were there.

"A token of demonstrating tolerance?" Captain Samuel repeated, as we informed him of all that was said at the Castle that morning. "Well, that's both

17

interesting and concerning. I think it would be best if you didn't return there. We don't want our curiosity to get us in trouble. Whatever this upcoming demonstration will be, it will no doubt be something we will want to miss."

"I think I might need to be there," I replied. "Only because of that one man, Judah, who seemed like his eyes were being opened, but he said he still felt trapped."

"I don't think he will go back there," argued Nathan. "He seemed like a man who was being called by the Great King. The Great King won't lead him back there."

"This may be hard for you to understand, my brother," I replied, "because you have never been a part of the Castle. For a person who knows nothing but the Castle, it is a difficult thing to see it for what it is. Even though your eyes are being opened, there is a tie and connection with the Castle that seems impossible to sever. It's as if you can't imagine life without it."

"I suppose you're correct," Nathan said. "I'm trusting you, for that kind of connection to an institution doesn't make sense to me."

"But it does to me," replied Captain Samuel. "I think you should return there, next King's Day, to find this man, but if you can, try outside of the Castle first. I sense that Castles will soon become a place that will be dangerous to us, that is to say, physically dangerous. It has been spiritually dangerous for years, more and more, but now I fear that we might be targeted as being intolerant, and therefore, the enemy."

"We were threatened today," I said. "You speak the truth."

"Such things are bound to happen," Justin said. "It shouldn't surprise us. Let us draw nearer to our families, to be the spouses and parents we are called to be. The hope for tomorrow is families who are aligned with the Scroll."

It always blessed my heart to hear Justin speak of the Scroll. He was a mighty man of the Great King and a skilled warrior. Only a year after he joined us, he married the widow, Joanna, and adopted her five children. She was the same woman who William and I saved the night the Northman attacked, though it cost William his life. How I missed that man.

"Justin speaks the truth," testified Captain Samuel. "Always turn your heart to home, and shepherd your family. Failure to do so is what led to the downfall of the Castles. They focused so much on being the Castle, and telling others about the Great King, that they neglected the most important thing—their family. Let us not repeat their error."

"Let us speak now of the swamps," Nathan said. "Have we any more information?"

"None," replied Captain Samuel. "Though we desperately need answers."

"Benjamin and Violet went to the village earlier this morning," I said. "I sent them to speak to the families of these victims. We know that most of them are as bewildered as we are, but I sensed that the answer might be closer than we think. Let us hope that my children are able to discover the truth."

"We might be overthinking all of this," Justin said. "What if the dragons are simply taking these victims to devour them?"

"There is always something more than that," I answered. "The dragons always have a greater purpose or strategy in mind. For example, when my wife and I were children, a dragon lured us into the forest to eat us, but with what purpose? Not simply one of destruction of human life but one of eternal consequence: destroying a prophecy that had come to its attention. Perhaps these victims are heirs to some kind of prophecy."

"I hadn't thought of that," Nathan said. "Maybe the Great King has plans for these people, and the enemy is getting to them first."

"Perhaps," said Captain Samuel. "But you must remember that no plan of the Great King can ultimately be thwarted."

"The ways of the Great King are indeed a mystery," I said. "But this is the bottom line: innocent people are being taken. Don't you remember the look on that woman's face in the swamp? Her horror was beyond description. She was likely a sweet woman, with her own dreams and ambitions, and now she is a victim of the enemy.

We must stop this at once, for the sake of those who are too weak to stand for themselves."

Daniel then entered the Oasis and was beside us in an instant. He was calm and not at all out of breath. He bowed in respect.

"Your children will be here in one moment," he said. "They wanted me to make sure you were all gathered together. They have news for you."

"What is the news?" I asked, eager for information.

"Your son insisted that he be the one to tell you," Daniel said.

Fortunately, Violet and Benjamin then entered the Oasis, sprinting and out of breath. They approached our council, and we could all see concern on their faces.

"What is it?" I asked. "What happened? What did you learn?"

"The victims," Benjamin said for all to hear. "It turns out that they aren't victims at all."

"What do you mean?" I asked.

"They are volunteers," he replied.

Chapter 4

"Volunteers?" I asked. "That's impossible. Didn't you see that woman at the swamp? Would you call her a volunteer?"

"Indeed she was," Benjamin replied. "She actually labored greatly for the right to be taken, for there are others that are in line."

I was shocked by what I was hearing.

"Are you sure?" I asked my son. "People volunteering to be taken by dragons? This is hard to believe."

"It is true, Father," Violet said. "The families themselves know nothing about this. It is mainly with their children. There are people, seemingly connected to the dragons, who make the idea of being taken by a dragon fascinating to the younger generation."

"Then we must warn them!" Captain Samuel said. "We must warn these people that being taken by dragons will lead to imprisonment in the swamp, or even death."

"We can try," Daniel replied. "But I do not think they will be convinced. As Violet said, they seem to be in league with the dragons. Something secret and evil is stirring."

"Do you know where they meet?" I asked.

"No," Benjamin replied. "But I do know where the reaping happens."

"The reaping?" I asked.

"Yes. It's where the volunteers are taken by the dragons. I'm not for sure when it happens, but I think that it may be tonight."

"Then we must go there, under the cloak of darkness and see this thing," I said.

"I agree," Nathan inserted. "Though, I'm afraid of what we will see."

As we dismissed the council, I noticed Daniel nod in respect and deference to Violet. She returned the gesture and turned toward home. She had now grown into a woman wrapped about with modesty and integrity. Daniel's eyes remained fixed upon her as she made her way. I knew the time had come to approach this young man, who in many ways was as a son to me. Jedidiah, his older brother had raised him well, along with their mother, but I had often assisted them in the discipleship of this young man in the ways of the Great King. He was quiet, and somewhat reserved, but his countenance was bold and manly, and the few words he ever spoke were filled with wisdom and power.

"Daniel," I said, getting his attention.

"Yes, sir," he replied genuinely.

"What are your intentions with my daughter?"

This question was a bit forward and sudden, and as soon as I spoke it, I wished I would have replaced it with more gentle words. But the question was spoken, and so I waited patiently for a response. To my delight, and affirmation of this man's qualities, he spoke with little time needed for contemplation.

"I plan to love her and respect her as a brother does his sister until the day you advise it to be further," he replied. "And if you allow it, and if she will have me, I plan to marry her."

I was unable to refrain from smiling and didn't mind manifesting my approval.

"Keep on being the man you are," I said. "And we will see what happens."

"Yes, sir," he replied with a bow of his head.

I then turned to seek out Benjamin, for we had preparations to make. I found him off to the side of the meeting circle, enjoying a conversation with Rebekah, Nathan's youngest daughter, who was seventeen years of age. This form of dialog was appropriate, but I noticed something special about the way they looked at each other.

Goodness, I thought to myself. Two romances in as many minutes.

Rebekah was a woman of great qualities, for she walked in the wisdom and character of her parents. Elizabeth and I had often considered this woman as a match for our son, as all parents should contemplate on such things. But there were quite a few wonderful young ladies amongst our people, and Benjamin hadn't yet revealed any intentions to us. My wife and I knew that one of the most vital steps in our commission as parents was to get our children to the marriage altar according the Scroll, and to give them in marriage to like-minded Scroll-followers. As I watched Benjamin and Rebekah speak, I thought I witnessed a sparkle in both of their eyes, but just as quickly, Benjamin bowed in respect and dismissed himself from the conversation. He then made his way to me.

"Enjoying yourself?" I asked, hoping to get a lead on his feelings.

His face was focused and determined. "I'm enjoying the idea of cutting off a dragon's head tonight," he replied. "Let's prepare."

Later that evening, Benjamin, Nathan, and I were hiding in the shadows around a grove in the forest where Benjamin believed the reaping took place. The glow of the waxing moon filled the glen with a dim pale light. We were all spread out, Nathan in a tree, myself concealed within the brush, and Benjamin behind a tree. It was getting quite late, and I was just about to signal to my brothers that we should return home, when a dim light appeared. It was a torch, slowly approaching through the forest in our direction. Four figures appeared. Three of them were cloaked and wore masks that were white, like specters, which made my blood run cold. One of the masks had a red triangle upon the forehead. The unmasked individual was a young man, dressed like a common villager. I thought him to be one of the *volunteers* my son had mentioned.

As they entered the grove, they continued to walk straight toward the edge upon which I had concealed myself. They came so close to me that I was certain they would see me, and just before they were on top of me, they turned and faced the grove, putting their backs to me. I breathed ever so quietly and slowly, that is how close they were to me. The masked man who bore the red triangle appeared to be a leader of some kind. He turned and addressed the volunteer.

"The time has come," he said. "Soon, we will leave you here in the middle of this vale, and a dragon will come and take you away. You have been tested, and you have overcome. You are now one of us. You are no longer in the dark concerning our agenda, as the others are. When you return, you will be one of the Enlightened Ones."

As the masked man spoke, his voice sounded familiar to me, like I had heard it before although I couldn't place it. He continued, "Remember all that I have taught you, Jacob, and hold true to our purpose. When you return, you will be a man of power, fame, and influence. People will admire you; women will flock to you. You will lead many to our cause and destroy those who stand in our way."

As he spoke, the volunteer, Jacob, looked to him with an expression of seriousness, devotion, and admiration.

"Remember," the masked man continued, "it all comes back to the question of authority. You must cause people to answer this question, *Who is my authority?*"

At this, one of the other masked men interrupted. "Yes!" he said. "And when they ask this question, you tell them that *we* are the authority! It is the Enlightened Ones who have the final say!"

In response, and to my horror, the masked leader removed a knife from his belt. Like lightning, and without explanation, he sank the knife blade directly into the heart of the man who had interrupted. It took everything within me to stay still and not cry aloud, for though I had seen many dragons fall, and some humans killed by dragons and raiders, I had never witnessed such a sudden and violent murder.

The man who had been stabbed didn't make a sound and fell dead at the feet of the other men. The recruit's face was filled with terror, but he remained still like a pillar.

"That man was a fool," the leader said. "I hope you will not repeat his error, for he was mistaken. You do not convince people to make us the authority. You must return from your training, able and ready to convince people that *they* are the authority. Whatever the topic or context, they must see themselves as the authority. When they ask the questions, *Who am I? What is my purpose? How do relationships work? How do I raise my children?...*" At this last example, the leader seemed to laugh to himself and then continued, "When people look to themselves for the answers, instead of the Scroll, they will crumble upon their own philosophies. It is the authority of the Scroll we must destroy. Even their good and moral ideas, if they are according to their own reasoning, will end in their downfall. Do you understand?"

"Yes, Your Excellency," the recruit answered, his lips trembling with fear.

"Very good," the leader answered. "The goal is for people to think independently, to trust in their own reason and moral conscience. But enough talk; you will learn everything soon enough. Be strong, my brother. We love you, and we will await your return. Go now. Stand in the middle of the circle and wait."

The man obeyed, and the other two masked men left, taking their torch with them. The light grew dim as they departed, and soon, only the moon gave light. The wind began to blow, as if a storm was coming.

I remained hidden in the shadows, watching the man standing in the middle of the grove, shivering from fear. I was unsure of what to do. I heard an owl hoot from across the circle, only, I knew it wasn't an owl, but was Nathan, signaling to me. He too, I was sure, was wondering what was to be done. I thought I heard dragon wings

25

in the distance. Was I really going to allow this man to be taken by a dragon? But if I stopped him, what would happen? We might become enemies of this secret society. And who was the masked leader? I knew him. I was sure I did, for his voice was from my past, but I couldn't place it. I heard another owl's hoot, this time from my son. Were those dragon wings I heard again, or just the evening breeze? Suddenly, all of these questions and reveries were interrupted by the voice of Benjamin. He was walking out to the man and speaking to him. The man started and looked around him as of one unsure of what to do. I quickly ran out into the circle, as did Nathan.

"You don't have to do this," Benjamin said loudly, speaking over the wind.

"Who are you?" the man said, shocked at the sudden appearance of others.

I spoke the man's name, and he spun around and looked at me.

"What are you doing?" he cried out. "What do you want? Leave me alone!"

"We want to help you, Jacob" I said.

"I don't want your help," he said.

"This is no time to reason with him," Nathan said. "What should we do?"

"Whatever it is, we must do it quickly," Benjamin said. "Should we kill the dragon?"

"No," I replied. A plan entered my mind, though it was only a flash of a plan, seen in a fraction of a second. I quickly ran toward Jacob, who began to run away from me in fear, and I tackled him within the edge of the thicket.

"What are you doing?" he asked, scared to death as a man who wasn't a warrior.

"Just give me your shirt," I said calmly. "But do it quickly."

He obeyed, and I quickly removed my shirt and put his on.

"Brother," Nathan said, observing my plan. "Are you sure about this? We need to think it through."

"There's no time to think it through," I said. "I can sense the dragon coming. We have less than a minute before it's here."

"What do we do with him?" Benjamin asked, pointing at Jacob.

"See him back to the village," I replied. "But conceal your identity."

"But then they will discover what has happened," Nathan said.

"True," I replied. "But that's something that can't be undone, for we will not harm this man or detain him in any way."

"Father," Benjamin said, "this scares me."

"Don't be afraid," I said. "Use your ability. You'll know what to do."

I then looked at Jacob. "Jacob," I said, "you are in terrible danger. Not from us, but from the people who brought you here. I will pray for you."

At this Jacob smiled. "You're a Scroll Follower. I should have known. You fool."

I could sense the dragon, only twenty seconds away. I dropped my sword and knife on the ground.

"Take him into the forest now, before the dragon smells you, and keep him quiet until we are gone!" I then looked at Benjamin. "Take care of your mother and sisters. Whatever happens, you know I love you. Follow the Great King."

I then sprinted to the middle of the circle. I heard Jacob attempt to yell and looked over to see Nathan and Benjamin pick him up, gag him, and sprint within the forest. I looked up and saw the dragon coming down upon me. I prayed in my heart, *I am in Your hands, oh Great King*. The dragon landed, scooped me up in its claws, and paused as if smelling the air. This worried me greatly. I also feared of a stray cry from Jacob. I knew if anything gave the dragon the idea of foul play, that I would likely be swallowed in an instant. The dragon smelled again, and then looking over its shoulder, it spun around. Reaching out its neck, the beast bit into the corpse of the murdered man and quickly chewed him up and swallowed him. The dragon's wings then flapped like a whirlwind, and within an instant, I was soaring high within the air, with the moonlit world far beneath me.

Chapter 5

I was experiencing what virtually few humans ever had. I was flying. I could see the village with its few midnight torches aglow. I could see the Castle, standing tall and proud, with a few dragons perched upon its summit, as was the latest custom. My gaze then fell upon the Oasis, and upon my home, for I was now passing overhead.

This homely image brought me back to myself. The events of the last few minutes had been so hastily done that only now did I begin to reflect upon them and ask myself, *What in the world have you done?* I was held in the claws of a dragon that at any time could cast me down to a certain death. I had left behind my son, my best friend, and a man who was sure to return to the murdering leader of his group and report that the dragon took the wrong man. How long would it take for that message to be relayed to the other dragons? I figured that Nathan and Benjamin, along with the other warriors, would come and keep watch upon the swamps, though that gave me little comfort, for soon I would be in the den of the enemy. What if the dragons recognized me? What if they knew the name of the one they were supposed to take? I decided, therefore, I would use the name *Jacob* if asked.

I then thought of Elizabeth, who would likely be waiting for my arrival, only to find I had been taken. I wondered if I would ever see her, or my daughters, again. My thoughts then turned to the murderer. I was certain that I knew him, but from where? I thought that if I could hear his voice again, I could pinpoint it, but now it was absent in my mind. I only knew that it was a voice from my past. And the thought that a man from my past, likely an acquaintance of mine, was a murderer and that his victim was decaying in the belly just a few feet from me, made me feel very afraid for myself and my family. He killed with such ease and with zero remorse that I was sure he had done it before.

Now I wished that I had not allowed the dragon to take me. I wished, so badly, that Nathan had kept himself quiet and that I had signaled to them to retreat deeper within the forest. I would have gone back to my wife and children and would have been able to protect them from any harm. Now I was in the clutches of the enemy. Fortunately, I was soon reminded of the fact that the Great King was sovereign and was able to work all things together for good. I only hoped and prayed that my choice was pleasing to Him and that He would protect me and bring me back safely to my family.

My musing was suddenly interrupted by a sensation that nearly made me cry aloud in fear, for I thought that the dragon had released me and I was dropping to the earth. I soon realized, however, that I was still within its clutches and that together we were dropping downward at an incredible speed. I perceived the swamp beneath us, approaching quickly. I cried out in fear as we plunged into the murky water. Then all was dark, and I slipped from consciousness.

When I awoke, due to some inner soberness and alertness, I remembered everything that happened and knew exactly where I was. I was with the dragons in their den, under the swamp. A flood of urgency swept over me, for I knew that it was only a matter of time until the news of what I did reached the dragons. This thought plagued me and made me wish that I would have commanded Nathan and my son to kidnap Jacob and hold him until I returned, though I knew in my heart such a thing was wrong.

Taking in my surroundings, I observed a room, carved out of rock, seemingly deep within the earth. I was upon a bed, the only piece of furniture in the room. The only other manmade object was a door of iron bars, like that of a prison, behind which I was trapped. I sat up and put my hands to my head. Was I in this prison because they knew who I was? Would I ever see my family again? I thought of the murdered man, stabbed in the heart without warning. Would I share his fate? I thought of the murderer. If a man would murder, in cold blood, one of his own followers, what would he do to my family if he found out who I was and what I had done? Fear began to enter my heart.

A still small voice from within me spoke, *Fear not*, it said, *for I am with you*. I shook off my fear, and rising to my feet, I walked to the door. It was unlocked. I was unsure what to do.

Just then I heard footsteps and backed away from the door. A hooded figure, wearing a black robe entered my room. Removing the hood, I was face to face with a beautiful woman. She was older than I was, likely around fifty years of age. Her face was stern and her eyes seemed almost empty. Her hair was short and as black as midnight.

"What do you call yourself?" she asked.

To my frustration and terror, I answered without any thought. "I am Caleb," I answered. As soon as the name left my lips, I felt like my heart was going to stop. What a fool I was! Wasn't she expecting me to say, *Jacob*? I froze and tried my best to hide my apprehension. To my surprise and relief, the woman didn't seem troubled in the least.

"Welcome, Caleb," she said with little emotion. "My name is Jade. You may call upon me for any questions you might have during your time here."

She then handed me a black robe which she had with her and turned her back to me. "Put that on," she said. "Quickly. For we have much to do."

I obeyed her command, and as I did, she continued to lecture me. "There is no room for hesitation or unloyalty," she continued. "Only a few days ago, a young girl from a nearby village arrived here. She was, supposedly, in allegiance with our society. It turned out to be too much for her. She tried to run. We retrieved her, and she was immediately sacrificed to our Master."

Fortunately, Jade's back was still turned to me, so she didn't see my reaction. I was sure it was the girl we had seen exit the swamp, and I was sure that my face was unable to hide my abhorrence at this news. I quickly calmed myself and put on a straight face as she turned back around.

"Very good," Jade said, looking at me in the robe. "Whenever you are outside of your cell, keep your face covered. That is our way."

I was pleased at this news, for it would conceal my identity from any humans or dragons that might recognize me. I put on my hood and followed Jade out of the cell. We walked down many corridors, all of which were underground.

"Your time here will not be long," Jade said as I followed her. "Not if you are apt to learn."

We were passing other cells, almost all of which were empty.

"Obviously," she continued. "Your being here is a sign that you have already learned much and have shown great strides in the cause which we fight for. If you work hard, you will be able to return above ground in three months or so. Where you return will be dependent on your qualities. I will be your main guide, responsible for your overall development. I answer to my superiors, so don't make me regret taking you on. I have already trained and commissioned nearly sixty representatives in my short time here, so I know what I'm doing. Listen to me, and you will become one of the Enlightened Ones."

"You've trained sixty people?" I asked curiously. "But I thought that around only forty people had volunteered."

"From your village, perhaps," Jade answered. "But that's only one village of many."

"How many volunteers are there?" I asked, shocked at her words.

I heard her laugh softly. "See for yourself," she said.

We then entered an extremely large cavern. If I had never seen it with my own eyes, I would had never imagined that such a cavern existed within the earth. A small village could have fit within it. The tunnel we had just exited was situated high above looking down into the cavern, like the view from the top of a tower looking down within a small village. The cavern was flooded with hooded figures. They were beyond count, like the sand on a seashore. Within the middle of the vast cave was a statue of a dragon, very large and formidable. In front of the statue was a cloaked figure holding something in its hands, though I couldn't make it out. Everyone was chanting the words, *Death, death, death*! The figure then held in one hand what I perceived to be a dagger and was raising it above the object in his other hand.

"What is that?" I asked Jade as I strained my eyes to see.

"It is a knife," she answered.

"What's in the other hand?" I asked with horror.

"It is a baby," she responded without emotion.

Chapter 6

My heart seemed to burst within me. I breathed in deeply, in preparation of shouting such a rage that would have silenced the entire assembly. But my shout never came. For instantly, just after Jade spoke, the knife fell upon the infant, and the entire assembly erupted in applause. I fell to my knees, unable to contain my heartache, though I did control my emotion to some extent.

Jade stepped beside me. "You disappoint me," she said. "Though, it isn't surprising. Some recruits are not yet so enlightened to embrace the first sacrifice they witness. Don't worry. It will get easier. It better, or else we will have trouble."

I choked back the tears and the anger and slowly rose again to my feet. I considered that child an innocent casualty of an ancient war. And I vowed that this child's blood would be avenged, though I knew deep within me that the Great King would be the one to avenge it.

"But it was a person," I said plainly, still not able to resist any protest.

"A person?" replied Jade. "Listen to me now and learn the truth. That was no person. It was a lump of flesh and blood, nothing more. An actual person has dreams and ambitions and friends and talents. That thing had none of these. It was still sub-human and was therefore a very insignificant sacrifice to the Great Dragon."

"The Great Dragon?" I repeated.

"Yes," answered Jade. "He is your Master now. This statue doesn't do him justice. Soon, when all things are ready, he will appear, and you will worship his true form."

"How often are there sacrifices?" I asked.

"It varies," she answered. "Sometimes we sacrifice an adult, usually a recruit who didn't measure up. Other times, our offerings are babies which we birth within these walls. We just had a baby born a few days ago, so you can expect another sacrifice soon. I hope you receive it better than you did this one."

By this time, the thousands of recruits were engaged in different activities. Some were sitting at tables for meals. Others were standing at attention, almost like soldiers, as another addressed them. Others, it seemed, were engaged in some sort of oratory exercise. They were in large groups, many speaking at the same time, like diplomats arguing. I could sense many dragons, not too far off, though none were visible.

"There are thousands of us, Caleb," Jade said as I looked out upon the scene. "After generations of being shut up, and shut out, and despised, now we will be the ones in charge. Society used to reject us, but now we will become the new standard. Fear not, my brother. You will no longer be looked down upon. You will be loved and adored."

She then led me down into the multitude. I could see very few faces, but the few faces I did see, shocked me. Almost all of them were young, around twenty years of age. Jade then brought me to a class that seemed to have just begun. The teacher was an older man with a long beard. I took my seat at the back of a gathering of approximately fifty people.

"Caleb," Jade said, whispering in my ear, "this is Dagon. He is one of our wisest teachers. Listen to him! I will check in on your later."

I was still overwhelmed by all I had seen in the last hour. I had been taken by a dragon to an unknown realm, witnessed a baby sacrifice, and was now surrounded by scores of strangers who had volunteered for such dealings. I turned my attention to Dagon.

"The strategy is simple," he said, "yet profound. There are two main targets that must be destroyed if we are going to win this battle. We must destroy the Scroll, and we must destroy the family."

I shifted uneasily in my seat. The man continued. "Let us begin with the Scroll. The Scroll is the foundation of the enemy's faith and doctrine and must therefore be reduced to a mere trinket or relic in the eyes of the people. How do you do this? You get them to question everything and then force them to answer based on their own thinking. Get them to question marriage and then get them to think it through based on their thinking alone. Every idea and theory are worthy of consideration in this age of enlightenment. Otherwise, it is intolerant. Get them to question morality. Ask them the questions, *What is morality? If something makes someone happy, how can it be immoral? Is there only one moral compass, or is morality subjective?* Get them to question the Great King. Ask them the questions, *Is the Great King real? If the Great King is real, why did He write such an intolerant Scroll? If the Great King isn't real, are there any absolute truths?*"

I wanted to jump up and shout aloud in righteous anger, though I knew it would be my final protest. I had never heard such blatant evil spoken in such a way. I didn't want to continue to listen, but I knew that I had to.

The man continued. "You must become a master of ideas and suggestions. Don't focus so much on changing people's ideas but rather what they base their ideas upon. As long as you can convince them to lean upon their own understanding, in the end, you will win. To base any ideas, even moral ones, on your own thinking is to begin a downward spiral for future generations. In other words, if you convince them to lean on their own understanding, then their children will utterly fail. The parents will demonstrate by their example that the Scroll isn't useful for practical living. This is our goal: to bring up a generation that claims faith in the Scroll but doesn't consult it regarding daily life. Does anyone have any questions?"

One man raised his hand. "What if they keep quoting the Scroll?" he said. "What if they just won't turn away from it? What do you do then?"

Dagon smiled. "You must make them feel foolish for consulting the Scroll," he replied. "Say to them things like, You really believe in a Scroll that says that women were made for men? Or say, I thought you were educated enough to not base your life on such an ancient manuscript. Be sure to get them around people who will also criticize them. The goal is to make them embarrassed and ashamed for acknowledging the Scroll."

Another person raised their hand. "What if they invite you to the Castle? Should you go with them?"

"Absolutely," Dagon replied confidently. "There isn't a better place to convince them of the hypocrisy and absurdity of the Scroll than a Castle. Find error in the captain's message or in someone's attitude, and use it as ammunition against the one who invited you. Make him feel embarrassed about his Castle. Or, you can always go a completely different direction and get plugged into the Castle, especially if it's one we already control. In that case, use your position there as a way to spread slander, gossip, and division. And make sure to do it all in the name of the Great King. Get the people there excited about community projects and building campaigns; anything except the Scroll."

Dagon paused for more questions and then continued.

"Let us now consider the demise of the family. This is imperative to our conquest. The strategy is simple: it's all about getting the children. We must convince society, more and more, to delegate their children to us. Then we can get their hearts.

Whether it's education, the arena, or the Youngling Guilds, we must convince the parents that we are the experts and they are not. In addition, we must attack the image of the patriarch, that is to say, the idea that the man is the head of the household. This is easy to do, for we can simply accuse them of being sexist. *Equality* is a powerful word; use it often so that if anyone speaks against what you say, you can accuse them of being against *equality*. Convince people that a patriarchal society is a custom for the ignorant and uneducated."

A person sitting beside me raised their hand. "Would this be a good context for gender confusion?" she asked. I was surprised at her female voice, for by all outer appearance I thought her to be a man.

"For certain," Dagon replied. "Nothing will bring about the demise of the family quicker than gender confusion, being that gender is the foundation of the family. We must raise up a generation of feminine boys and masculine girls. Convince young ladies that being female is a curse, that marriage is slavery for women, and that motherhood is a burden. This will make the girl ashamed of her body, as well as the idea of a Great King who created her that way. For when she begins to blossom and looks at her body and sees that it is equipped to please her husband, grow a baby, bring forth that baby, and feed it, she will utterly despise being a woman and will turn against her Maker. Likewise, convince boys that responsibility and leadership are burdensome. Surround them with activities that promote self-focus and immorality. Get them addicted to entertainment and games. Convince them that the easiest and best path for them is that of abdication. Give them hobbies that promote slothfulness and selfishness."

All this time, I was in shock, for I had never heard such blatant heresy. It was as if the Great Dragon himself was leading the conversation. And yet, even in my shock, I had to acknowledge the strategy of the enemy. His plan was a good one. Nothing would destroy the followers of the Great King more than the demise of the Scroll and the family. The thing that amazed me the most was the fact that I had seen both of these things happen in the Castle, yet the Castle didn't recognize it. It was like they had been defeated but didn't know it. They thought that they followed the Scroll and that their families were functioning according to the will of the Great King, yet in reality, they were falling apart. The Scroll had been reduced to something cited at times to appease one's conscience instead of a manual for daily life. The family, likewise, had been altered to fit into the modern practices of age-segregation and gender confusion.

Dagon was then approached by a hooded individual. They whispered back and forth for a moment, then Dagon spoke. "My students," he said, "we have a special visitor today, a man much more gifted than I. I present to you, Gramsci."

Everyone seemed to marvel and talk to each other. Obviously, this man was someone special in that place.

"Greetings," Gramsci said as he stepped forward. "I have just come from the presence of the Great Dragon himself." At this everyone gasped and awed. "I have for you here a doctrine, a philosophy, that will crush the enemy. It is already being implemented by some of my closest followers, many of whom are in charge of castles. With this new weapon, we will be unstoppable."

Chapter 7

"Pay attention," Gramsci continued. "You will not want to miss any of this. What I am about to tell you is the future of our doctrine and power. It doesn't yet have a name, but the idea is constructed and firm and will indeed become our foundation. As I told you, many of our greatest infiltrators are already using it, and its success is unparalleled with any of our previous schemes. As the future builders of our empire, you must learn it and wield it well. At first, this will sound like something that isn't that dangerous to society, but that's the point; it seems harmless. The truth is that this idea will unravel everything that our master hates about society, the Scroll, and the Castle. What I am about to tell you is indeed his greatest masterpiece."

Everyone waited in eager anticipation. Gramsci continued.

"It is a new history of the world," he said. All remained still and contemplative. "It is a history of the world that denies a Creator." He paused to let this sink in. Everyone was quiet and still, and the audience seemed to be unsure of the strategy.

Gramsci repeated himself. "Listen to me as I say it again: History, the origin of all life and existence doesn't begin with the Creator. There is no Creator at all."

Someone raised his hand. "Teacher," the man said with an attitude of great respect, "if there's no Creator, then how did the world and everything in it get here?"

"Excellent question," Gramsci replied. "Now, my loved ones, prepare yourself for the answer. Here it is: The world made itself."

The room remained quiet, though a part of me wanted to laugh out loud. This is their masterpiece strategy? I asked myself. To tell people that the world made itself? Who in their right mind would believe such nonsense?

Another student seemed to have similar thoughts, for he raised his hand and asked the question, "With all respect, sir, do we actually expect people to believe this?"

"Absolutely," Gramsci replied. "For you, it seems like a longshot, but that is because you've always heard a history that included a Creator. The children of today will grow up with a different history. They will grow up being taught and believing that everything just appeared here by chance."

"Sir," another man motioned with his hand, "how can everything just appear? Isn't that impossible?"

"Think about it this way," Gramsci replied. "No one was there when it happened, so how can they disprove it? And remember, people are like sheep; if they are continually around others who think it, they will conform. No one wants to be thought of as an outsider. Neither do they want to be thought of as a fool."

Another student raised her hand. "But only the first few lines of the Scroll deal with Creation. The rest of the Scroll speaks of other things. How will attacking only a few sentences of the Scroll help our cause?"

"My dear sister," Gramsci replied, "if you disprove even one line of the Scroll, it invalidates the entire thing. Either it is all true and from the Great King, or it isn't. If we can convince a generation to deny the first line of the Scroll, then their children will deny it all."

These words struck me and made me reconsider this scheme of the enemy. What first appeared as a joke was now beginning to look very dangerous.

Gramsci now held up a scroll. "I have the new history of the world right here," he continued, "and it doesn't include the Great King." The people around me began to get excited. "Not only that," he continued, "but humankind doesn't come on the scene until after many, many years. Instead of humankind being something purposeful and important, we are now a random addition that is unimportant! You will also notice," he said as he held up the scroll, "that there are animals here that aren't seen anymore. They will be described as ancient animals, animals that pre-date history itself, animals that never walked the earth at the same time as mankind."

He then began to list off some animals. A hand went up. "But many of those animals were eradicated by our forefathers, only a few generations back," a student said. "They don't pre-date history."

"People don't remember such things," Gramsci said confidentially. "Besides, people believe what is published more than what is spoken by their grandparents."

"But what will the idea of an older earth accomplish?" someone asked.

"Don't you see?" Gramsci explained, enjoying the revealing of the plan. "If the world is older than can be numbered, and if people were made late in the process, then the words of the Scroll are false. It says, very clearly, that the Great King made mankind in the very beginning to rule this earth with Him. If we instead propagate the idea of an old earth and a young mankind, then it goes against the Scroll. They will believe people weren't made to rule over the earth. We instead came upon the scene late in the game and are, therefore, more of a burden than part of an integral plan."

"Remember!" Dagon said, chiming in. "If we can get the next generation to simply deny the first few words of the Scroll, then it will discredit the whole. Even if they go to a castle, and even if they sing songs and listen to eloquent messages, if they don't see the Scroll as authoritative, then they will not live according to the Scroll. And if that is the case, then we will have them."

I sat back in amazement. *This was indeed the Great Dragon's masterpiece*, I thought to myself. The strategy was genius. They weren't flat-out attacking the Great King or His teachings when He was on this earth. They were just changing the first few lines of the story. And in doing so, they would destroy the very foundation of our faith—the Scroll.

I knew it was a heresy easy to counter for someone trained in such things. But for the average person and for the average castle-goer, they would easily fall prey to such thinking. And if that happened, if society as a whole embraced such foolishness, then there would be no basis for any moral or spiritual absolutes. The moral guide would no longer be the authoritative words of the Scroll but instead the reason of mankind. Reason would be worshipped instead of the Great King! *But again*, I thought to myself, *who would believe such nonsense? Surely people would see that such an idea is impossible.*

I couldn't help myself. I had to ask the question. I raised my hand and was called upon. "With all respect," I began, "is there any plan on making this believable? It's a wonderful strategy, but I just have a hard time believing that people will embrace such an illogical idea that everything made itself."

"A very good question," Gramsci said. "Yes, we do have a plan. First of all, I must quote one of my favorite mentors. He would always say to me, *If you tell a lie long enough, loud enough, and often enough, the people will believe it.*

"I have here," he continued, motioning to a man who came forward from the front row, "I have here one of my disciples, Karl. He is a teacher in a village. Men of the village look to him as a specialist in all areas of learning. He is one of us, and he is embracing this teaching and promoting it to the people of his village. Like I have done with Karl, we must get ahold of the specialist. Society used to hang on the words of captains, but now they do more so with specialists. This is our greatest strategy in implementing this idea. All people look to the specialists with great respect. They believe anything they say. If they say that the earth made itself then people will believe them. Not only that, but it is the specialists whom people send their children to, and children are so impressionable. Win the specialists, and you will win the children. Win the children, and you win society."

Everyone applauded.

"Something else," Dagon added, "that you must understand, is the reason why this teaching will be so attractive to people. Listen carefully. With the idea of the Creator comes the idea of a Judge. By its very essence, if you have a Creator, then He is the Lawgiver and is therefore the Judge. What idea is more attractive to the guilty, who have broken the law of the Great King, then the idea that He doesn't even exist? If they hear that the Judge doesn't exist, then it will bring them great joy and ease. Law-breakers don't like to think of one day giving an account. They want freedom. This is what this doctrine offers."

"Well said," Gramsci complimented. "At this point," he continued, "I thought it a good idea to have a skirmish, as is our fashion. Karl here will be fighting for this new doctrine, that the earth made itself long ago. I need a volunteer to fight on the side of the Scroll, that the earth was made by the Great King only a few thousand years ago. Any volunteers?"

I was at this point sick to my stomach and overwhelmed at all I had heard. I quickly stood to my feet, hoping to get away in some corner to pray and be alone when Gramsci's words struck me like a hammer.

"You there!" he said with enthusiasm. "Wonderful!"

I had no idea what he was talking about, and quickly looked his way, hoping he wasn't talking to me.

"Yes, you," he said, motioning at me. "Thank you for volunteering. Alright everyone, let us prepare the area. We are going to have a skirmish!"

Chapter 8

My body froze solid, and I stood there, half-turned, looking at the man.

"Form the circle!" Dagon commanded. Everyone jumped up and started moving the benches to the outer edges of the area.

Gramsci then came my way. "You are new," he said. "What is your name?"

"I am Caleb," I replied.

"And what did you think about what you've heard here this day?" he asked, as the other students continued preparing the area.

"It was very informative," I replied, trying my best to put on a smile.

"Very good," he answered. "I feel, Caleb, that you are going to be an extraordinarily gifted apprentice. You are a bit older, but you have a charisma about you."

He seemed to be waiting for a response, so I thanked him for the compliment. He continued. "We are now going to have a skirmish, which in this place, is another name for a debate. We call it a skirmish because words are powerful, and with them, we fight." He then turned to his students. "Brethren!" he shouted. They all turned and bowed in respect. "This is Caleb," he said, motioning to me. "It is his first day."

Everyone laughed and began cheering for Karl who in their mind would easily annihilate the newest recruit. Throughout all these interactions, I was nervous about seeing someone I knew, though this was a bit unrealistic. As I stated before, there were thousands of people.

"Now," Gramsci said to us all. "Karl will be fighting for the belief that the Scroll is a forgery, seeing as the Great King isn't real, as well as for the belief that there is no Creator. Caleb will be fighting for belief in the Scroll and the Great King."

Gramsci then spoke to me privately. "Sorry to put you on this side of the debate, but it is customary to let the more skilled party fight for the truth. So, despite the fact that you don't believe in either the Great King or the Scroll, put forth your best effort, so as to give your brother a good exercise in debating his point."

"I'll do what I can," I replied, feeling a bit stuck. For on one side, I welcomed the debate. On the other, I was in disguise as a heretic and didn't want to blow my cover. I decided, therefore, to give a few good points and then let this man win the debate.

But just as we were about to begin I felt a voice within me say, *Even here, even now, you must defend Me.*

I knew, without a doubt, that it was the Great King speaking to me, though I didn't like what I was hearing. In my heart, I replied by saying, *But if I defend You, and win, they may kill me.*

I then sensed His reply: *Then die.*

This response didn't surprise me and was in a way actually comforting. Scores of recruits encircled us as we began. Karl approached me with a smile.

"So," he began, "are you a follower of the Great King?"

"Of course," I replied. As I acknowledged my faith, I suddenly felt a huge burden lifted from me. Despite the fact that I was within the pits of the enemy, surrounded by scores of blasphemers only yards away from the drying blood of a human sacrifice, I felt at complete liberty to speak freely.

"You fool," Karl said, trying to get control of the skirmish. "There's so much evil and suffering in this world. How could an all-powerful and all-knowing Great King allow such pain?"

"Your question is beautiful," I said, "for it has assumptions built into it that prove His existence."

Karl looked at me with surprise and confusion mixed together. I continued, "When you speak of *evil*, doesn't that mean that there is also such a thing as *good*?"

Karl paused. "Well, of course," he said, trying to be confident in his answer. "We all know that there is such a thing as good."

"So, if there is good and evil, doesn't that mean that there is a moral law by which we differentiate between the two?"

"A moral law?" he repeated.

"Yes," I said. "For you to call something *good* or *evil*, you must have an objective, moral standard to judge it by."

I could tell that Karl felt trapped. He knew I was leading him into an intellectual corner. I decided to speak for him. "The reason you are finding it hard to answer," I said, "is because you know that there must be a moral law. Without it, there is no morality. But you don't want to admit that it exists because that means that there was a Great King which made the law."

"Ha!" Karl laughed. "The Great King made the moral law? How do you know? Where you there when He wrote it? No, you weren't. You, therefore, live by blind faith."

"We all live by faith," I replied with a smile. "But mine is not blind."

"I don't live by faith," he rebutted, "but according to facts."

"Really?" I asked. "Then how do you account for the origins of this world? Where did it all come from?"

"It came from itself," he replied, trying to proudly promote their new doctrine.

"It came from itself?" I repeated. "So then, the world made the world. Is that what you're saying?"

"Well," he replied, "not exactly. There was an explosion."

"An explosion?" I repeated. "What exactly exploded?"

"Nothing," he replied, trying hard to seem confident.

"Let me just make sure I understand you," I said. "In the beginning, there was nothing. Nothing exploded. And that explosion made everything?"

"Absolutely!" he said, angry at my pointing out how ridiculous this doctrine was. "You don't understand how it worked because you aren't a specialist!"

"Ah," I said. "I see. Well, anyhow, going back to my original statement, you do indeed live by faith. Clearly you weren't there when this miraculous event happened. And so, you take that stance not from fact, as in something you can see, but by faith, and a very blind faith at that. By faith you believe that this world made itself, or as you say, that it came from nothing—a very illogical idea if you think about it. How can a world make itself? How can nothing make something? But back to my original point. You, Karl, live by faith, just as I do. The only difference is that my faith isn't blind; it is based on good logic."

"Ha!" replied Karl. "Your faith is built on logic? What is logical about the idea that there is a Creator?"

"There is much logic involved," I replied confidently. "It is just as I've told you. With a Creator comes rules, morals, truth, and purpose. Without a Creator, all of these disappear."

"What a silly notion," he replied. "I believe in love, truth, and morals. I don't need a Creator for those things."

"But who decides what is right or wrong?" I asked. "Is it you, the individual? Is it the majority? Or is it something else?"

He hesitated. "Each person decides for themselves what is right or wrong," he replied.

"Really?" I asked. "Well, what if, to me, killing you seemed like the right thing to do?"

"Then you would be put to death for murder," he replied in anger.

"Why?" I asked. "By what standard can you judge me?"

"The majority of us know that murder is wrong," he replied.

"You still haven't answered my question," I said. "You say we all know it is wrong. But how do we know it? You will not answer me, for you know that your answer will acknowledge the Great King."

I then looked at them all with anger in my eyes. "Hypocrites! So, you believe murder is wrong? What about that dead baby only a hundred yards away?!" I shouted in controlled rage. I knew that I might be crossing a line, but I didn't care. "Deep down in your soul you know it's wrong to kill that baby! You just go along with it like mindless sheep because you're too insecure to admit the truth! That you are all murderers!"

At this, all the students began to raise their voice in hostile opposition. Dagon ordered them to step back. "The skirmish is between Caleb and Karl!" he shouted. "Stay back!"

I decided it best to calm down. Karl hesitated.

I could tell he was thinking of something to say. I wasn't ready to give him the opportunity to do so.

"I'm still waiting," I said. "I'm still waiting for one logical point to how your worldview makes any sense. But you can't answer me, because it doesn't at all. In your worldview, there is no logical explanation for love, good, evil, justice, or any moral action. In your worldview, we are just the result of time and chance. Therefore, if I want to kill you, you can't say it's wrong. There is no such concept of wrong in a world of time and chance. In my worldview, however, good and evil make sense. Justice, law, punishment, and love all make sense. My beliefs are logical and they give me answers for all of these questions. You, however, have no explanation for your worldview. Therefore, you must borrow from my worldview to simply function in this world."

"What?" Karl replied with anger in his voice. He was trying not to appear taken back from my argument, though I could tell his head was spinning. "How do I use your worldview?"

"It's exactly what I just told you," I said patiently. "When you say that something is right or wrong, you are stealing from my worldview. When you say that something is good or evil, you are stealing from my worldview. To truly live according to your worldview, there would be no good or evil. How can good or evil exist in a world made by chance? The truth is, you couldn't function one day without my worldview. It brings you back to logic, sound reason, and purpose. So, you see, your life is one big contradiction. With your lips you deny the Creator, but with your actions, you prove His existence."

Everyone seemed to be silenced. Karl was looking around at his fellow recruits for some kind of help.

"Attack the Scroll," Gramsci finally suggested.

Karl regained some of his confidence.

"You are a sexist and a bigot," he said, with some true signs of aggression in his voice. "Your Scroll contradicts love, putting boundaries on who can show intimate love together. At the same time, it reduces the female to the mere property of her husband. Marriage was created by your ancestors in order to legalize the slavery of women. And then they put it into a Scroll, supposedly written by a Great King, in order to make it unquestionable. What have you to say now?"

"Pay careful attention," I said, "and I will clearly show you your lack of understanding. The Creator of all things, since He made all things, is the ultimate ruler and authority. He says how we live, and how we love, and what is appropriate, and what is not. To be physically intimate, outside of marriage, isn't love; it's lawlessness. You can argue with the Judge all you want, but in the end, you will find yourself in His

49

prison and won't be able to argue any longer. Regarding your notions of marriage, you are sorely mistaken. Marriage is wonderful. It was instituted in the beginning by the Great King and cannot be redefined or reordered. The Great King made men to be masculine heroes, who sacrifice for women and children. He also made women to be feminine and beautiful and to love their husbands and children. The greatest fulfillment for a woman is to be a follower of the Great King, who serves her husband and is devoted to her children."

At these words of mine, all those listening erupted with anger and shouting. Dagon raised his hands to calm them.

"Remember," he said to them all, "that Caleb is pretending! He is our brother."

I didn't wait for any permission to continue.

"Your arguments are invalid," I continued. "They are merely your ideas, based on nothing factual, historical, or logical. And once again, your very argument steals from my worldview. How can you speak of right and wrong and slavery when you don't even believe in truth? Go back to your studies and try again. You will fail. Why? Because the foundation of your worldview lacks any authority. What authority is there in a world made by mere chance? You are basing all of your ideas upon the mere opinions of men, men who have been poisoned by the empty philosophies of the Great Dragon, whose goal is to destroy mankind. Once again, my worldview makes sense. I have answers for your questions. But you are unable to answer any of my questions with clarity or reason."

"It doesn't matter!" Karl shouted. "It doesn't matter what you say! You're wrong!"

I couldn't help but smile. "What an amazing argument you've supplied." I then looked at the students who surrounded us. "I'm sorry to disappoint you, for you had hoped to see a skirmish, but instead, you witnessed a slaughter. It will always be so, when someone embraces such an empty and foolish philosophy. But let me end this skirmish by explaining one last piece of the puzzle. You all claim to believe that the

Great King doesn't exist, but deep down, you know the truth. You all know, if you're honest with yourselves, that the Great King is real. That isn't the issue. The issue is, you don't want Him to be real because you hate Him. You want to justify your sin and lust, and so you try to dismiss the Judge from your thinking. Don't be deceived. You will all one day stand before His throne. And on that day, you will wish that you could come back to this time and change the path you've taken, but it will be too late."

Karl was beside himself, as were his associates. All were quiet for a time and just looked at me. The sound of hands clapping broke the silence. They were the hands of Gramsci.

"Well done!" he said. "We have a recruit already ahead of the game! You will be a teacher soon!" He then turned to all the others who had heard the debate. "I want you all to listen to this man," he said, pointing at me, "for such a man who can argue for the enemy in such a way can clearly do more when arguing for the Great Dragon."

Karl came and shook my hand, as seemed to be expected, and quickly departed. Everyone was then dismissed, and it was announced that there would be no more studies for that day. In all the activity, I felt something squeeze my hand. I turned around but saw no one. I looked down and found a piece of paper in my hand. Opening it, I read the following: *cell P139.*

Chapter 9

I looked around again. Who gave this to me, and why? Was it a trap? I knew that I had to pursue the meaning of this note, and quickly, for I still wasn't sure how long my true identity would remain unknown. I left the main cavern and began to look for cell P139. As I searched, I passed uncountable cells, and it seemed to me that various rituals were beginning. I saw acts of witchcraft taking place, which I knew they would soon try to teach me if I couldn't escape first. I saw other activities in my peripheral vision, things too shameful to be even named, impurity that knew no limits, perversions from the pits of the Great Dragon. It was as if they were trying to invent new acts of wickedness. I had discovered all I needed to. I understood the purpose of this place. The enemy was training up a generation of warriors. If not for the threat on my life, I might be tempted to stay and learn more. But the immorality that was now rampant, all around me, was too much. I didn't know that such vile and immoral behavior on such a large scale could ever exist. I had to escape.

I continued my search. Unfortunately, I found myself in an endless maze of passages and sin. I couldn't find P139. I needed directions, but I dared not ask anyone around me, for to do so I would first have to interrupt the rampant immorality.

Eventually, I came upon a cell that wasn't filled with immorality, at least not at first glance. It was a cell that seemed more in order and tidy than the others. There was a man in its center, seated at a tiny desk and writing hastily. He seemed to be more aged than most I had seen in that place.

"Hello," he said, seemingly excited to see me. "Come in, come in."

I obeyed, and quickly observed that his small table was covered in numerous pages which were either written or drawn upon.

"Yes," he said. "You have come to see my work, haven't you?"

I was a bit curious, and wanting to play the part of the heretic, I took an interest.

"What is this?" I asked, motioning at the scattered pages.

"This is my greatest strategy yet!" the man answered with enthusiasm. "I'm almost finished, and when I present these to my superiors, they will call it the best of its kind yet produced."

I picked up a few of the top sheets and began to read. They were a few pages, covered with both sketches and paragraphs. It seemed to be a simple story about a girl and her friends.

"This is a work of fiction?" I asked. "A story?"

"Oh yes," the man answered, "but it's more than that! It's a teaching, a doctrine, hidden within the story. You see, the target audience is younglings. That's why it has pictures, though not all of my works do. You have to get them when they're young, but you already know that. The stories are simple and entertaining, yet in them, the doctrine of our people is implanted within the mind of the youngling."

I was skimming through the story and came to the ending. The man allowed me to take my time studying the story. He stood next to me, his eyes fixed upon my face as he rubbed his hands together in anticipation of my reaction.

"I don't fully understand," I said after some time. "This is a story about a young man and woman who fall in love and get married. It seems that they live happily ever after. What doctrine of our people is communicated in that?"

The man laughed with pleasure. "Exactly!" he said. "It seems so innocent and pure and wonderful. But if you had carefully read the story, you would have seen that the girl rebels against her parents and also compromises her purity at one point. It is subtle, and in the end, she is reconciled with her parents, but the seed is still planted. Through the guise of entertainment, Scroll-followers will experience the systematic chipping away of their resolution and faith. Eventually, rebellion, impurity, and selfishness won't shock them. They will be desensitized. Worldliness will be normal and expected. Eventually, parents won't even expect their children to follow the Scroll but will instead think that rebellion is normal. Ha! And how ironic will it be that the very weapon that defeated them was implemented through things they chose to put before their very eyes because they wanted to be entertained. Ha, ha, ha! Eventually, the stories will be more outright and forthwith in their rebellion against the Scroll. But first, we must numb them bit by bit. Take this story for example," he said, as he handed me another stack of pages. "This one is about a simple peasant who makes his living as a goat herder."

The man paused, waiting for my reaction.

"That sounds harmless enough," I replied.

"Precisely!" he exclaimed. "But throughout the story there is a side character, the man's brother, who is a lover of other men."

I looked at my new acquaintance with shock. "But that is forbidden and unnatural!" I shouted in horror.

"Of course!" he replied cheerfully. "Once again, we see that by reading such a story, the reader will grow calloused to such perversions. For the sake of entertainment, they will put such wickedness before them, until the day comes when they are desensitized to it. Normality breeds acceptance. They will open their hearts to the Dragon, and it will all come through the guise of my work. Morals will be compromised and lives ruined simply because people want to be amused!"

I stood there, dumbfounded, not able to hide my shock and disapproval. I thought to myself, Surely. Surely the followers of the Great King wouldn't fall for such a trick. Surely they would utterly reject such entertainment for the sake of the Great King and for the sake of their children. I feared for those in the Castle, however. I feared that even those with the best intentions might be led into this deceit, and that in doing so, their children would be led far away from the Great King. This man was talented; his stories pulled me in right away and made me want to read more. I concluded at that moment that the best way to protect my family was to draw a line in the sand: We would only engage in entertainment that was written by followers of the Great King.

My thoughts were then interrupted by remembering my former errand. After a few more examples of his blasphemy, which would undoubtedly send him to the pit of fire, the man directed me in the direction I needed to go. Half an hour later, I stood before the cell marked P139. Finding the door open, I slowly entered. A hooded figure sat on the bed, motionless, and quiet.

"Hello," I said softly. "Who are you?"

"I have the same question for you?" the person retorted. It was the voice of a woman, though she sounded young.

"I'm Caleb," I said plainly.

"That's not what I mean," she continued. "I know what you are. You are one of them, aren't you?"

I didn't know what to say. Had I overstepped my boundaries in the debate? Had I made it too obvious what side I was really on? I had trusted the voice inside of me that told me to be bold. Was that a mistake?

"And what if I was one of them?" I asked. "You would no doubt turn me in immediately, wouldn't you?"

The woman hesitated. "No," she said at last. "But what if you weren't one of them? What if you were tricking me, as is customary in this place? What if I shared with you what I know, and then you betrayed me?"

"It sounds like we must simply choose to trust each other," I said.

"There is no such thing as trust down here," she answered with pain in her voice.

"Show me your face," I said. "That is a good first step to trust."

The woman removed her hood and I was shocked, for she couldn't be any older than my eldest daughter.

"How old are you?" I asked.

"I am only fifteen."

"Fifteen?" I replied. "How in the world did you end up here?"

"I'm an orphan," she explained. "At least, I have been since I was around nine years old. My father was a dangerous man and ended up getting into the wrong crowd. We found him beaten to death one morning. Not that it mattered much to me. My mother ran from man to man, and eventually, never came back home. The Illuminated Ones took me in."

I decided to bear my soul to this girl, for she reminded me of one of my own daughters.

"What is your name?" I asked.

"Sarah."

"We have much in common," I said. "For I too am an orphan, both my parents died when I was young. I will not keep the truth from you. You are correct, Sarah. I am one of *them*. I am a true follower of the Great King. How did you know?"

"It was when you were debating with Karl," she said. "Your words did something to me, inside of me. I have been here for nearly a year. And in that time, I have done things, many things, too horrible to tell. Your words made me afraid, more so than I was already, of the wrath of the Great King."

As she said these words, she wept bitterly.

"Don't be afraid, Sarah," I said. "The Great King has brought me here for this very purpose. He wants you to know that He will forgive you, and cleanse you, and make you new. All that you've done, all the evil, will be forgotten. You must pledge your allegiance to Him. You must forsake the Great Dragon, and this place, and join with the Great King."

"What you say seems too good to be true," she said, tears streaming down her cheeks.

"It is the truth," I said. "The Great King's words are true. You can count on them. He promises to forgive all those who will follow Him."

I watched Sarah weep, though through her tears I could see in her eyes that she was counting the cost of what lay before her. She then stood to her feet with resolution.

"Then I am His," she said. "With all my heart, I will follow the Great King. I renounce all of my sin, deceit, and evil ways. I will only walk in the ways of the Great King for the rest of my life."

I smiled and thanked the Great King for His mighty ways of providence. For had I not been obedient to Him by speaking freely and truthfully in the debate, this young girl would not have been convicted of her sin. I now saw my mission in that place as complete, and now only escape entered my mind.

"Sarah," I said, "we must get out of here, together. You've lived here for nearly a year. Is there any way to escape?"

"Most of the passages are guarded by dragons," she said. "But I have heard of people making it out, though it is rare."

I thought of the young girl coming up out of the swampy waters and her fate. I fought back the fear. "The Great King will make a way for us," I said. "We should leave tonight, after all have fallen asleep."

"Asleep?" she said. "This place is never asleep, for evil is most rampant at night. Can't you feel it? Lawlessness is everywhere."

"Why do they do that?" I asked. "Why do they promote such perversion?"

"To destroy our souls," she said. "Once you indulge in such sin, your soul goes numb and you become dead on the inside. This is the first time I've felt alive in my entire life."

Sarah's comment made me smile, and she smiled too. The creases in her face made me think that she hadn't smiled sincerely in a long time.

"This place will not overcome the Great King," I said. "They are training up worldly philosophers. We are training up Kingdom philosophers. And though they outnumber us, one of us can silence a hundred of them, just as I did today with Karl."

Sarah's face grew sober. "It isn't only philosophers and debaters they are molding," she said.

"What do you mean?" I asked.

"Come with me," she replied.

I followed Sarah down many different passages. I pulled my hood further around my eyes to guard them from the depravity of that place. I could then sense in my spirit that we were nearing dragons.

"Sarah," I said, "is this a good idea?"

"Trust me," she said.

I had never sensed such a presence of dragons. It was so thick that I had a hard time putting one foot in front of the other. We then came to a passageway that was guarded by a small dragon who seemed to beckon us to halt.

"We come to see the harvest," Sarah said plainly.

The dragon then stepped back, allowing us to pass. We entered a large cavern, like the one I had entered earlier that day. Except this one wasn't filled with volunteers. It was filled with dragon eggs. They were beyond count. We walked to the edge of a precipice and looked down upon them. The many torches in the cavern afforded just enough light to see the piles of eggs at the bottom of the pit. I stood there, speechless, thinking myself in a nightmare.

"What are these for?" I asked softly to Sarah, who was beside me.

"They are for the war that is coming," she answered. "They are due to hatch in only a few weeks."

I couldn't believe it. The number of dragons we had faced in the past had never numbered more than twenty at a time. There had to be more than ten thousand eggs in that pit.

"Come," I said, taking her hand. "We must leave this place now. The Great King will show us a way out of here together."

"There's one more thing," she said.

"What's that?" I asked.

"There's someone that must escape with us," she said.

"Who?" I asked.

I then saw a tear come to her eye.

"My baby," she said.

Chapter 10

"A baby?" I said. "Here?"

"Yes," she answered, returning to her tears. "It is only five days old. I was nursing it, but they took it away and told me to return to my training. Today was my first time back, just in time for your debate. They tell me that it will be sacrificed soon."

Her cries had now turned to sobs and were so loud I feared that the dragon sentinel might be suspicious. "Come," I said. "Let's go back to your cell where we can talk in private."

We made it back and locked the door.

"Is it a boy or a girl?" I asked.

"A girl," she said.

"And what is her name?" I asked.

"Her name?" Sarah asked, sounding puzzled. "She doesn't have one. They say it isn't human yet, for she has no dreams or ambition. They say that she will never be human; she is to be sacrificed very soon."

"These things they are telling you are lies," I said calmly, yet with authority. "The Scroll clearly says that she was a human at the moment of conception. In the Scroll, when a woman discovers she is pregnant, it says that she is *with child*. Search your heart, Sarah. Do you really believe that such a beautiful baby girl isn't a human? Isn't that very concept ridiculous?"

"Yes," she hastily agreed. "I believe you are telling me the truth. Please. Please help me. I don't want to lose her."

"You won't," I said resolutely. "By the power and grace of the Great King, I tell you the truth: You will not lose your daughter."

My mind was made up. The Scroll taught that men should lay down their lives for women and children. I would either get Sarah and her daughter out of this place alive, or I would die trying. There was no other alternative. If I was to die, at least it would be as a man of honor, interceding for those who weren't able to defend themselves.

"Would they let you take your baby?" I asked.

"No," she said. "They guard her."

"How many people guard her?" I asked.

"Only one," she replied. "A woman. They don't suspect that anyone would take the baby, so the woman is only there to nurse and care for the baby until the sacrifice."

"Very good," I said. "Tomorrow morning, I will meet you at your cell. Then we will go together to the baby's cell, and I will tell the guard that I have orders to move the baby. I'm sure I can convince her."

"And then we will escape?" Sarah asked.

"Yes," I replied. "I will need your help for that. Do you know of a way out?"

"I know of a few possibilities," she replied. "But as I said, they are almost always guarded by dragons."

"That shouldn't be a problem," I said. We spoke for another half an hour about the details of our plan. We also prayed together. Exhausted beyond measure, I went to my room and quickly fell asleep.

Early the next morning, I was awoken by Jade.

"Good morning," she said, though she didn't give me an opportunity to respond. "You have already made quite an impression," she said. "Dagon considers you to have more potential than any previous recruits on their first day."

"I hope I will make you proud," I said.

"I'm sure you will," she said. "Now hurry along. There is a special appearance today by a very extraordinary dragon, followed by a baby sacrifice."

"A baby sacrifice?" I asked, trying to hide my apprehension. "So soon?"

"Yes," she said. "Do you think you are in a better place now than you were yesterday? I hope you will embrace it as you should."

"I hope I will indeed embrace it," I said, after which Jade left me alone.

I quickly hurried to Sarah's cell. It was empty. I didn't know what to do. I was just beyond the point of desperation when I saw her running toward me weeping.

"We are too late!" she said. "I couldn't wait for you. I went to check on the baby and two men arrived and said that they were to take her for today's sacrifice!"

"Take me to them!" I said. "Quickly!"

I followed Sarah, and as we ran along, I tried to calm her down as much as possible. After she dried her eyes and gained her composure, we rounded a corner. There were two men conversing, one of them holding the infant.

"Stay calm and follow my lead," I said. We then approached the two men. "You there," I said, with some aggression in my voice. "I'm afraid there's been a mistake."

"What do you mean?" one of them asked, looking upon us with disapproval.

"Is this the baby for the sacrifice?" I asked.

"Absolutely," the other answered. "We have strict orders, and it will be our necks if it doesn't happen."

"Well, of course," I said. "But plans have changed a bit. This baby is to be sacrificed, but this girl with me is supposed to do the sacrifice. Give her the baby."

"Are you sure?" one of the men asked.

"Of course," I said. "I have my orders as well. Now give the girl the baby so we can get on with it."

"But this is the baby's mother," the one man said, recognizing Sarah.

"Of course it is," I said. "That's the point. The Great Dragon wants us to see mothers killing their own babies. Think of how much honor that will bring him. Now, are you going to be part of the problem or part of the solution? We have a schedule to keep. There's a special appearance today by a dragon and we must be ready."

The two men looked at each other for some form of approval and reluctantly handed the baby to Sarah, who was thankfully playing the part this entire time.

"Thanks," I said. "I'll see you later."

We then walked away from the men.

"What now?" she whispered.

"Conceal the infant in your cloak as best you can," I said. "Which way do we go to get out of here?"

"We must go through the main cavern," she said.

"Seriously?" I asked with frustration. "Very well. Keep your head down and stay close to me."

We entered the main cavern, which was flooded with robed figures. It was overwhelming, in so many different ways, and I wondered how these people did it day after day. We were about half way through the cavern when something happened. A horn blew. It was loud and piercing, and everyone was immediately quiet and still, to the point where Sarah and I had to do the same, though we tried to inch our way through the immense crowd without making a scene. A stray voice made an announcement.

"And now," the voice said. "One of our greatest leaders, the forerunner of the Great Dragon himself. I present to you, Gadreel."

Everyone applauded, and to my astonishment, an enormous dragon entered the cavern.

What amazed and shocked me wasn't the size of this dragon; it was the fact that this dragon was missing its left eye. It had been cut out—by me! It was the same dragon that had kidnapped Elizabeth around nineteen years earlier. The same dragon who had lured Elizabeth and I, as children, into the forest to destroy us. I quickly lowered my head and continued to inch through the crowd with Sarah beside me, but it was taking a very long time. Soon it would be time for the sacrifice, and then they would know what happened. I was also starting to hear the baby fuss.

"My brethren," the dragon said, its voice nearly shaking the walls, "I come here today to bid you tidings concerning our master. The time for his reappearing upon this earth is at hand. It is nearly here. As you know, our army of dragon hatchlings are almost ready to appear, and then..."

But the dragon didn't finish its thought, but paused and looked around with concern. The dragon then inhaled, deeply and slowly, through its nostrils. My heartbeat quickened.

"Well," the dragon said, smiling, "someone is here with us today, someone who shouldn't be."

The dragon inhaled again, deeply and slowly.

"There is a traitor in our midst," it continued, and everyone gasped at the announcement. "A follower of the Great King is here."

It inhaled again, deeply and with enjoyment, like someone smelling their favorite meal.

"Oh," it said, "how I've longed for that scent, and how I now long for the taste. Where are you?"

Everyone was now looking about them.

"Where are you, Caleb?" it said.

Chapter 11

To say I was afraid is an understatement. I was in the pits of the enemy, surrounded by thousands of the enemy's followers, detected by the largest dragon I'd ever seen, and my only allies were a fifteen-year-old girl and her infant daughter. We were still far from the tunnel leading us away from the cavern, and people were now looking for a man named Caleb.

"Hey," someone said, "is it that man?"

I couldn't see who they were referring to, but I was sure it was me.

I then heard other voices, saying, "Stop! You there!"

I kept holding on to Sarah's free hand and leading her on. A hand grabbed my shoulder and spun me around. It was Karl.

"I thought that was you," he said with a smile. "Looks like you have an appointment with a dragon," he said mockingly.

I cast my fear aside. "At least now you know why I beat you," I said. "It wasn't because I was pretending."

"Well," he said, "at least now I will have the last laugh."

"Oh, I don't think so," I said. "Just wait. You will eventually die, Karl, and when you do, you will stand before the One you tried to disprove. And on that day, you will wish so badly that you had been on my side. For all eternity, you will wish it!"

My words seemed to impact Karl, for he stood still and didn't speak. His companion, however, did. He turned toward the dragon and shouted aloud, "Hey! We have the man! He is here!"

As he spoke another man touched me on the shoulder and whispered in my ear. "Found you," he said.

I knew the voice at once. It was my son, Benjamin. I quickly turned to him. "What are you doing here?" I gasped.

"No time for that now," he said. "Here."

He quickly handed me my sword. "This girl is with you?" he asked, noticing Sarah.

"Yes," I said. "And her baby. It's only the three of us, and you, but now we are done for."

A mob was approaching us.

"It's not just us," Benjamin said. "Most of our army is here."

Benjamin then lifted his sword and shouted, "Now!"

Many things happened, all at once. Around twenty soldiers, all around me, cast aside their black cloaks and unsheathed their swords. At once they began to escort us in the direction we needed to go. Nearly two dozen women, led by my wife, also appeared and quickly released their arrows upon the dragon, driving him backwards. The dragon shook off the sudden attack, and quickly approached us, trampling men underfoot. All sorcerers were likewise ordered to attack.

A bolt of lightning suddenly shot forth and struck the dragon, knocking it upon its back. I knew it was Justin using his ability. Chaos broke out everywhere. People were shouting, running, and being trampled. Suddenly twenty dragons, so it seemed, poured into the cavern. Fire, arrows, smoke, shouts, all of these filled the air. Some of the more skilled sorcerers had now reached our position. One of them was Jade. Her eyes were filled with hatred.

"Defend yourself," I shouted above the chaos. "But don't strike down any human. Kill only the dragons!"

The sorcerers were hitting us with a form of fire, but it was weaker than dragon's flame. Benjamin pointed out the tunnel we sought, and we were nearly upon it when the Gadreel came upon us. I stood my ground, and now with both sword and shield, I battled the dragon. Its fire beat down upon my shield, and my sword cut into its flesh.

"Everyone into the tunnel!" Nathan ordered. All of our soldiers obeyed his instruction as I held off our final opponent at the entrance.

My enemy seemed to recognize Sarah and called to her as we fought. "Sarah!" the dragon called out. "Have you been so deceived that you go with the enemy?!"

Sarah turned and addressed the dragon. "I have been born again!" she said. "I am now a follower of the Great King, and my daughter will follow in my footsteps! You desired to kill her today! She will live!"

"No!" the dragon cried in anger.

"You fail, yet again!" I said. "You try to thwart the plans of the Great King, and you prove to be His pawn! Now flee, or else I will cut out your other eye!"

But something happened then that none of us were ready for. Hiding within a small cavity of the cavern wall was a dragon only fifteen feet in length. And desiring to please its master, it sprang upon Sarah and lifted her high within the air. The infant fell from her, providentially landing in the arms of my wife, Elizabeth, who had just come to my side.

The creature then flung Sarah into the grasp of Gadreel, who looked at me with sinful pleasure. "Ha!" it said mockingly, holding Sarah in its right hand. "It looks like you are the one who has failed."

Sarah looked at me with a look that is hard to describe. It was sad, though content. A countenance which reflected on a life of misery but was now ready for a life of love. "Rachel," she said. "Name my daughter Rachel. And tell her that her mother loved her. And tell her that her mother was a follower of the Great…"

But before Sarah could speak another word, the dragon crushed her to death within its grasp.

Chapter 12

It took Nathan, Benjamin, and Jedidiah to keep me from rushing back into that cavern, for my desire for vengeance was paramount. In the end, they were wise, for we were being overrun by both humans and dragons. Reluctantly, and full of rage, I turned and followed the army down the narrow tunnel.

"All present and accounted for," Levi reported to his father.

"Good," Nathan said. "And the tunnel?"

"It is shut behind us," he replied. "Jedidiah brought it down. The enemy will not follow us."

"Not from under the ground," Nathan said. "But still, perhaps, from above. We must hurry."

For nearly three hours we hurried along, and during this time, little dialog took place. My brethren had questions, and so did I, but they could tell that I was in mourning. Sarah was young, like one of my own daughters. My wife, as always, could read me like a book.

"She is with the Great King now," she said. "And her baby is safe."

"It is now our baby," I said.

"The Great King be praised," my wife said, tears flowing down her cheeks. "We will raise her as our own, and she will bring great glory to the Great King and to her first mother."

We finally came to an exit which led to the forest above. Waiting to greet us was Captain Samuel and the rest of our brethren. The sun was shining, for it was only midday, and by nightfall, we were safe within our Oasis. We quickly gathered to pray and debrief all that had happened.

"How did you find me?" I asked. "And what happened once I was taken by the dragon, two nights ago in the grove?"

"Benjamin found you," Nathan said. "He simply took your advice. You told him to use his ability. He could sense that you were in immense danger and was immediately drawn to your presence. Within only four hours of your being taken that evening, Benjamin and I found the tunnel. We scouted it out and found that it led right to the heart of the dwelling under the swamps. We returned with the brethren, found a storage room full of black cloaks, and the rest you know."

"Regarding Jacob," Benjamin said, "we bid him to repent and leave his path of darkness, and then he left us, silent and without emotion. We haven't seen or heard from him since."

"Tell us your side of things," Captain Samuel said.

I relayed all the details I could remember. The council was shocked that such wicked training was happening on such a broad scale.

"They are killing babies," I said. "We must get back in there and stop them immediately."

"I'm not sure we can," Captain Samuel said. "Not with so many people and dragons involved. They will be ready for us next time."

"But we can't just sit by and watch it happen, either," Justin said.

All were quiet for a while, deep in thought. Eventually Captain Samuel broke the silence.

"This we must give more thought, while we trust and wait on the Great King," he said. "He rescued one baby today and put it into a family that will raise it in light of the Scroll. We must pray for this to happen more. In the meantime, we must turn our heart back to our homes. We must make sure that our marriages are pleasing to the Great King and that we are raising our children correctly, in homes full of joy and full of the Scroll's light."

I then relayed the image of the dragons' pit and the countless eggs.

"This can mean only one thing," Captain Samuel said. "The final battle is near, and the Great King will soon return."

"Are we sure that He will return?" one of our number asked.

"Absolutely," replied Captain Samuel, "for the Scroll says it to be so. At the beginning of the war against human and dragon, over six thousand years ago, the Great King drove the Great Dragon into hiding and detained the dragons to the forest. He then wrote the Scroll which we treasure so dearly. It says that one day the dragons would exit the forest, lead the world astray, and there would be a final battle. When that battle happens, He promises to appear."

"Then let us be encouraged," Nathan said. "This will be a time of difficulty and of testing, but it is bringing us one step closer to the arrival of the Great King. We must be in a constant state of readiness."

"Do you think they will look for you, Caleb?" Captain Samuel asked.

"Yes," I replied. "I think they will. I fear I have endangered everyone here."

"Our location is still a secret to most, though," Justin said. "Unless they have ties with the Castle of Ravenhill, we may be free from danger."

"Considering my first impression of Captain Asa," Nathan said solemnly, "I'm guessing that the enemy is within the ranks of Ravenhill Castle."

"We must be on constant guard then," Captain Samuel said.

We sat in silence for some time. Then Nathan spoke. "It is almost King's Day," he said, then turned to me. "Are you sure, Caleb, that you want to return there?"

71

"My conscience persuades me to go," I said soberly. "That man, Judah, seems like a lost sheep. What if you never reached out to me, Nathan? What would my life look like?"

Further plans were discussed. After the meeting, Captain Samuel pulled me aside. "Be wary of the Castle," he warned. "You are known now to the underground followers of the Great Dragon as a rogue and a spy. And you never know if any of them will be at the Castle. It is very likely there is some overlap there."

An hour later, I was reclining in my home with my family. All of us were loving on little Rachel, our new daughter. There was weeping, laughter, and thanksgiving.

"You see, children," Elizabeth said, "the Great King is able to work all things together for good. Nothing is beyond Him, and His ways are perfect."

My three daughters were especially fond of the baby and were taking turns holding her.

"This will be good practice for each of you," Elizabeth said, addressing her daughters. "Since you are girls, what is your destiny?"

"To be a wife and mother," they all said smiling. "Just like you."

"And what amazing wives and mothers you will be," I said. "Just like your mother, you girls will so bless your husbands. Remember that the Great King made you to complete your husband. He is waiting for you, and needs you, for without you, he is still not whole. You will fulfill him and make him strong. Through your reverent submission, diligent service, and unfailing love, you will set your husband up for immense success."

Elizabeth smiled with new tears emerging, and she turned to me. "I have been wanting to be pregnant again, but to no avail. But now the Great King has blessed me with another child outside of my womb, a daughter."

"The Great King is so good," I said smiling.

The next morning, I was up early, for a sense of urgency was building within me. I had been within the ranks of the enemy, and I knew their schemes. My son Benjamin was sitting within the middle of the Oasis with both Jedidiah and Levi. They were putting wood upon the ashes of the fire pit, trying to restore the flame from the previous evening.

As I approached, they rose in respect. I bid them to sit down, and I took up a seat beside them. The sky was brightening with the new day and birds were singing praises to the Great King.

I then motioned to Jedidiah, "Is your brother on patrol?"

"Yes, sir," he replied. "He left only a few minutes ago."

I looked within the forest around us with concern written upon my face.

"Don't fret, Father," Benjamin said. "He is fine. I would sense if it was otherwise."

I nodded with a grin. "So," I said, "what brings you men out here so early?"

"It's something we have been doing the last week or so," Levi replied. "Trying to meet before the sunrise, to pray and talk about the Great King."

I thanked the Great King for such moments. To see my son and other men, on their own initiative, seeking the Great King put a joy within me beyond description. I thought back to the mediocre expectations and happenings of the Youngling Guild. My heart broke for those families.

"Well, I think I will seek out Daniel and join him for a time," I said.

The others laughed. "If you find him," they jested.

I decided to enter the forest upon the eastern edge of the Oasis, and in doing so, I passed closely to my home.

The day was now lit, and I was pleased to see my wife and daughters up and doing chores outside the home. My youngest, Lily, noticed me and called out, "Hello, Daddy!" she shouted. "Where are you going?"

I smiled and motioned with my finger for her to keep her voice down. I then came near to my family. My wife gave me a gentle kiss. "Good morning, beautiful ladies," I said. "I'm on my way out to the forest to do some patrolling."

"Oh, can we come?" Rose asked. Violet and Lily asked the same.

I looked at my wife and her smile reflected a principle that I had learned well; it's always good to take your children along. Even if they slow you down, or even if you want to be alone, the discipleship of your children is more important than whatever other pursuit you have before you.

"Of course you can come," I said cheerfully. "But we will be training," I said, somewhat seriously. "So be sure to get your bows and quivers."

The three girls jumped up and down with excitement, especially the two younger ones, and were quickly assembled and ready.

"Shall I come with you?" my wife asked.

"We should be fine," I said. "Thank you though."

The four of us exited the Oasis, into the dense woodland. The morning sun diminished behind the canopy of trees. My three daughters walked with arrows notched upon their bow strings.

"Remember," I said as we walked along, "we must always stay alert and sober minded."

"Father?" asked Rose. "When will we discover our abilities?"

"That will happen when it is the proper time," I replied. "You must be patient."

"Do you get to choose your ability?" Lily asked.

"No," Rose answered her sister. "The Great King chooses."

"Is she right?" Lily asked me, her sweet little voice blessing the forest around her.

"Yes," I said kindly. "Your sister is correct. However, there is nothing wrong with asking for certain abilities."

"You mean in prayer?" Rose asked.

"Precisely," I said. "You can do it now, as we walk along. Tell the Great King what ability you would want."

The girls were quiet for a time. Rose broke the silence. "Mighty Great King," she said. "I would like to heal people."

"Amen," I said. "That prayer, I believe, is in alignment with the will of the Great King, for you, my dearest, have always been inclined to help the sick and wounded."

"Mighty Great King," Lily said softly. "please give me the ability of seeing in the dark."

"Oh," I said. "What a wonderful prayer. So be it. Open her eyes, oh Great King, even in the darkest places."

We now waited for Violet's request, and just about when I thought she was avoiding the topic, she prayed. "Mighty Great King," she said, "please help me save the men I love, so that they will not have to die."

The immediate lump in my throat forbid me to comment, for I knew where that desire came from. Of us all, Violet was the only one with her twin brother, Isaiah, when he died. She had a bond with him that may have even been greater than that of Elizabeth. I think in her mind, logically, she knew that there was nothing she could have done to save her brother; it was the will of the Great King. But in her heart, I wondered what she really felt about the events of that fateful day.

"Amen," I said finally, not wanting to hurt her by my silence. "That is a good prayer, my dearest."

"Thank you," she said thoughtfully. "I hope it is answered. Otherwise, I will die."

This confused me. "What do you mean?"

"I simply mean that I will die before I see a brother of my heart fall before me again."

I remained quiet and thoughtful.

We continued to walk slowly and at full alert, for even though I didn't sense any dragons, I was still compelled to be at the ready. I then noticed off to my left a set of young dragon tracks.

"Look at these tracks," I said, my girls kneeling beside me, close to the ground. "What do you see? Remember, you must be observant and aware. Use all of your senses."

The three girls studied the tracks.

"It is a young dragon," Violet observed. "Around a year old."

"Very good," I replied.

"These tracks are old," Rose added. "I would guess around one week."

"Correct again," I said.

"It was a scout," Lily commented. "Look at its inner claw, on the back legs. Only scouts have those."

"Well done," I said to my girls. "You all made very correct and insightful observations. One thing you missed, however, is that the dragon who left these tracks is now dead."

My girls all looked at me with confusion on their faces. "How can you know that?" they all asked.

I answered, "Because I was here in this precise spot a week ago. I followed these tracks a mile from here, found the beast in its den, and killed it."

The girls all smiled. "Daddy," they said with laughter, "was it easy to kill?"

"No," I replied with a smile. "It was a bitter foe. I needed the help of two other men to bring it down."

"Who helped you kill it?" Violet asked.

"Daniel and Jedidiah," I replied.

"Oh, Daddy," Rose said, "when are we going to kill a dragon?"

"When the Great King wills it," I replied. "I would think soon though."

"Daddy?" Violet asked. "Can you tell us more about when you and Daniel killed the dragon?"

"Your father did all the work," a stray voice said. We all jumped at the surprise. It was Daniel, leaning against a tree trunk, only a few yards away. "Forgive me," he continued. "I didn't mean to startle you."

He came closer to us, and we were relieved to see him, for in the forest, the more allies you have with you, the better.

76

"Regarding the dragon," he said, "I only distracted the beast. It was your father and my brother who made the killing stroke."

"How did you distract the dragon?" Lily asked.

Daniel came close to Lily and bent down a bit to be at her height. "I ran in a circle around the dragon, over and over again, until it was so dizzy, like a dog chasing its tail, that the beast fell over from sheer exhaustion."

We all laughed at the tale. Daniel then took a good careful look at the girls.

"You have the look of warrior archers," he said, "fit for the service of the Great King."

The girls beamed with pleasure, especially Violet.

"Have you scouted the area around the Oasis?" I asked.

"Yes, sir," he replied. "Many times now. There are no dragons or people anywhere around us."

"Very good," I replied. "For the next few days, we should be more on guard than normal. I fear that the enemy may retaliate soon."

"Consider it done," he said, and I sensed that his response was not only directed to me, but also to my eldest daughter.

For a moment I felt a stirring in my spirit. Had Daniel won my Violet's heart? If so, he had done so without any dishonor or worldliness involved. It would be his character, manliness, courage, and integrity that she would esteem, not anything external. And though I didn't know for sure how she felt, I trusted that Providence would reveal her true feelings in due time.

"Well," I said, addressing Daniel, "my daughters and I could use an escort as we continue to track dragons. Could we have your service?"

"It would be an honor," the young man said with a bow of his head.

We continued on for another half an hour, taking opportunities as we were able to instruct my daughters. We then decided to head back home. We had only just begun when I sensed something.

"What is it?" Daniel said, reading the expressions on my face. "Is a dragon coming?"

"No," I said, with a quizzical look upon my brow. "It is odd. Something I've never before experienced. And it is fast, extremely fast."

I didn't have enough time to alert them to the reality of the situation. Suddenly, and to everyone's shock, a beast burst forth through the undergrowth around us, colliding directly into Daniel and myself. Fortunately, our shields took most of the impact, though our bodies were lifted high into the air. The creature itself was also knocked down by the impact and rolled across the ground until it was stopped violently by a tree trunk.

I looked up to see something completely foreign to my vision. It was like that of an enormous lion, around twelve feet long. Yet it had the scales and head of a dragon.

"It's a fire hound!" Daniel shouted, rising to his feet.

The hound turned to Daniel and quickly blew from its mouth a strong blaze of fire, much hotter and faster than most dragons. Daniel's speed moved him quickly out of the way. The hound, frustrated and full or rage, turned quickly to the three girls who were huddled together and without shields to protect them. The girls pulled back their arrows courageously and let them fly, but the arrows barely penetrated the extra thick hide of the hound, not affecting him more than a splinter would. He opened up his mouth to breath fire, but as quick as lightning, Daniel ran into the beast's side with his shield, causing the hound to be violently thrown down to the ground in pain.

I was now upon my feet and began running toward the hound to finish it off; Daniel also approaching. Then, unbeknownst to me, for I was so focused upon the enemy that I was unaware of my surroundings, two more fire hounds ran within the fray at such speeds that Daniel and I were barely able to put up our shields before we were once again upon our backs from the impact.

"Daddy!" I heard my girls cry. I looked over to see Violet, not far from me, for I was thrown towards her and the others. Daniel, who seemed to be either unconscious or dead, was now about to fall prey to the three hounds who were coming upon him side by side. His fate seemed sealed. Violet then separated herself from her sisters and began to run towards Daniel.

"Wait!" I called out. "Violet, wait!"

She didn't slow down at all, but just gave me one brief glance over her shoulder as she continued to sprint towards the man who now had her heart.

My heart was filled with fear and shock mixed together. What shocked me, however, wasn't that she was advancing upon three fire hounds, but rather something that happened when she looked at me over her shoulder, for I had beheld her eyes. Instead of her blue eyes, like the brightest oceans, her eyes were dark red, like a raging fire. And I could have sworn that actual flames were where her pupils should have been.

Chapter 13

I was paralyzed. I wanted to get to my feet, but I was in immense amounts of pain, and my heart was choked by a fear that I had never before experienced. Even though my son and wife had been in perilous situations, it was different with Violet. She was my daughter, and her brother's survivor. She crouched before Daniel, in between him and the enemy.

"Stay back!" she shouted with fury in her voice. "Stay back or I will kill you all!"

The beasts seemed to laugh, taking their time and enjoying the drama of their kill. She lifted her voice again as she remained unmoved before her true love. "In the name of the Great King, who created all things, you have no rights to this man!"

As she invoked the name of the Great King, something happened. Her face and clothes and hair began to burn, yet she wasn't burning up. Soon her entire body was aflame with red, blue, and purple flames, rippling gently across her clothing and skin. The hounds were no longer reveling in the moment, but quickly, out of fear and rage, blew their flame upon Violet. She remained where she was, unmoved and unburned before the man she loved. The hounds blew their fire harder and brighter. Nothing happened. Their flame reflected off of Violet as it would a shield. Violet then fitted an arrow to her string, and let it fly.

Her arrow soared forward, completely ablaze, like a firebrand of glory. The arrow exploded upon impact, sending the three hounds in all directions and in various pieces. Violet remained standing, bow in hand, calmly breathing. She was beautiful, like an angel of fire, whose face burns with flame, yet whose kiss would be as cool and soft as a flower petal in early spring. The fire then left her body and all was still.

At that moment, there was no doubt in my mind. Daniel had won my daughter's heart.

I slowly, and with some difficulty, rose to my feet. And coming to both her and Daniel, I found him still motionless with Violet holding him in her arms and sobbing uncontrollably. Rose and Lily also came near and were also weeping. I slowly removed Daniel from Violet's grasp and laid him upon the ground.

"Is he dead?" Violet asked amidst her sobs.

"No," I said. "He is breathing."

"Someone is coming," Rose said, commenting on the footsteps which echoed throughout the still forest.

"I'm sure it is your brother," I said calmly. "And also likely your mother."

My guesses were both correct, for Benjamin, according to his ability, had sensed our danger. And running to our aid, he passed close to our home, therefore sending my dearest Elizabeth with him.

"Everything is alright," I said aloud, desiring to calm them.

Just as they came upon us, Daniel awoke. He was a bit disorientated but seemed to be without any major injury. Violet sighed in relief, and being overwhelmed with emotion, she rose to her feet and ran within the arms of her mother.

"What happened?" Elizabeth said calmly but with great concern.

"Your daughter became a woman today," I said. "She saved the life of Daniel, and likely, the lives of her father and sisters."

Benjamin was examining the remains of the enemy.

"What were these creatures?" he asked.

"Fire hounds," Daniel said, who was by now in his right mind.

"Fire hounds?" Benjamin repeated. "I've never heard of them."

"Few know of them," Daniel replied. "Indeed, I believed them to only be a myth. They are the quickest and deadliest scouts of the enemy. They are able to follow scents from hundreds of miles away. There is little doubt in my mind that they were seeking out Captain Caleb."

I then helped Daniel to his feet. He was beaten and sore but was alright. He looked at the scene around him and then turned his attention to Violet, who was now somewhat calm, still in her mother's arms.

"Sister Violet," he said respectfully, "you saved my life. I am forever at your service."

Violet released herself from her mother and took a few steps towards Daniel. "And you, sir," she said, "saved my life and the lives of my sisters. I am forever at your service."

We all stood there, still and quiet, reveling in the serenity and sincerity of the moment. But alas, urgency was needed.

"Beloved," I said at last, "we must return to the Oasis. In another hour, the Castle will have its service, and I must be there. After the service, we must make drastic plans, for I fear our home is no longer safe. Let us hope I'm wrong, but the enemy may soon be upon our doorsteps. If that happens, may the Great King give us wisdom."

After a hasty return, Nathan and I quickly made our way to the Castle. I posted Justin and Levi halfway between the Castle and the forest in case we needed assistance. I also stationed Jedidiah and Benjamin at the edge of the forest to relay any news. The men of the Oasis were all on the lookout. Tensions were high. Nathan and I entered the building on the northern end therefore avoiding the main hall and the *Act of Tolerance*. I was curious to see what it was but was more purposed to find Judah. I had hoped to find him in the northern entrance where he had been lingering last King's Day. However, I didn't see him until the service began, and he was on the opposite side of the sanctuary. The group began with an introductory song, after which Captain Asa took the stage and was welcomed with applause.

"My friends," he began, "today we make history! The Great King has been turning us away from hatred and towards love, and today is the final step. It is written in the Scroll, *Love your enemy*. Our greatest enemies had always been dragons, and now, they are our friends and allies."

Everyone applauded.

"How can this be anything other than wonderful?" he continued. "It makes all the sense in the world! The Great King begins by saying, *Dragons are the enemy*. Then He says, *Love your enemy*. How complicated is it to see what the Great King ultimately intended? We now see and understand His infinite wisdom and plan. The dragons were never the enemy but were instead the pathway to understanding what the enemy really is. Tell me, army of the Great King, what is the enemy?"

"Intolerance!" everyone shouted.

"Yes!" he said. "And, therefore, what is our main weapon for good?"

"Tolerance!" everyone shouted.

"Yes!" he said. "And today, everyone will see just how tolerant we have become! In the great hall of this castle is a memorial, a place of offering, just like in the temple of the Great King that stood long ago in Salem. Each of you is asked to go and offer a pinch of incense to this memorial. It is not a worship, of course. We only worship the Great King. It is a sign of your tolerance and love for all people, regardless of their choices, allegiance, or lifestyle. We must stop allowing our preferences on certain issues or our lifestyles from dividing us. We must unite under the banner of love!"

Everyone cheered.

"Now," he said, "some have asked, curiously, what happens to those who refuse to show this simple pledge of tolerance. Let us say, simply, that such people are a disease on this earth and that we are the cure."

Everyone cheered, and a new song began, which spoke of the new age of tolerance. I was beside myself, yet understood the fact that when someone compromises the Scroll, the levels of perversion and heresy they attain shouldn't be a surprise. Everyone stood to their feet and began filing into the main hall. I was curious to see this *memorial of tolerance,* but Captain Asa's final words made me all the more eager to get out of there.

"Let's leave while we can," Nathan said, motioning to the northern entrance.

I looked about us and spotted Judah. He was going along with the flow of the crowd, toward the main hall, though I guessed that he didn't want to go that way.

"Let's catch up to Judah first," I said.

Nathan was reluctant but followed my lead. We made our way as best we could toward Judah. I then heard the northern gate lock behind us.

"That's not very reassuring," Nathan said.

"There are many ways out of this castle," I said, trying to comfort my brother.

We were now near to Judah, so as to get his attention. He looked back at us with a look of confusion and concern.

"Why did he come here?" I asked in frustration.

"I'm asking the same question about us," Nathan replied.

We had now entered the main hall and were able to see the monument. I couldn't believe my eyes. I wanted to shout to everyone to stop what they were doing, though I knew that it would do them no good at all.

Chapter 14

Upon the northern side of the main hall, there hung a new banner. It read *Tolerance, love, and freedom for all*. Directly below the banner was the monument. In hindsight, I shouldn't have been surprised by what I saw. I knew that the Castle had been influenced by the world for decades, but now, it was completely taken over. Erected there was a statue of a dragon, looking much like the statue I had seen under the swamps. In front of the dragon was a bowl with a flame smoldering within, where the incense was offered. It was heartbreaking to see.

We had now finally caught up with Judah. "Brother," I said to him, "are you sure you want to do this?"

"No," he replied with fear in his eyes. "I most certainly do not!"

"Then what are you doing here?" I asked, though I knew he could ask us the same question.

"I don't know," he said. "I feel trapped and alone."

"Come with us," Nathan said. "We will teach you how to follow the Great King according to the Scroll. It will cost you everything, but this atrocity will cost you even more."

"I will go with you then," he said, forcing a smile. "But how will we get out of here?"

"We will walk out," I said. "Follow us."

The flow of the crowd was taking everyone to the front of the monument and then swinging them out by the entrance. Taking Judah by the hand, we went against the flow and were soon at the southern entrance. As I suspected, both Eric and Captain Asa where there waiting for us.

"Friends," Captain Asa addressed us, seemingly trying to get the attention of those around us at the same time, "I trust you aren't going to leave without first offering a sign of tolerance."

Nathan and I looked at each other uneasily. Nathan spoke up, "That monument is nothing less than a shrine to the Great Dragon.".

Those around us gasped aloud with offense.

"You see!" Eric said to those around us. "They are intolerant!"

"We are very tolerant!" Nathan argued. "We just won't be forced to do something we don't want to do!"

Captain Asa asked, "But what is wrong with a peaceful and harmless sign of love?".

"This isn't love," I replied. "It's allegiance—allegiance to the Great Dragon. We stay loyal to the Great King."

Captain Asa's expression of love and peace left his face. "You fools!" he said. "You are impossible to talk to! You don't understand the simple truths set before you. You are legalistic, fundamentalists, and haters!"

"We love everyone," I said calmly. "And we therefore tell them the truth."

"Oh, I see," said Captain Asa mockingly. "So, you are the saviors of the people, eh? Are you going to save this man?" he asked, pointing to Judah.

"Only the Great King can save us," I replied. "But I will help this man, as long as he wants it."

"You will only corrupt him," Captain Asa said. "You will make him just as much of a prejudice, judgmental, and phony man as yourself. I can't allow you to do that."

I could see a look of determination and resolution in Captain Asa's face. He had something in mind, and it didn't look good. Everyone present could sense the tension. Nathan pulled on my arm, encouraging me to continue our trek. I understood his mind. We would walk away and hope that nothing further happened.

"Stop!" Captain Asa said in a commanding tone.

We continued. He repeated the words, louder than before, but we didn't obey. I then felt something across my chest. I looked down and saw his sword.

"Not one more step," Asa said crossly.

I looked at him. "That's a bad idea," I said. "Are you sure you want to do that?"

"Why wouldn't I?" he asked mockingly.

"Because it might hurt a bit," I replied in controlled anger.

Nathan put his arm on my shoulder in an effort to calm me.

"I'm determined that you won't leave here until you offer incense," Captain Asa said resolutely.

"That will never happen," Nathan said.

"This is my final..." Captain Asa began, but he was cut short.

"We don't need any final offers," Nathan said firmly, yet gently. "We aren't going to offer incense. Can we leave now?"

Captain Asa hesitated and looked from side to side at the crowd. Then his eyes fixed back upon us, and they were full of darkness and hatred. "No," he said. "You cannot leave."

"And what exactly are you going to do to stop us?" Nathan asked, communicating with his eyes that Captain Asa was making a terrible mistake.

"Me?" he replied. "I won't do anything. But they will."

He then motioned to six dragons that were standing guard directly behind us. Their eyes were fixed on us, and their jaws wide open with anticipation. I looked at Nathan. His eyes were full of a similar aggression to what I felt in my heart.

"Understand," Captain Asa said, "those dragons aren't just dragons. They are my allies. My brothers. If you harm them, then you harm me."

"If you have bound yourself to the enemy, that's your affair," Nathan said. "Those dragons are the enemy. If you've allied with them, then you're making yourself an enemy of the Great King."

"You narrow-minded fools," Captain Asa said. "You'll never understand."

As the conversation was happening, the dragons were creeping closer and closer to us. Scores of people were watching, and they all seemed to be likewise aimed at our destruction.

"I suggest you withdraw your sword and let us pass," I said to Captain Asa.

Two of the dragons had now made their way to our front, blocking us from the path leading away from the Castle. I could see Justin, Benjamin, and Levi beyond us, walking our way, for though they were far off, they could sense what was happening, especially Benjamin.

"Very well," Captain Asa said, removing his sword. "Don't let them leave," he ordered the dragons. "Not until they offer incense."

I looked at the dragon across from me.

"I'm not even going to ask you," I said, putting my hand on my sword. Nathan followed suit. The dragons stood their ground. Simultaneously, Nathan and I unsheathed our swords, and simultaneously, the dragons in front of us fell to the ground lifeless and headless.

Nathan and I then ran, along with Judah, as fast as we could, for we knew we had little hope of fighting off the rest of the dragons without the aid of Justin, Benjamin, and Levi who were now running toward us.

"Keep an eye out for dragon fire!" Nathan said, looking over his shoulder as we ran.

I glanced back and saw nearly a dozen dragons coming after us, though the shock of what we did to their comrades bought us a few precious seconds. I now saw a bolt of lightning fly over our heads from the sword of Justin. It didn't hit an opponent, but it did slow them down. We had now caught up with some of our allies. I looked back, and I couldn't believe what I saw, for there were countless dragons coming after us. It was as if the Castle had been stocked full of dragons for such a time as this.

"We must continue running!" Benjamin said. "Hurry!"

Judah was screaming out loud and frantically running. We were only two hundred yards away from the forest, but I could tell that we wouldn't make it in time. "We will have to turn and fight!" I shouted.

"There are too many!" Nathan objected.

I looked back. They were nearly upon us. I prepared to stop and turn. But then, to my surprise and pleasure, I saw our entire army racing out of the forest to meet the enemy. Elizabeth was running right towards me, her eyes filled with alarm and passion. She suddenly planted her feet, fitted two arrows to her bow, and fired. The two arrows came within inches of either side of my face. I turned back to see them lodged into the eyes of the nearest dragon to me.

"Dragon fire!" Nathan shouted.

We then turned and put up our shields. Captain Samuel came to our side. "All special abilities, use them now!" he shouted.

"Lightning, fire, ice, and intercessory shields all shot out from our forces within the approaching horde. The enemy was now interlaced with us, and there was warfare all around me. Fire, swords, arrows, and claws were clashing everywhere. Slowly, we fought ourselves into the forest, a place which had ironically become more of a refuge for us than for the enemy. The enemy halted at the forest's edge and eventually retreated. I scanned the battlefield. No dead humans—only dead dragons.

"We made it!" I said with a thankful heart. I looked over to find Judah. He was safe but frightened to death. I could understand. He had never seen a battle with the dragons. "You are safe now," I said to him. "And you stayed true to the Great King."

Many were binding their wounds and helping each other. Benjamin was carrying Susanna, the daughter of a noble family from the Oasis; it seemed that he had saved her life. He set her down upon the ground and called Rebekah over to help him tend to her wounds. Rebekah came to his side. I could see, so I thought, a look in Rebekah's eyes, a look of admiration for my son. It wasn't just *any* look; it was *the* look. It was the look that Elizabeth gave to me every day of my life. At the same time, I could also see it in Susanna's eyes, as she looked up at her hero. I then monitored my son. It was clear to me that he was feeling something similar; the question was which of the two ladies did he admire?

I then noticed Elizabeth running towards me, her eyes full of tears.

"What's wrong?" I asked.

"It's Captain Samuel!" she said.

"Is he injured?" I asked.

"No!" she replied. "He's gone! The enemy took him!"

Chapter 15

"What do you mean?" I asked.

"He's gone," Elizabeth said again. "Some of our brethren saw them take him. They've led him away like a criminal."

"Where to?" I asked with fear in my heart.

"I don't know," she said, her eyes downcast. "But I know what they will do to him. I know it in the depths of my being."

"You think the dragons will take him to the swamps to be sacrificed?" I asked.

"No," she replied. "The people will take him to the village square. And then they will do what their wicked hearts' desire."

I quickly started making my way towards the village, though staying near to the forest's edge, and many others followed me. A dark sense of evil seemed to rest all around us. And the closer we came to the village, the feeling heightened. I could now see a mob of people in the village square, though we were too far away to see what was happening.

"We can't all go there," Justin said. "They will surely attack us."

"But we can defeat them," Benjamin said. "We can rescue Captain Samuel."

"Killing humans is forbidden," Nathan said. "We can't go against the Scroll."

"I will go and see what's happening," I said.

"Stay concealed," advised Nathan. "And stay far away from the mob."

Within a moment, I was concealed upon the roof of a barn only fifty yards from the square. All eyes were on what was happening, so it was easy to remain hidden. They had Captain Samuel upon a stage and were surrounding him with sticks and brush. I could scarcely contain myself. Were they really going to burn him alive? There were two dragons which stood to each side of him, as sentinels. I readied myself. I would come to his defense. I would reason with the mob. I opened my mouth, and was just about to shout, when Providence met my eyes with Captain Samuel's.

He was looking right at me. He shook his head, slightly, and I immediately knew his heart. He was telling me to remain concealed. I don't know whether it was reason or the insight of the Spirit of the Great King, but I suddenly understood the situation. Captain Samuel was going to die, and if I tried to save him, I would die as well. The wrath of this mob was unquenchable. I then remembered all I had heard and learned during my time in the enemy's camp. This was their agenda. And who knew how many of their agents were intermingled amongst the people?

Captain Asa now stood upon the stage. "Behold the price of intolerance!" he shouted, and everyone erupted with unquenchable lust for blood. It was as if they were possessed with evil itself. "These people," he continued, "these religious, cultish, legalistic fanatics are the only disease remaining in humanity. And we are the cure!"

Everyone shouted vile words of hatred at Captain Samuel, whose eyes were still fixed upon me.

"Let me now invite up our Administrator of Justice," Captain Asa declared. "I give you, Simon."

Everyone cheered. Simon then ascended the platform and motioned for silence. He addressed Captain Samuel. "You have been accused of intolerance, heresy, and dragon slaying. This court finds you guilty, for the evidence is paramount. Your punishment is death by fire. Do you have any last words?"

I perceived a smile form on Captain Samuel's lips. "I will keep my last words brief," he began, "for I am eager to meet my King. First of all, in keeping with the Scroll, I forgive each of you for the wrongdoing you now commit. I also warn you, in sincere love, of the deceitful path upon which you now travel. Repent, and turn to the Great King, and follow the teachings of the Scroll, that you might not fall into judgment. Lastly, I would address any fellow brother who may now be listening. Stay the course. Don't give up. Never turn aside from the Scroll. The end is near." As Captain Samuel continued, I felt that he was speaking directly to me. "Listen, my son, you will travel, in the end, to your roots. You will know when. That is all I have to say."

Simon motioned to the two dragons, who each took in a deep breath.

Captain Samuel lifted his voice one last time. "All praise, glory, and honor be to His majesty, the Great King!"

No sooner did the words leave his lips than the dragon fire utterly consumed him.

At that moment, only two sounds echoed through the village. The first was the steady sound of dragon fire. The second was the voice of Captain Samuel, crying out in excruciating pain. Just as the dragons ceased their fire, and just when it seemed that Captain Samuel's body was reduced to a pile of bones, his two strong arms shot high into the air and clapped three times. And his voice echoed throughout the village, "Those who follow the Great King will never die!"

His body instantly collapsed into a heap of bones and flesh.

Chapter 16

All was silent in the square. I perceived that some tears were being shed amongst the bystanders. Others nodded in approval.

Captain Asa returned to his place upon the platform. "Behold the price of intolerance!" he shouted, and many cheered with him. "Now," he continued, "shall we end with only this man? At first, I wanted to let this send a simple warning to those who would oppose us. But now, I am persuaded to go the full measure. Why put up with such heresy? Why not extinguish it once for all?"

The crowd had now reverted to a mob and were again hungry for blood.

"My sister," Captain Asa continued, "whom many of you know, has come to us in our time of need. She has informed me that this group meeting in the forest is more dangerous than we had ever imagined. Today they beheaded many of our beloved dragons; tomorrow, it will likely be our children!"

To my horror, I now saw a woman step upon the stage that I never thought I would see again. It was Jade. She was dressed like a member of the Castle and armed with sword and shield.

"Come by, brethren!" she shouted. "You have your weapons with you! Hasn't the Great King equipped you for such a time as this? Come also faithful dragons! We march into the forest to rid it of these infidels!"

I quickly got down off of the barn roof and sprinted to the few brethren who were waiting for me.

"Did you hear that?" I asked with fear in my voice. "They are coming for us! To kill us all!"

"What should we do?" Justin asked, his face full of panic.

I hesitated. Rage began to enter my heart. "We must fight them," I said.

"Fight them?" Nathan repeated. "They are people. That is murder, and it is against the Scroll."

"They threaten our families," I said. "We must protect our beloved. That is not murder. It is defending our families, which is also in alignment with the Scroll."

Nathan hesitated.

"We don't have time for this!" Justin said. "We must do something, now!"

"We must run," Nathan said. "We must leave the Oasis."

In my heart, I knew that Nathan was correct, although I didn't want to admit it.

"Captain Samuel is dead," Nathan said, looking at me. "I leave the decision in your hands, Caleb. The enemy is approaching. Every second counts. Tell us what to do."

I took a deep breath and looked around me. My eyes fixed upon Justin, and I thought back to when we first met.

"Greystone," I said. "We must all flee to Greystone."

"Greystone?" Nathan asked.

"Yes," I said. "It is far from here, but that is the point. It will be far from the enemy. Justin's wife, Joanna, is from there and knows the brethren there."

I then turned to Daniel. "Hurry," I said. "Run to the Oasis and tell all the people to flee down the western path."

I looked to see the mob descending to the forest edge facing the Castle.

"There is no time to waste," I continued. "The mob will be within the Oasis in half an hour. And they have dragons. Tell the people to only take their weapons and Scrolls. There's no time for anything else. We will have to trust the Great King for all other provisions. You must convince them of the urgency, Daniel, and you must lead the women and children down the path. The rest of us will cut through the forest and meet them. At that point, Justin will continue to lead them to Greystone, for he knows the way. The rest of the men will guard the rear end of our people in case we are followed by the enemy. Hurry now, Daniel! Go!"

He was away like lightning.

"And what if the mob follows us down the path?" Benjamin asked. "What if they track us? What will we do then?"

"We will fight them," I said solemnly.

We sprinted into the forest. We knew we could not outrun the enemy to the Oasis; only Daniel could do that. Our goal was to meet with everyone on the western path, which was nothing more than a deer trail that cut across to the open country to the northwest of Ravenhill. We only hoped that Daniel was successful and everyone made it out in time. All of our thoughts were upon our families. The thought of more fire hounds coming upon them made my heart shudder.

"Benjamin," I said, "let me know if our people are endangered."

"Their hearts are anxious," he replied, "but not in peril. I sense that they are already on the move."

As we continued to sprint together in silence, my thoughts turned to Captain Samuel.

I expected myself to be weeping at his loss, but for some reason my eyes were dry. I couldn't explain why, for Captain Samuel had been like a father to me. I began to imagine, however, my wife and children joining him in his fate, and it made my eyes water. I knew that being a martyr for the Great King was the most honorable of all deaths but beholding the death of Samuel left a fear upon my soul.

I then thought of Captain Samuel's final words. He spoke of traveling to my roots. I wondered what that meant. Much had happened in the last week. I had witnessed a man murdered at the hand of someone I knew but couldn't seem to identify. I had also witnessed the sacrifice of an innocent baby. I had rescued and adopted another baby, though at the expense of her mother. I had just witnessed the execution of our eldest captain. And now, we were trying to save our families from blood-thirsty mobs and dragons.

We soon came upon the path.

"How do we know if they've already passed us?" Nathan asked.

"Don't worry," Benjamin replied. "They are near, and unharmed, though their hearts are broken and fearful."

We soon saw them coming, women and children, weeping and frightened. Daniel was at the head of the line, with my wife and daughters behind him.

I embraced my family with a heart of gratitude.

"Is it true?" Elizabeth asked with eyes full of tears. "Is my father dead?"

"Yes," I replied. "I'm so sorry, dear."

She put her head upon my chest and wept.

"It was a good death," I said soberly. "He is a martyr."

I then turned to Daniel. "Hurry, Daniel, and see if the enemy pursues us. I will meet you at the end of the line." Daniel sprinted within the thicket.

"Justin," I said, addressing my old friend, "I have asked you to lead this group, but your blade and ability are too valuable. I need you to come with me."

I then turned to my bride, trying to arouse her from her grief. "Elizabeth, you must lead this line of people. Be strong. Encourage the women. We will send Joanna to help you with the way. We go to Greystone. Be strong."

The men with me and I quickly made our way to the rear of the line of roughly one hundred and twenty people. Daniel and the other men were waiting.

"They are destroying the Oasis," Daniel said, pointing to the billows of smoke that we could see through the leaves of the trees.

"Are they following us?" I asked.

"No," he replied. "They've sent out some scouts in different directions but mostly away from us."

I released a sigh of relief. "The Great King be praised," I said.

I then turned to Justin. "How many days on foot will it take us to reach Greystone?"

"With all of us," he replied thoughtfully, "moving as one, it will likely take us five days."

"Very well," I replied. "There is a creek not too far up the path. We will quench our thirst there. I see that some of the women grabbed water jugs in their haste. This is a blessing. We will need them. After the creek, we must hike on late into the night, to separate as much space between us and the enemy. Tomorrow, we will hunt and forage. For now, speed and secrecy are our main objectives. Men, spread out amongst the line with your family and be ready. Daniel, I am sorry to put this burden upon you, but you are our best scout. I will need continual updates regarding our situation."

By the grace of the Great King, the rest of our journey was uneventful. We found food to nourish our bodies, and the weather was kind. Despite the fact that our homes were destroyed, our hearts were lifted and we pulled closer together. Judah, who had only been among us for a few days, remained very quiet. I wasn't sure if he was glad how things had fared, but I had to trust the Great King, not man. He had chosen to join us, and if he felt otherwise, he was able to leave us if he pleased.

As we traveled along, I opened up to those dearest to me about the last words of Captain Samuel. I recounted that he said I would travel to my roots. What did that mean? Was that what I was doing now? I was going back to Greystone. But those weren't my roots; Ravenhill was. No one seemed to have any answers, and we devoted the matter to much prayer.

We finally camped off of the edges of Greystone. Rising before the sun, with much joy in our hearts, we approached the village. In the black darkness of the early morning, we could see small fires shining through windows and slats in the walls of homes.

"Look, Daddy," Lily said pointing. "There's a Castle over there."

"What do you mean?" I said kindly. "It's nearly pitch-black; none of us can see more than a few yards in any direction."

"I know," she said sweetly. "But I can see it. It's far away, but I can still see it."

Justin and his family were near to us so I asked Joanna about it.

"The girl is correct," Joanna said. "The Castle of Greystone should be about a quarter of a mile that way, upon a hill."

I was shocked. I then remembered Lily's prayer.

"The Great King has heard you," I said with enthusiasm. "You can see in the dark."

My wife and children rejoiced with her. Then a grave notion entered my mind.

"Lily," I said gently. "Do you see anything on top of the Castle?"

She peered into the darkness. "Dragons," she replied. "There are many black dragons. They look like they are sleeping."

Even here, I thought to myself. *Even here the enemy has come.* I expected such happenings in a larger village like Ravenhill, but Greystone was a smaller and more traditional village.

"There are other buildings," she said. "They are very large, but I don't recognize them. They are upon the hill close to the Castle."

"What do they look like?" Benjamin asked his sister.

"One is round, with tall walls. The other, shaped like a crescent moon, with a great platform at its center."

"That's interesting," Nathan said, whose family was traveling near to ours. "I wonder what they are."

His son Levi, who spoke seldom but always with great wisdom, said, "They are an arena and a theater."

"Really?" I marveled. "Do you think so?" I was shocked at this suggestion, for though arenas and theaters were growing more popular, I couldn't imagine that they would have built them in Greystone.

"Does it really surprise you?" Levi asked respectfully. "Dragons are upon the roofs of the Castle. For that to be accomplished, minds must be led astray. The arena and theater are an excellent tool for doing such. They were both built in Ravenhill, and only five years later, the dragons began to perch upon the Castle there."

After another twenty minutes of walking, the day began to shine forth. Our hearts lifted as we saw the quaint homes all nestled together. For me, it was an emotional experience, for there was the home of William, the man who raised me in the latter half of my youth. It had clearly been taken over by another man and was still a blacksmith shop. It had been twenty years since I had seen that village, though it looked almost exactly the same.

Joanna was leading us on our way, holding Justin's hand, with her other hand upon her mouth to silence the mixed emotions that were stirring within her. We clung to the river's edge, and followed it about a quarter mile. We then came to a pile of burnt rubble. We stood there quietly. Finally, I spoke.

"Joanna," I said softly, "what is this place?"

"This is our destination," she said with a pale look upon her face. "This is where the brethren used to train."

"But where are they?" I asked.

"I don't know," she said, her eyes filling with tears. "There are dragons upon the Castle, and this meeting place is in ashes. I'm guessing that our brethren are all dead."

Chapter 17

Our hearts were empty. We stood there, still as statues, for a few moments. Nathan broke the silence, "The day is waking up," he said. "And if the people of this village are as hostile as the mobs of Ravenhill, we are about to find ourselves in the same situation we tried to escape from."

I didn't know what to do. I thought of moving on to another village, but our provisions were low, and none of us knew the way to any other village that was far from Ravenhill. I thought of hiding within the forest, but there was no Oasis filled with homes awaiting us within the forests around Greystone. All eyes were upon me.

"Our situation is dire," I said, "and I know we should be concealed soon from dangerous eyes. But let us first seek the Great King in love and humility."

We clustered together, all embracing, and prayed quietly. We were at the end of ourselves. We were broken. I knew it was right where the Great King wanted us to be. After we prayed, I decided to move us away from Greystone, for even though we were on a far edge of the village, if anyone saw our numbers it would cause alarm and bring us unwanted attention. We had just turned to the west, to quietly make our escape, when I noticed a young boy, likely ten years of age standing directly before us.

He was dressed poorly, his garments dirty and torn. Upon his shoulder was a bag of supplies. He looked at us curiously. I had in mind to simply circle around him, but then he spoke. "What are you doing here?" he asked, with both curiosity and fear mixed together.

I hesitated.

He spoke again. "Who are you? What were you just doing?"

I hesitated once more. I then remembered the lesson I had learned deep within the pits of the enemy: to be honest and to speak without fear. If I was able to be bold in such a place of darkness and evil as the pits of the enemy, couldn't I answer with honesty a child's question?

"We are followers of the Great King," I answered gently. "We were praying."

The boy was quiet for a moment. "Why don't you go and pray in the Castle?" he asked, pointing in the direction of the stone structure to the south.

I chose my words carefully, "We follow the Scroll in a manner that is a bit different than those at the Castle."

"Really?" the boy replied. "How so?"

There I was, leading a band of a hundred and twenty souls, in a foreign land, having a conversation with a boy about the differences between the Castle of men and the Castle of the Great King.

The boy waited patiently for my response.

"We don't conform our beliefs to match that of the ever-changing society around us," I said plainly. The boy looked a bit nervous, which seemed to spread to all of those present.

"Who amongst you wields the sword?" he asked. "And who amongst you wields the bow?"

I looked around me at my brethren and then returned my gaze to the stranger. "Our men wield the sword, and our women wield the bow."

Some kind of realization seemed to come to the lad, for he looked about him uneasily.

"Come," he said with urgency in his voice. "Hurry, before they see you!"

He then turned and ran for the forest that was upon the river's edge.

I looked at those around me with a question of uncertainty.

"We prayed for the Great King to lead us," Benjamin said. "Let us follow the boy."

We quickly hurried after the lad. Daniel asked for permission to run ahead and scout for an ambush. But I bid him stay close to me, for I felt that it was indeed the hand of the Great King leading us.

We followed the boy down many winding trails for nearly half an hour. At last we came to a small opening, only large enough for three tiny cottages all nestled together. A man and a woman were sitting there around a fire and didn't notice us until we were upon the edge of the grove. They sprang to their feet in both fear and amazement. They stood still, their eyes going back and forth from the boy to our assembly. Finally, a voice broke the silence. It was Joanna's.

"Luke! Mary!" she shouted with joy in her voice.

She then ran from among us directly into the strangers' arms. About a dozen others came forth from the huts. They were tattered and torn, but at the same time, the glory of the Great King shone upon their faces. Everyone present now understood the situation. Two fellowships from distant villages had now come together.

We were introduced and many hugs and handshakes were exchanged. I gave a brief explanation as to why we had come and what had happened in Ravenhill.

"Things are no better here," Luke said. "The Castle has abandoned the Scroll, nearly entirely. They began preaching a false message of tolerance for dragons. Their captain, a woman named Jezebel, introduced other teachings that are too shameful to mention."

Many of our fellowship gasped at the mention of a female captain.

"Our fellowship was accused of heresy," Luke continued, "because we wouldn't accept their new teaching. They burned down our meeting place, killed many of our number, and took many others as prisoners."

"Prisoners?" Nathan asked. "Do you know where they are?"

"We don't even know if they are still alive?" Luke replied.

"Well," I said humbly, "we have come to you, without warning and without any real provision. I fear we come as a burden."

"On the contrary," Luke said smiling. "Your coming to us is an answer to our prayers. There are only eighteen of us left here. And our chief captain is quickly fading into the world to come."

"Can you take me to him?" I asked kindly.

I called for Angela, our healer, as well as Rose, for I wanted Rose to be near what may be her ability. Together we went with Luke and Mary into one of the cottages.

An old man, his beard long and white, was lying still upon the bed, awake but unaware of our entrance. Mary sat beside him and got his attention. "Captain John," she said softly, holding his hand, "there are visitors here to see you."

The man seemed to come back to us, as if he had been in a faraway place. He fixed his eyes upon Mary. "Visitors?" he asked. "From where?"

"They are our brethren from Ravenhill." she replied.

"Ravenhill?" he repeated.

I then came forward and introduced myself. He bid me to come to his side. "Captain Caleb," he said. "You are young. Who were your superiors?"

"I was trained under Captains Samuel, Enoch, and Benjamin."

The old man smiled. "My friends of old," he said, closing his eyes as if wanting to dream.

"They all found good deaths," I said.

"Ah," he said. "And death is soon to find me."

"I don't believe so," I said. "I have a sister here with me who is able to heal."

"No healing will happen today," he replied kindly, "at least, not with me. It is my time. You come at the perfect hour, for I feel that the Great King has so ordained this meeting. Listen to me, son. These people here with me are good. They love the Great King. Captain Luke is a good man, but no one man should bear the weight of leadership alone. Please help him. I entrust them into your care. Feed them. Protect them. Love them."

"It will be done," I replied. "I, and the captains with me, together with Captain Luke, will love them as our own. The two flocks have now become one."

The old man smiled.

"Before you depart this world," I said gently, "I have a question for you. Captain Samuel died only a few days ago. He died a martyr of the Great King, murdered at the command of the mobs of Ravenhill, mostly of the Castle."

"Ah, Samuel," Captain John said, his eyes closed with weariness and peace mixed together. "I wish I could have been there to see it. Or better yet, I wish I could have been there dying next to him."

I nodded understandingly and continued, "His final words were directed, I believe, to me. He said that I was to seek out my roots."

At this, Captain John's eyes seemed to look into the world to come, and his countenance was fierce to behold. "Roots," he said stoically. "You must travel to your roots."

He continued on like this for some time. I sensed that he was fading and would soon be gone. All of us who were around his bed waited in eager anticipation for an explanation.

"What does it mean?" I asked.

"I don't know," he said, barely able to whisper. "But I know it is from the Great King. You must find out what it means. There is no doubt that Captain Samuel was speaking to you the very words of the Great King. This is a message not just for you but for all our people."

"How do I find out what it means?" I asked desperately.

"Eli," he said calmly. "You must seek out Eli. Captain Luke knows where to find him. He will know. He is the wisest of all who remain upon this earth."

Captain John then looked at both me and Captain Luke and smiled with a face full of joy. "I go now to my final home," he said softly. "Show yourselves to be men, my dear sons. The time for courage and faith is now. I bid you farewell. All praise and glory be to the one Great King."

He closed his eyes and was gone.

Mary fell on her knees beside him and wept. I kissed him upon his brow and prayed the Great King receive him. I then stood and spoke to Captain Luke, "I am with you, my brother."

"And I with you," he replied. "You need to know where to find Eli. I know where he dwells. It is far from here."

I paused and considered all that was before me. I was certain that the Great King was paving a way for me to receive His truth and that Eli was the final step. But there was great need all around me. "I thank you," I said to Captain Luke. "But my journey to see Eli will have to wait. There is much to be done here."

"What is that?" he asked eagerly.

"We must build up this place to be a dwelling for our people. This will be our New Oasis. Your people are famished and cold. Together, we will bring the light and provision of the Great King to this place."

Captain Luke's eyes teared with gratitude.

"And there is one more thing," I said. "The prisoners that were taken. Where are they?"

"We have no idea," he replied. "If they are still alive, they are locked up somewhere."

"Not for long," I said confidently. "We're going to get them back."

Chapter 18

"Do I have your permission to lead these people?" I asked Captain Luke with much respect.

He smiled. "You have full liberty, my friend. We are with you."

I exited the small hut and addressed all the brethren, "Captain John has passed on to the life to come. We honor him, and tonight, he will be buried and our prayers will go with him. Captain Luke will see to this noble task. The two groups which have met today are now one. We are united in vision and purpose, under the leadership of the Great King. Our first task is to secure this location and make it capable of suiting our needs. The work before us is a hard one but very rewarding. All men come forth."

I divided the men into three units. One for clearing trees. The second for turning those trees into usable lumber. The third for hunting. The women immediately began to help lay out the New Oasis, forage for food, and prepare places for cooking and washing.

We buried Captain John at sundown. All mourned his loss, but at the same time celebrated his life. Before we were dismissed, Captain Luke encouraged the brethren, "Those of us who have dwelt in Greystone owe much to this man we bury today. We would not be who we are without him. He devoted his life to the ways of the Scroll and stood up for what was right. Such great men do not appear out of thin air; they are made. There are sons gathered here who will one day be such men, if we form them to be so. There are daughters here who will one day stand beside such men, if we help them to do so. Captain John's favorite saying was this: *Stay close to the Scroll.* Let us continue that legacy, so that the leaders of tomorrow will be there when we need them."

Upon daybreak the following morning, we continued our work. The women began constructing gardens and planting them. A small creek ran near that place, but I also decided to task some men with digging a well. Within a few days, the area was transformed, and we all anticipated that in only a few days more, we would all be in cozy homes, enjoying the peace that comes with such blessed community.

In addition to building our dwelling, we also resumed our training. Captain Luke was a gifted teacher, and together, our two bands of soldiers quickly learned to fight as one. Judah also began his training, and we were happy to have him. He was about thirty-five years of age and quickly bonded with my son, Benjamin. This made me glad, for Benjamin needed someone to mentor. He was at the perfect age to do so, and Judah gave him the opportunity.

I commissioned my son, along with Daniel and Levi, with the task of going into the village to try to discover what had become of our captive brethren. I chose them according to their abilities. Daniel would be able to relay to us any messages. Benjamin would sense if fear came near to us. And Levi could discern truth and error in any testimony they received from others. I didn't dare send Captain Luke or any others who were from that village, for they were known to all as being heretics.

Upon our fourth day of being there, about midmorning, I was eating a late breakfast with my wife and daughters when Lily spoke up.

"Why is it wrong for the captain of the Castle to be a woman?" she asked, in her innocent and sweet tone. "I know it's wrong, but I don't understand why."

"It's really simple," Violet said with a smile, excited to educate her dear sister. "The Great King created both male and female with different purposes and callings, and with those are different strengths for the tasks before them. Men were created to lead. They are called to lead society, the Castle, and the family. This is why Father is the head of our family. Women, in comparison, were created to be a helper to man. So, when you get married someday, your husband will be the head of your family, and you will be his helper, just like Mother is a helper to Father."

"Does that mean you will be Daniel's helper?" Lily asked.

"Lily!" Rose said with frustration and embarrassment. "You can't say that."

"It's alright," Violet said, as she smiled and blushed. "Now," she continued, "this is why it is inappropriate for a woman to be the captain of a Castle. It isn't because she isn't capable or smart enough. It is simply out of order. If a woman is to lead the Castle, it will make women question their roles as wives and mothers and helpers. And this is why many families within the Castle are falling apart. They don't understand that attached to gender is a purpose. They don't understand that the Scroll addresses all of these questions and must therefore be obeyed with all due diligence."

I listened to my daughters with exalted joy. I couldn't think of much else that brought me such jubilation as listening to my children explain the ways of the Great King with respect and truth. To see your children equipped to defend their faith, and to do so with confidence, is indeed one of the greatest gifts the Great King gives to parents.

"Very well said," my wife commented, who was also delighted at her daughter's words. "The questions that distinguish us from the Castle are these: *Does the Great King call us to live however we want to, just so long as we love Him? Or does He have commands for every area of our life?* The modern Castle thinks that as long as you claim allegiance to the Great King, it really doesn't matter how you do things. If you think the woman should be the head, that's alright. If you think that your children should be separated from you during the gathering of the army, that's alright as well.

We, however, answer differently. We believe that the Great King has given us principles and precepts that are to be followed in every area of our life. He doesn't tell us to do as we please. He instead says, *This is how you are to worship Me and be a family and be My Castle.* This one simple distinction is really the foundation of all our differences. The modern Castle sees the Scroll as dealing with only certain specific areas of life, whereas we believe the Scroll speaks to every area of life."

"Amen," I said graciously. "Your mother is teaching you the doctrine of the Sufficiency of the Scroll. We believe that the Scroll is sufficient to teach us everything we need to know. We don't need the opinions of men, or the latest cultural shift, to know how to live. We have the Scroll."

While we were still speaking, Nathan and Luke approached. Benjamin, Daniel, and Levi were with them.

"Forgive the intrusion," Nathan said, "but our scouts have news."

"We have found the prisoners," Benjamin said. "There are five of them, three men and two women, and one is with child. They are being held in a small prison on the northern edge of town."

"Is the prison heavily fortified? Is it guarded?" I asked, eager for good news.

"It is very heavily fortified," Levi said sadly, "with both dragons and men."

"The dragons don't bother me," I said as I stood to my feet. "It is the question of the men that brings me concern."

"You know my view," Nathan said. "We cannot shed the blood of men, only of dragons."

"Yes," I said gravely. "I know your view, my dearest brother, and you are likely correct. But these tyrants came and took our brethren away from us."

"We must trust in the providence of the Great King," Nathan said.

"True," I agreed, "but the ways of the Great King are often unsearchable. Perhaps, instead of an all-out offensive, we could send in only a few men for a secret rescue."

"That will be difficult," Benjamin said solemnly. "Time is against us."

"What do you mean?" I asked.

"They are scheduled to be executed at dawn," he replied.

Chapter 19

Immediately as the words were said, Captain Luke left us weeping. We stood quiet and unsure of what to do.

"There must be a way," I said at last. "We have to save them."

"I fear we can't," Levi replied. "The people expect an attempt to be made, and so they have taken all necessary precautions. If we all marched out, I think we would have a chance, but it would require the deaths of many villagers as well as many of our brethren."

I stood still in frustration and helplessness.

"There is one thing we can do," Benjamin said. "We met a man who works in the prison who said that he would allow a time of visitation for any loved ones of the prisoners."

"Can this man be trusted?" I asked Levi.

"Yes," he said confidently. "He spoke the truth. It would need to happen tonight though, under the cover of shadow, for the other guards cannot be trusted."

I was unsure of what to make of the situation. The thought of going to my brethren who were imprisoned, and be able to reach out and embrace them, and yet not be able to free them, made no sense to me at all. Captain Luke had now returned with his wife Mary and was asking Daniel questions about all that was being said.

"I don't know," Nathan said to me. "I trust my son's ability, but the situation is still too dangerous. We would be risking our lives with no guarantee of saving theirs."

Captain Luke then approached us. "I have just been informed of the situation," he said, "and I'm going to see my brethren."

"You can't," Nathan said to him. "The guards will recognize you and likely kill you on the spot."

"I will travel concealed then," he said resolutely. "And my wife is coming with me. We must comfort our brethren."

I could tell that Captain Luke would not be persuaded otherwise. Within an hour, Levi had found a villager with a wagon of hay in which to conceal Captain Luke and Mary. "This villager will deliver Captain Luke and Mary to the prison at the correct time," Levi assured. "He will not betray them. But I will go; for this to work, the timing must be perfect."

"You are a brave soldier," I said to Levi, "made in your father's image. But I ask you to let me go instead. Even though it would be safer for my people for me to stay here, I feel like the Great King desires that I do this."

I said farewell to my family, and many tears were shed. Many men, including my son, wanted to come with me, but I would not add to our risk of loss. I gave instructions to Nathan and Justin and began my journey. It was by now midafternoon, only a few hours before dusk. I concealed both Captain Luke and Mary in the hay and took my seat next to the conductor of the wagon.

"What is your name?" I asked the man.

"I am Robert," the man replied. He was an older man, around fifty or sixty years old.

I looked at him and then took another glance.

"Robert?" I asked, digging into my memory. "I know you, sir. For I lived here, twenty years ago, and worked for William. I delivered nails to your business if I remember correctly."

"Nails?" the man repeated. "You are the young man who worked for William the blacksmith, then. I remember you. The last time I saw you, we were fighting the Northmen during their raid that one fateful evening when William was murdered."

"I left the very next day," I said. "It is good to see you, sir. How are you?"

"Oh, as well as I can be, I suppose," he replied. "I don't do much these days. Don't have any family really to speak of. Just living life day to day."

"Are you a member of the Castle?" I asked.

"No," he replied. "I've never really gotten into that stuff that much. They say they've tamed dragons, and that is all fine with me, as long as the beasts stay away from my home. They seem to hate the people you are with, and I don't really see why, but I kind of stay to myself and stay out of such affairs. Things are changing though, that's for sure. People are changing. Children are different. When I was young, the word *youngling* didn't exist. Families seem to be different too. Not as many people are getting married these days, neither are they having children. These are different times. I really don't understand it, but like I said, I just stay to myself and mind my own business."

"You are very observant," I said kindly. "Allow me, if you would, to explain to you briefly how things have changed."

"As you wish," Robert said curiously.

"Look over there," I said, pointing to the arena and the theater. "You see those buildings? Those weren't here twenty years ago."

"That's true," he said. "They seem to be popping up in every village as of late, so I hear."

"And it's not by accident," I said. "There is a battle of ideas going on in this world, and those two buildings are often tools of the enemy."

"Really?" he said, surprised at my words. "But they're only places for games and plays!"

"Plays which are written by whom?" I asked.

Robert thought for a moment. "I have no idea," he said.

"Most people, likewise, also have no idea," I said. "They are entertaining plays with wrong ideas interlaced within them. Trust me. I've been deep within the camps of the ones who write them. They have an agenda. They want to destroy things like marriage, purity, masculinity and femininity, the family, as well as the Scroll. They chip away, bit by bit, at these resolves until they are no more."

"Well," said Robert in deep thought, "that actually makes sense. I've been to a few of the plays, and I noticed that there were some bad things displayed. I think, though, that most of us excuse it because the rest of the play is so entertaining. But what about the arena? What's wrong with playing games?"

"There's nothing wrong with games, in and of themselves," I said cheerfully. "Just like there's nothing wrong with the idea of entertaining people. It's a matter, however, of content, time, and focus. Regarding the games, they begin being seldom and small, but eventually they overtake everything. I saw it in Ravenhill. At first, the games were once a month or so, and the athletes only practiced a little. But then, because of the demands of the crowd and oftentimes because of pride and selfishness, the games took over people's lives and families. People literally devoted the majority of their time to mere games. Not only that, but the games became more violent. They awoke within people a deep and hidden lust. And when lust is mixed with pride, bad things happen.

"And so, through these two institutions, children became consumed with the things of the world. The Great King and the family no longer had any place in their daily lives. The meal table, for example, which for centuries was a daily place of family interaction, was by and large abandoned. No one cares about families eating together anymore. But they care very much about games. The Castle, likewise, conformed to this pattern, just as they had with the local schoolhouses. Now, when the Castle gathers, they separate their children from the parents, just like in the schoolhouses. They entertain the assembly, just like in the theater. And after the meeting, everyone hurries to the arena to watch their favorite idols perform.

"So to finish my brief explanation," I concluded. "Family was no longer able to function and flourish as it was designed to. This led to a new generation which saw no use for either marriage or children. All they want to do is serve themselves."

Robert listened patiently and remained quiet for some time after I had finished speaking. I had learned to not be afraid of silence. Twenty years earlier, I was on a similar wagon with Justin. He was the one talking while I was being quiet. And in the midst of that silence, I had decided to follow the Great King.

"You've definitely given me much to ponder," he said with much contemplation. "More than you know."

Darkness was creeping in around us, and we had now reached the prison. There were many soldiers camped there, roughly sixty. Fortunately, the few dragons who were stationed there were curled up in giant heaps sleeping. I asked for a man named Mark, who was summoned.

"I'm a friend to Levi," I said softly, "whom you spoke with earlier."

"Of course," Mark said. "Looking about him a bit uneasily. Is it just the two of you?"

"No," I replied. "There are two who are concealed in the hay."

Mark nodded and led us around the corner of a stone wall where we were more hidden. The only light now that shone around us were those of torches and the dim starlight shining down from on high.

Mark looked about him. "It is the perfect time," he said. "Get your two friends and follow me."

I quickly hopped down from the wagon and removed Captain Luke and Mary from the wagon. We dusted the hay from them and hastened after Mark, as Robert remained still and quiet upon his wagon. We followed Mark down a short hallway and came to a middle-sized cell which concealed the five individuals, two women and three men.

"Captain Luke!" one of women exclaimed.

"Quiet down," Mark said sternly. "You have five minutes. That's all."

I then thought of the wagon and the hay. "Mark," I said, "you're obviously doing this because you have a good heart. Couldn't we hide them in the hay, just as I did this man and his wife? Couldn't they escape?"

Mark's face became angry. "Don't act like you know me or anything about me," he said sternly. "The soldiers will check that cart when it leaves. Besides, if the prisoners are missing, it will be the heads of me and my men. You have four and a half minutes left. Now see to it, and leave me alone."

Captain Luke and his wife were embracing their beloved through the bars of the cells and weeping. Another cry was then heard. It was the cry of a baby.

"What is that?" Captain Luke asked.

One of the women, a young girl named Joy, had been lying in the corner. What we hadn't seen, was the young infant wrapped in cloth lying next to her.

"Joy!" Mary exclaimed as quietly as she could. "Your baby has come!"

"Only an hour ago," a man named Paul said.

"For pity's sake," I said to Mark, "please let us at least take the baby."

Mark stood in thought. "The new talk, as of late," he said, seemingly thinking out loud, "is that these babies aren't really people until they grow up a bit." My heart sunk with these words. Mark then looked at the infant. "But I don't buy it," he said resolutely. He nodded, and Paul and the other woman named Abigail prepared the baby to come with us.

"Farewell," Joy said to her baby boy, with tears flowing down her cheeks. "I will see you another day. Until then, live for us both."

119

She then looked at Mary. "Name him Titus, after his father, whose death only a few weeks ago, has given me the courage to endure all this."

Mary received the baby and held him close. I had hastily been introduced to everyone, and they were all told about our coming, for which they rejoiced.

"I'm so sorry," I said to them, weeping slightly, "that I couldn't save you."

"Don't fret, my brother," Abigail said with sincere contentment upon her face. "The Great King is with us, and He has called us to this task, and we embrace it freely."

Mark scoffed. "Hmph. Really?" He then looked at Joy, still laying upon the hard-stone floor. "You have suffered this evening in childbirth. Are you now ready to suffer more in the morning?"

"What I suffered this day was because of the curse given upon my gender through the fall of our first parents," Joy replied. "What I suffer tomorrow in the arena will be because of my love for the Great King."

"Suffer?" I said. "Arena? I thought they were to be beheaded!"

"They chose instead to feed us to wild beasts in the arena," Paul said with a courage unimaginable. "The crowds desire blood, so they will get it."

"No," Captain Luke said. "This cannot be."

"Don't worry, our dear captain," Abigail said. "We will endure. You have taught us well."

Captain Luke looked at his wife, and they nodded to each other. "This only reinforces what we have already decided," he said. He then turned to Mark, "Open this prison door, please."

Mark put his hand on his sword. "You dare try to rescue them?"

"No," Captain Luke said smiling. "We aren't going to rescue them. We're going to join them."

Chapter 20

"What?!" I exclaimed, taken back at Captain Luke's words. "You can't do this!"

"We can and we will," Captain Luke said resolutely. He then turned back to Mark. "In the name of the Great King, I command you to open this cell, and let both me and my wife enter."

To my amazement, Mark did so without hesitation.

"But what of the baby?" I asked.

"He will go with you," Mary said, handing me the infant. "Deliver this baby to Joanna."

"Joanna!" Joy said with amazement. "Of course. She's back from Ravenhill. Oh, how I love her. Please tell her that my son is now her son."

Captain Luke and Mary entered the prison, and the door was shut. I stood there, baby Titus in my arms with both shock and amazement on my face.

"Why do you look so surprised?" Captain Luke said with a smile. "These are our sheep, and we were commanded to feed them and care for them. You yourself said, this very morning, that the ways of the Great King are higher than our ways. This is

His way. Farewell, Captain Caleb. It has been such a joy to know you. You now return to your people and I to mine, to see them through this task, until the end. Don't come and watch us in the arena. Don't try to save us. Only remember us. We go to the Great King. We deposit this little life, Titus, into the world. Justin and Joanna will raise him in the light. May he live according to the courage of his mother and father."

"Times up," Mark said. And as he did so, his voice cracked slightly.

I returned to Robert and took my seat beside him in the cart, the baby Titus concealed under my cloak. We easily made it through the guard check, as they only prodded our cargo and did not examine us. We rode in the darkness of the night in silence. I cradled baby Titus in my hands—the newborn life that would never feel his mother's embrace again.

"Are you alright?" Robert asked gently.

"I am more than alright," I said quietly. "I am amazed by the majesty of the Great King, which He demonstrates in the faithfulness of His chosen ones."

We returned to the edge of the forest where Daniel, Levi, and Benjamin were waiting for us. I gently lowered myself to the ground with Titus in my arms.

"Caleb," Robert said solemnly, "I didn't ask about what happened to the man and woman you brought with us because I knew when I first saw them what they had in mind. I didn't know Luke well, but I knew he was a good man. I wonder if I might come back tomorrow and visit, maybe even stay with your people."

"Dear Robert," I said sincerely, "if you embrace the Great King and His Scroll, then you are one of our people, and we welcome you with all sincerity."

I returned to the New Oasis and relayed all that happened to the people, and many wept. Justin and Joanna humbly and gladly received Titus, and the following day was devoted to prayer and mourning for our comrades. The following week was one of continued efforts for building our dwelling, and soon, all was finished. Our normal way of life seemed to be resuming.

One evening as we were dining together as a family, with Judah attending, my wife shared a wonderful announcement. "It has pleased the Great King to give us another child," she said. "I am pregnant, and we will see if my prophecy is true, but I'm convinced it is a son."

I was overjoyed, for I would now be the father of seven children. Baby Rachel and this baby would be less than a year apart. This was a special blessing, and we praised the Great King all the more.

"The Scroll says that children are a blessing from the Great King," I taught my children that evening. "And that is what each of you are: a blessing. Your mother and I wouldn't trade any of you for all the gold in the world. Learn from us. Obey us, and you will be blessed. Remember, your life purpose is defined for you in the Scroll, and it is three-fold. First, to be in covenant with the Great King. Second, to marry and fulfill your marital duties as described in the Scroll. And third, to parent your child in the ways of the Great King."

I then addressed each of my daughters. "Somewhere out there is your husband," I said. "You will complete him. You will be his most precious and desirable treasure. Of all he has, he will give thanks most for you. You will find your true fulfillment in devoting your life to the plans and purposes of your husband. The Great King will give him a vision. You are his number one helper for fulfilling that vision."

I then turned to my son. "Somewhere out there, my son, is your wife. She is waiting for you, thinking of you, and longing for you." As I said this, my wife smiled at my words. "You must prepare yourself for her," I continued. "You must become the man that the Great King desires you to be, a man worthy of your wife. You must be strong for her. You must love her, serve her, and listen to her. Follow her wisdom, for she will help you. You must lead your children also. Teach them. Spend ample amounts of time with them, always trying to have them with you."

"You have been a wonderful example to me, Father," Benjamin said. "I'm excited to have a family of my own someday; soon I hope."

I then turned my attention to Judah. "All of this also applies to you, Judah. Continue your training. Continue to study and follow the Scroll, and the Great King will supply all of your needs."

Judah bowed his head humbly. "I thank you for your wisdom," he said. "How did you know?" he continued. "How did you know that your wife was the one?"

"That's a good question," I replied. "There is much to our story but suffice it to say this: I knew I wanted to marry her because I didn't want to live life without her. It's actually easier than you might think. You marry your best friend. You find a woman that loves the Great King and loves the Scroll and who has similar convictions. And if the Great King brings your hearts together, and if you find yourself captivated by her, then she's the one."

"And when did you find yourself captivated by your wife?" Judah asked, seemingly fascinated by the topic.

I turned to my wife with a smile, and she returned the same. "As a child, she already had my heart," I said. "Then, when I first beheld her as a young woman, she stole my heart again. Once I saw her—though I didn't know it was her at the time—kill a baby dragon, and even then, I was completely captivated by her."

"You saw her kill a baby dragon, and you didn't know it was her?" Judah asked, his face lighting up with wonder.

"Yes," I replied. "There were five younglings from the Castle. Well, some of them were from the Castle. And as I was spying upon them, a stranger in a hood crept forward and shot the dragon through the neck. It turned out to be my Elizabeth."

"Is it really that simple, Father?" Benjamin asked. "You find a girl of like-mindedness, who loves the Scroll, and if you are captivated by her, then she is the one?"

"More or less," I replied. "But don't forget what I've told you and your sisters about the necessary steps in that discovery. The parents have a key role, and prayer is essential."

Benjamin smiled and nodded his head, and I wondered which woman was occupying his thoughts.

I then dismissed my children. My girls went to spending time with Rachel, who had just awoken from her nap. Benjamin and Judah began a chess match, as had quickly become their custom. This left me free for time alone with my bride.

"A son?" I asked hopefully.

"I am sure of it," she said, a tear coming to her eye. "It is a son to replace Isaiah."

I put my arm around her. "Isaiah could never be replaced," I said gently.

"You know what I mean," she replied. "It's just that, I miss him so much."

"I miss him too," I said. "We all do."

"He would be sixteen years old," I continued. "A grown man. I miss him dearly."

"Tell me again," Elizabeth said in a whisper, so soft that I could barely hear her. "Tell me again why the Great King took him away from us."

"I don't know why He took him away," I replied. "But I know that the Great King loved our son, and I know that He is good."

"Amen," she said, encouraged at the sovereignty of our King. "It was a good death."

"It was indeed," I agreed. "It has given all the young men amongst our brethren an example to follow."

Elizabeth then turned to me, wiped the tears from her cheeks and looked into my eyes. "So much has happened as of late, and so quickly, that I haven't had the chance to tell you how proud I am of you. On the day that my father Samuel died, you became the leader of our people. Now you have another tribe upon the death of Captain Luke. They all will look to you now more than any other."

"I don't think I'm ready," I said, overwhelmed at the responsibility.

My wife smiled. "You are more than ready," she said. "You've already been an amazing leader. You rescued us all from the enemy in Ravenhill. Led us to this place. Brought back Titus to live and grow strong. The Great King is with you."

"I will give it everything I have," I said humbly. "I only hope I do well, especially as a father."

"You are a wonderful father," Elizabeth said, "and an amazing husband."

"I hope so," I said. "I just want to see them all follow the Great King, marry well, and then raise up our offspring in the ways of the Scroll."

"The Great King is with us," she said. "They will marry well and walk in His ways. Violet seems destined for Daniel, a wonderful man of Scroll vision."

"Indeed," I agreed and then hesitated. "I believe that our son will also soon marry."

"Really?" she said. "To whom?"

"I'm not sure," I replied. "I think it might be either Susanna or Rebekah."

"Hmmm," my wife replied thoughtfully. "They are both wonderful girls, very like-minded to our family. I will speak to Violet later this evening about it. She knows both Susanna and Rebekah well. We will gain much by her insight. We must remain diligent in prayer, both for Benjamin and for Violet. When do you think you will allow Daniel to marry her?"

"Soon, I believe, though it is a strange feeling. I've always longed for the day to see my eldest daughter united with a man of the Scroll. But now, the thought of her not being here when I rise in the morning or around my table in the evening is difficult for me. My heart is filled with joy for her and with sadness for me at the same time."

My wife caressed me gently. "I know how you feel. But try to picture the joy upon her face as we visit her in her new home. And imagine she and Daniel and their children coming to visit, and the children sitting around their grandfather, hearing his words of wisdom. Imagine your children's children slaying their first dragon."

My heart was stirred at my wife's words, and I looked at her with much love and appreciation. She had always been a rock for me, a constant source of provision and confidence.

"Yes," I agreed. "That stirs my soul. It is time for her and Daniel to become one. But first, I need his assistance on a vital mission. Our people are here and safe, and all is in order. It is time for me to seek out Eli."

"Eli," my wife repeated. "I've heard of him, but the reports I've heard make me frightened at the idea."

"He trained Captain Enoch, long ago," I replied, trying to encourage her. "That should count for something."

"But last I heard, he is no longer with his people."

"That is true," I said. "He is exiled on an island."

"An island? Caleb, the sea is dangerous. There are dragons in those waters that we have never had to face here. They are an entirely different breed and are said to be more lethal than black dragons."

I held my wife close to my chest. "I'm certain, my love, that it's the only way."

Chapter 21

The following morning, I arose with the sun. Nathan was waiting, for we were still discussing who should come with me. In the end, we decided that he and Jedidiah should stay to lead and protect the people. Even though I understood the need for this, I was grieved to not have them with me. The warriors who would accompany me would be Justin, Benjamin, Levi, and Daniel.

Benjamin and I were outside our home preparing and packing our provision when Susanna approached us. I remained where I was, pretending to be preoccupied with what I was doing, for I desired very much to hear her interaction with my son.

"Farewell, Benjamin," she said. "I brought you some food for your journey. A few small cakes of figs and raisins."

"Thank you," my son replied kindly. "They will be a nice treat along the way."

"Do you know how long you will be gone?" she asked.

"Unfortunately not," he said. "Though I hope it isn't too long."

"Well," Susanna replied, "you will be missed. Farewell."

"Farewell," he replied and watched her walk away.

My son returned to where I was with a thoughtful expression upon his face.

"Susanna is a good girl," I said, trying to get him to share his feelings.

"She is," he replied, "a very good girl."

I then noticed Rebekah coming to us, her modest form pushing aside the morning mist.

"It seems you have more than one good girl coming to see you," I said quietly with a smile.

Benjamin put down the provisions he had just received from Susanna and went to greet Rebekah, who received him with a humble bow.

"Forgive me," she began. "I know you are busy with preparations for your journey. I just wanted to let you know that my family and I will be praying for you every day."

"Thank you," my son replied.

"I also brought you this," she continued, handing him as embroidered piece of cloth. "It reads, *Though a thousand come upon you, they will not harm you.* It is from the Scroll."

"Did you make this?" Benjamin asked.

"Yes, sir," she replied gently.

"It is lovely," he said.

"Thank you kindly," she replied, and bowing low, turned to leave.

"Sister," my son called to her, "I have hope that I will return."

"I have no doubt of that, brother," she replied. "You are an exceptional warrior, Benjamin. Even the mightiest serpent of the sea will be no match for you."

Rebekah bowed once again and turned away. My son turned back to the house, and coming near me, picked up both his gifts: cakes in one hand and a Scroll cloth in the other. I was greatly impressed by both ladies and prayed that the Great King would lead my son's heart.

Elizabeth and my daughters said farewell to us one last time before we left.

"Father," Violet said. "Are you sure I can't come with you?"

129

"I am sorry," I said to her. "You would be a great addition, but everything has been decided."

"Please tell Daniel," she said, "that my heart goes with him."

"I will," I said kindly. "And you may be assured," I said with a smile, "that on our return, your heart and his will soon become one."

Violet gasped, and tears came to her eyes instantly. She threw her arms around me.

"Thank you, Father!" she said. "Thank you so much!"

I held her close and gave thanks to the Great King as the other sisters also embraced her.

"Please be careful," Elizabeth said. "I have grown accustomed to you fighting dragons in the forest but not in the waters."

"I know," I replied. "But remember what the Scroll says: *When you pass through the waters, I will be with you.* You also take care. Nathan will look out for you, but be on the lookout none the less. These are evil times."

My ladies embraced their two men, and together we prayed. My company then departed. Nathan walked with us for the first hour.

"Farewell," he said at last. "Daniel knows the way. I hope that you find the meaning to Captain Samuel's riddle."

"We will," I replied, "if it pleases the Great King. We must. For I believe that without it, we will fail to find the will of our King."

"And what if we are attacked?" Nathan asked. "What then? Aggression for our people seems to build within the Castle and the village every day. The people are hungrier than ever for blood."

"You will have to decide how to face such circumstances," I replied. "Whether you stand and fight, or run and hide. If something does happen, Benjamin will sense it and we will hasten our return and find you. Be strong, brother. I put our people, and my family, in your hands."

We prayed and parted ways. It was a five-day trek through the forest to the sea, and we didn't know what dangers would await us as we traveled. We were now going to places I had never been to. Fortunately, Daniel had scouted out much of the area before, and so I sent him ahead to warn us of any danger.

As the four of us walked along, I visited with my son. "That was kind of Susanna and Rebekah to bid you farewell," I said.

"It was," he agreed. We continued to walk in silence for some time. I waited, for I knew that his mind was busy at work.

"Father?" he said after much thought. "Is it possible for you to feel strongly for two people at the same time?"

"It is," I replied. "There are many loveable people in our community. Indeed, I love them all. But there is a part of your heart that is reserved for only one woman. The kind of love that a husband is supposed to have for his wife is a love that can only be given to one woman."

He was quiet for a time, then spoke again. "Do you know why I asked you that question?"

"I think so," I replied thoughtfully. "You are like a man trying to choose between two swords. They are both incredible and skilled in the making, yet you can only wield one. You must choose, and yet, you feel like you can't, for they are both so wonderful."

"Exactly," he said. "That is how I feel, though, deep down I think I know."

"Then you must seek confirmation," I began. "You must try to discern which one fits you best. You are pulled to both because of their beauty, personality, and kindness, but what about their hearts? Which heart attaches with your heart? That's the question you need to answer. Your mother and I are praying for you."

"I know what the proper steps are," he said. "Do you approve of the options set before me? For if you didn't approve of one of them, it would be the confirmation I seek."

"Your mother and I approve of both ladies," I said. "Though I must agree, I believe that you know which one is for you, just like you said a moment ago. The reality that is confusing you is that in order to say *yes* to one girl, you must say *no* to another. And to say *no* to such a wonderful girl makes you feel guilty. Don't let this trouble you, my son. You must trust in the Great King. He will take care of His daughters."

"My mind is becoming clearer," Benjamin said.

Levi and Justin were able to hear our conversation. Levi, who had recently married, joined in.

"Forgive me for intruding," he said, "but allow me to add this to the discussion and give my dearest friend counsel. When considering a wife, you mustn't let outward beauty persuade you, for it is fleeting. The main issue is simple: *Does she love the Great King with an undying love?* In addition, *Does she consult the Scroll in every area of her life?* This is what you must focus upon, for she will become not only your wife but also the mother of your children. What kind of mother do you want your children to have? One who is beautiful, or one who holds to the Scroll?"

"How about both?" Benjamin jested, and we all laughed together.

The rest of our journey to the northern shores was uneventful, with the exception of a few red dragons we encountered. They were formidable foes, but our combined skill was no match for them. A warrior should never travel alone. Upon our fifth day of our expedition, we exited the forest and looked upon the rich and fertile coastlands of the north. There was a village there, and we sought out boatmen who would help us cross the waters to the island we sought.

I noticed, as we entered the village, that the agenda of the enemy had already permeated that place. The men seemed to be lazy and disconnected with their families. Many of the young people were walking about, treating others as only spouses should, yet shamefully. Immodesty was normative. We even saw people of the same gender acting as if they were one. The darkness was so thick that I felt I could cut into it with my blade.

"Caleb," Justin said, his voice trembling, "the teaching you told us about, which you learned of in the pit of the enemy, it must have been implemented here. They have been convinced of a different history. How else could such darkness exist?"

"This is true," Levi commented. "One must put the Great King out of their mind to embrace such treachery."

We quickly found a dock and spoke to the chief boatman. "A prophet?" he said. "On an island? Ha! More like a crazy man he is. Around here, he is simply known as the Exile. He was banished to a small island, about a day's sail away. Not sure how many years he's been out there now; actually, I'm not even sure if he's alive. But you'd have to be as crazy as him to try to go there. Leaving the inner bay is a death wish. Too many sea-serpents out there."

"We have silver pieces," I said. "It should be enough for a good boat and a master to sail it."

The man looked at our silver and scratched his head. "I think I have a mate who will be willing, but I'll only be willing to give you my worst boat. It will float, but I ain't willing to watch one of my chief boats sink to the bottom of the sea."

The next morning, we set out. Our guide was a man named Ishmael, who seemed to be a very quiet and hardened man. He was likely fifty years of age, though, I thought that his appearance might be due to hardship instead of years. Our vessel was beaten and aged by the sun but seemed sufficient. It was about twenty feet in length and had only a small compartment in the hull for any storage or shelter. Upon the front part of the boat was some kind of weapon, resembling a giant crossbow. For all of my companions and me, it was our first time upon any body of water. Fortunately, the sea was calm and the winds pleasant.

"This is wonderful," Justin said. "It makes me wish that I could live by the coast and everyday sail upon the waters."

"In the life to come," Daniel said joyfully. "Then, we will have all of eternity to enjoy such pleasures."

"Ha!" Ishmael said, overhearing us. "If you believe in such things."

"What do you believe in?" I asked kindly.

Ishmael looked at me, his cold gaze piercing into my heart of flesh. "We ain't nothing but dirt," he said. "Soon we will return to being food for the worms."

"But in the Scroll it says..." I began but was interrupted.

"The Scroll!" he exclaimed. "I should have known. I used to be a good castle-goer like you folk. But the hypocrisy was too much for me."

"I'm sorry to hear that," Levi said. "But hear me, my friend. You mustn't allow the bad examples of some to destroy your view of that which is good. Just because there are pirates on the waters doesn't make every sailor dishonorable. It is the same with the Scroll. It is perfect, despite what so called followers of the Scroll do in its name."

Ismael took in a thoughtful breath and went back to his work.

It was now midday, and we were all greatly enjoying our voyage. We were now far enough from the shoreline where all we could see was water. It was an exhilarating experience.

"How long until we reach the island?" I asked our guide.

"Probably five hours or so," he replied. "It's just starting to come in our sights ahead."

I gazed in the direction Ishmael pointed, and I thought I could barely make out a speck of land.

"Daniel," I said, "you have the gift of vision. Can you see it?"

Daniel peered out over the waters. "I see it," he said. "Though, I have a hard time believing anyone lives there. It is quite desolate."

"It's likely that no one's there," Ishmael said. "I haven't heard of the Exile for some time. But look on the bright side: If he is gone, we won't have to spend the night and can hurry back home."

Doubt entered my heart. If Eli wasn't there, then I was back to square one. The final words of Captain Samuel were gnawing at my mind. I knew that within them was the future of our people. We sailed on for another two hours. I was now able to see the island quite well, for it was only a mile or so away. The blue waters were gentle and the breeze kind.

"Oh no," Ishmael said, interrupting my peaceful state of mind.

"What's wrong?" I asked, following his eyes out upon the waters.

"It's a serpent," he said. "Three points off the starboard bow, and it's a big one."

I looked but couldn't see anything.

"Can you sense it?" Justin asked me.

"I sense nothing," I replied.

"It's getting closer!" Ishmael said, as he began loading the giant crossbow. "Look at the ripples in the water! Get ready, you fools! You have weapons! Prepare to use them!"

Then I thought I saw an object coming toward our boat, submerged under the surface of the waters. It was extremely large.

"It's a leviathan!" Ishmael shouted. "What curse have you men brought with you upon this water? Curse you all!"

The creature now rose its head out of the water. It was like a giant snake, only larger and with rows of sharp teeth. It was gray, slimy, and its mouth was large enough to swallow all of us whole. Its eyes were solid black and it was likely eighty feet in length. Ishmael fired his giant crossbow. The four-foot-long arrow ricocheted off of the monster, which now returned below the surface, circling around for a second pass. Ishmael began to hectically refit his weapon. The beast raised up over us again, its mouth open to devour us whole.

"Justin!" I shouted.

My friend raised his sword and lightning shot forth. There was a bright flash of light and the leviathan cried out a deafening cry. The attack from Justin didn't kill the beast; it only seemed to fuel its rage.

"Oh, Great King!" Ishmael shouted. "Help us now! Help us!"

Levi—as only he could do in such a circumstance—lightly commented, "So, you're able to talk to the Great King now, are you?"

The serpent then came upon us at full speed and rammed the boat. The jolt was intense. I felt my body lift high into the air, and I peripherally saw all four of my companions fall into the water only a moment before I did.

Chapter 22

The water was icy cold and salty. I still had both sword and shield in hand. The shield, being made of wood, was manageable. But the weight of the sword began to quickly pull me under, and so, after a short moment of struggle, I had to let it go. I then began to swim as fast as I could toward the boat, which appeared to be empty. My heart was filled with fear, for I expected at any moment to be pulled under the water and devoured by the enemy. I could hear voices crying out in pain, but I couldn't see them or recognize them. I reached the vessel, and with much difficulty, got myself back upon the boat and dropped my shield upon the deck. I was so exhausted that I had to struggle to rise to my feet. Upon one side of the boat were Benjamin and Levi, also weaponless, swimming as fast as they could toward the vessel. I quickly took hold of the deck rope and tossed it to them. As I pulled them into the boat, I saw the leviathan emerge just behind them with Ishmael in its mouth. It had bit into his leg and wasn't letting go. Ismael yelled aloud in both fear and pain, just before he was submerged back within the water.

"Levi!" I cried. "Man the crossbow! Shoot at the beast when it comes back!"

Meanwhile, Benjamin and I scanned the water for any sign of Daniel and Justin.

"There!" Benjamin shouted. "It's Justin!"

I looked to see Justin, seemingly unconscious, about ten feet under the water. What I also witnessed, deeper within the sea, was another sea serpent swimming straight for him. Without hesitation, I grabbed the end of the deck rope and jumped.

"Pull me up right away!" I shouted before I hit the water. I dove straight for Justin, holding on to the rope with one hand while reaching for him with the other. Just as I grabbed hold of him, my son was faithful to start pulling us in. We were returning to the surface, but I knew it wouldn't be fast enough, for the sea serpent was nearly upon us. We were coming toward the surface of the water as the serpent began to open its mouth to devour us. Just then I saw an enormous arrow penetrate the water and sink deep with the forehead of the giant snake.

Levi and Benjamin pulled us into the boat. Justin immediately began to cough and sputter out water. Meanwhile I jumped to my feet. "Where is Ishmael?" I shouted. "Where is Daniel?"

"Ismael is dead," Levi said. "I saw the beast finish him off. I'm not sure if it will return."

"How many creatures are there?" I asked.

"At least two," he replied. "The one that got Ishmael and that one." He pointed at the dead sea serpent that was now half floating upon the surface of the water. Tears came to my eyes. "Daniel!" I shouted. Levi quickly reloaded the crossbow while Benjamin and I continued to scan the water for our dear brother.

"Daniel!" I shouted again. No response. I thought of Violet and the devastation that would come to her heart at another loss of a dear brother. We had begun to give up hope when we heard something. It sounded muffled and distant, and yet, near at the same time. To our surprise and shock, we saw the blade of a sword shoot out of the flesh of the dead leviathan. A few seconds later, Daniel's head popped up, sputtering and gasping for air.

"Daniel!" we shouted together, after which we cast him the rope and helped him into the boat. He was covered from head to toe with gunk, blood, and other unclean elements. He sat for a moment, quiet and breathing, with his eyes closed.

"I'm alright," he said at last. "Did we lose anyone?"

"Ishmael," I said gently.

"Then may the Great King have mercy upon him," he replied.

It seemed that, for the time being, we were safe. Fortunately, our mast and sail had been undamaged and we were still heading in the direction of the island. Levi took over the steering of the boat as we helped Daniel recover.

"What happened?" I asked.

"I'm not sure," he said. "It all happened so fast. I remember landing in the water and immediately seeing the open mouth of a serpent. I think that I reacted with such adrenalin, that according to my ability, I swam so fast within the creature's mouth that it didn't have a chance to bite me. I simply swam straight within its belly. It was dark, and I had enough wits about me to know where I was. I was able to, somehow, from time to time, get a breath, though it was very strenuous. I had lost my sword in the ordeal, though not my shield. Just when I thought I had no strength or air left, I felt my sword connect to my hand. The rest you know."

"Incredible," Justin said, fully recovered from his own experience. "The Great King was protecting you."

We then remembered Ismael. "The thief comes to steal, kill, and destroy," I said. "I wish we could have spoken to Ishmael more, to minister to him. It clearly wasn't the will of our King. We honor, however, the bravery of that man and the skill which he possessed to bring us here."

Daniel washed briefly in the ocean. Within another hour, we reached the island. We found a gentle inlet and docked the vessel, after which we began to search the isle. It was small, only the size of our new Oasis. A few trees were upon its edges, and in its center was a small mountain which rose high into the air. As we scanned the mountain, there was a large opening, high above, and within that opening was a robed figure with a staff in one hand and the other one stretched out toward us.

"Be warned!" he said. "Great danger awaits you upon this island!"

Chapter 23

We weren't sure what the man was referring to. Between the five of us, we only had one sword and shield.

"Who are you?" the man called to us. His beard was long and grey, and his eyes seemed aged and profound.

"We are followers of the Great King!" I shouted up to him.

"Very good," he replied. "Come! Come and dine with me."

We noticed a path leading up to the entrance, and within a few minutes, we were within a small cave of sorts which had an opening on both the east and west side of the mountain. Within the abode were large stones which seemed to serve as a bed, chair, and table for the man. I also noticed six fish cooking over a bed of coals.

"Now I understand why the birds brought me extra fish this morning," the man said as he turned the fish over. He then motioned for us to sit down on a long stone which served as a bench. The view from that place was extraordinary, for you could see miles upon miles of the ocean, so much so that you could see it bend around the curvature of the earth.

"You are Eli?" I asked the man.

"I am," he replied as he offered us cups of water.

"It is a pleasure to meet you," I said. "We have come to receive your help."

"Yes, yes," he replied. "I know you have questions, but they are not the right ones. You need help that you don't know you need. Everyone wants an answer; *teach us about the truth*, they say. But they don't realize that with every ounce of truth is more accountability to the Great King. They see Him as kind but not dangerous. He is dangerous!" he shouted, causing us to flinch. "It is dangerous to search out the thoughts of the Great King! For He is the Maker and Judge of all things!"

He spoke quickly, so much so that it was hard to follow his words. He paused for a moment and then continued. "You don't understand, do you? I told you this island was dangerous, and you still don't know why. It's because of this!" he shouted. He pulled the object out of his cloak so quickly that we nearly leapt to our feet in fear. But then, as we looked, it was clear that the object was a scroll.

"A scroll?" I asked. "We must fear a scroll?"

"Not *a* scroll," he explained. "*The* Scroll. The words of the Great King."

We relaxed a bit. "Yes," I said kindly. "As I explained to you, we are followers of the Great King."

"And you think this makes your situation less dangerous?" the elder asked. "You think you know the Scroll? My brothers, listen to me. You have barely scratched the surface. You must eat it, not with your mouth, but with your mind and heart and soul. It must reside upon your lips, like honey on the lips of a child. It must travel along every drop of blood that pulses in your veins."

I then realized, as the old man spoke, that he never focused his vision upon us. I studied his eyes and realized that they were gray and dark, though filled with a beauty and wonder beyond this world. He was blind, yet, he seemed to see more than any of us.

"You are in the presence of the very words of your Maker," Eli continued as he held up the Scroll. "And the more you hear them, the more accountable you are. You will not be able to say to Him, *we did not know.*" As the man spoke, his countenance was fearsome to behold. "On the contrary, when you stand before the Great King, on that Day, you will do so as men without excuse. For you read His words, and you learned His ways. Fear then, my friends, not walking in His light. Fear then, having even one area of your life unaligned with the Scroll."

He then returned the Scroll to his cloak and bowed his head in reverence to his King.

"They say you were exiled here by your people," I said.

The old man laughed quietly. "Is that what they say? Exiled? Perhaps. By my people? I think not."

"Are you able to help us?" I asked, eager to find the answer to our riddle.

The old prophet then appeared very serious. "That's what I'm trying to do," he said. "You think you came here to have your question answered. The Great King brought you here for so much more than that. He is trying to open your eyes."

He then walked over to where the fish were cooking and one-by-one served them to us upon simple wooden plates. "Now," he said, "tell me about the Great King. Who is He?"

The simplicity of this question seemed to catch us off guard, and we hesitated.

"Well," Daniel replied, "He is the Ruler of the Universe."

"Indeed," Eli said. "Continue."

"He is the Maker of all things," Justin commented.

"Amen. More."

"He is good," I commented, "and just and holy and all-powerful."

"Yes, He is," Eli confessed. "Well done. You have spoken truth, but let me make an observation. Of everything you've said, the Great Dragon could say the same thing."

My companions and I looked at each other. "What do you mean?" I asked.

"It is quite simple," he replied. "The Great Dragon could say that the Great King is all-powerful and good and that He is the Ruler of the Universe. The Great Dragon could say it."

"Why does that matter?" I asked.

"Why does that matter?!" he repeated. "It matters because it means that your view of the Great King has nothing to do with relationship. They are just facts that any dragon or dragon-breeder or castle-goer could say."

That point stuck with me. I was saying things about the Great King that anyone else could say, even the dragons. That bothered me. But what else was there? How could I say something that they couldn't?

"Very well," I replied, still trying to understand the connection. "How would you answer the question? Who is the Great King?"

"He is my Rock!" Eli replied thrusting his hands in the air. "He is my Fortress, my Strong Tower; He is my Bread and Water. He is my shade from the heat. My Shepherd. My Light. My Comforter, Counselor, and Helper. You see, my friends, those are terms that reveal a true relationship. The Great Dragon could never say that the Great King is his rock or light or shepherd. Neither could your average castle-goer. You speak of the Great King with abstract and lofty ideas, and thereby, you see Him as abstract and lofty. Therefore, He is distant, uninteresting, and impractical concerning daily life. I speak of Him, however, with pictures that have been given to us in the Scroll; pictures that communicate to us aspects of His character. Therefore, my King is near and real and tangible. He is in every personal aspect of my daily life, of my very being."

I began to understand the words of Eli. It was so common to turn the Great King into a concept, a doctrine, or a distant entity. Instead, He wants us to know Him as a Person who is near and desires real, practical relationship. And these were terms I could use that others couldn't. I could say to Captain Asa that the Great King was my

Fortress, and yet, he could not. It was a name I could give because it was based on experience and relationship which I possessed and he didn't.

"Are your eyes opening?" he asked. "They must if you are to fulfill all that is ahead of you."

"I see it!" Levi exclaimed, startling us by his sudden emotion. "It is so beautiful! He is *my* Rock! He is *my* Bread. He is *my* Bright and Morning Star!"

"Yes, my boy!" Eli said joyfully. "With every name of the Great King, there is an invitation to know Him better. You must stop skimming the surface of His being and dive down into the fullness of who He is."

Eli was now quiet and thoughtful and seemed to be looking about the open cavern with the eyes of his soul. I was at the point of surety that this man was a prophet of the Great King. Why and how he was upon this island I knew not. I was only thankful that I was there with him. If time permitted, I would have stayed there for months, not uttering a word but simply listening. And then I considered, perhaps, that he was upon that island because it kept him separate from the world. His perspective wasn't clouded by the latest opinions of man or the trends of society. All he had was the Scroll and the Spirit of the Great King.

I was then overwhelmed with the reality of how far I had to go in my pilgrimage with the Great King. It was so easy to simply compare myself with others and feel good about myself, yet in that moment, all I compared myself to was the Scroll. I was looking upon it, as in a mirror, and I was seeing what was lacking in myself. Yet at the same time, I was also seeing what was true about me because of the grace of the Great King. He was working on me, and my need for transformation was immense, yet He loved me. He was standing over me, great and mighty, yet He was gently caressing my head as a mother would.

"Tell me," I spoke without thinking, for my lips were simply transmitting the desires of my soul. "Tell me, brother, what is the most important thing for me to be the man I'm supposed to be, the husband and father I'm supposed to be, the leader I'm supposed to be; what is the most important thing?"

Chapter 24

Eli smiled, and walking near to me and my companions, he gently fell upon his knees before us. "The most important thing, my fellow soldiers, is the Great King Himself. What comes into your mind when you think of Him? Who is He? What is He like? How you answer these questions will determine your path.

"Hear me. Listen to my words! At whatever point your thinking of the Great King is incorrect, at that same point, your ability to follow Him correctly is forfeited. To follow Him correctly, you must know Him correctly. You think you know Him correctly? Forgive me for being so bold: you don't. Your view of Him determines your view of the Scroll, as well as your view of yourself. It determines all things. There is no context of life that is unrelated or not connected to Him. This, therefore, is your chief endeavor: to know Him correctly so that you may follow Him correctly."

This explanation that Eli had given to us was extremely impactful; for me, it summarized the many conflicts I'd experienced with the Castle. Every area of heresy or failure within the Castle, and within my own life, could all come back to our idea of the Great King. It was just as the Scroll said, *This is the true life; to know Me, the one Great King.* It broke my heart, as I reflected on all I had seen within the Castle, how distracted and confused people were, when all they needed was embodied in the Great King and His Scroll.

"Let me explain," he said gently. "If you want to be a good husband, it all comes back to your idea of the Great King. If you see Him as unengaged, distant, and not concerned with the simple details of life, then you will be a husband in the same fashion. If you want to be a good parent, and yet, you see the Great King as someone more concerned about buildings, programs, and the praises of other adults, then you will be a lousy parent indeed. You must see that the Great King is a good Father and that He is passionate about your wife and children. They are, according to His Scroll, your greatest ministry. You must engage your wife and children in the same way the Great King engages you—fully and with all of your heart. If you see the Great King as someone more concerned about attendance than allegiance, or more concerned with religion than relationship, then you will truly be set up for failure."

The old man then lifted his arms into the air to emphasize his following statement. "Every single misconception or misapplication, every single one, comes back to a misunderstanding of the Great King. I cannot stress this enough, for when you understand it, you will be very strategic in your life and purpose. Your life will all be about knowing the Great King correctly, according to the Scroll, instead of the ideas of men."

Could it really be that simple? I thought to myself. That every error in a person's thinking stemmed from a misconception of the Great King? In my heart, though it seemed too simple to be true, I believed it.

"This is why," Eli continued, "you must consult the Scroll above all else. The Scroll is the revelation of the heart and mind of the Great King."

When I arrived upon that island, I thought that I valued and loved the Scroll. But at that moment, after hearing the words of Eli, a greater fire than ever burned within me. It consumed me. I hungered and longed for the truths of the Scroll. I envied Eli, there upon that island with nothing but the Scroll and the presence of the Great King.

And yet, I knew that my circumstances, though different to Eli's, were exactly what the Great King wanted.

"Do you understand what I am saying?" Eli asked.

We all nodded in gratitude.

Eli then paused reflectively, "You say that you understand, and yet, you traveled all this way, and through many dangers, to ask me a question. Didn't you ever stop to consider that the answer was with you all this time?"

Like nearly all his words up to this point, this took me by surprise. "What do you mean?" I asked. "How has the answer been with us?"

The old man slowly lifted high the Scroll.

"The Scroll?" I asked. "The answer is in the Scroll? Where?"

"How would I know that?" he said smiling. "I don't even know the question."

I paused, being both confused and slightly embarrassed. "That's my point," I said respectfully. "If you don't even know what the question is, how can you know that the answer is in the Scroll?"

Eli came toward me, ever so gently and humbly. "My son," he said tenderly, and yet at the same time, gravely, "do you still not understand? This is the Scroll of the Great King. Every question you could ever ask is answered within it."

I didn't know what to say. I was inspired and at the same time, ashamed. All this time the answer I was seeking was in the Scroll.

"Excuse me," Benjamin said to Eli, in the deepest tone of respect.

"Yes, my son?" Eli replied.

"I know that what you speak is true," Benjamin said. "But I don't understand it. There must be some questions that the Scroll doesn't answer."

"Try and give me one," Eli said sincerely.

"What do you mean?" my son asked.

"Try to give me a question that the Scroll doesn't address in some way," Eli explained.

I could tell my son was uncomfortable, for he didn't want to challenge his elder, so he thought of an issue that would be easy to ascertain.

"Well," Benjamin said respectfully, "what about the question, *Should we go to the theater and watch their plays?* Many people have pointed out to me that the Scroll speaks nothing of the theater, so they say that we can't know the answer."

"What a wonderful question!" Eli replied, filled with excitement. "I love this game! You should play it often with your brethren. Let me show you how." He then began to walk around his abode in a large circle as he quickly reasoned aloud. "Well, the Scroll doesn't speak for or against such places, so we must look deeper. What goes on at the theaters? Entertainment, which of course, is filled with ideas and worldviews. The Scroll says to be wise about what is good and innocent about what is evil. It also says that bad company corrupts good morals, which, of course, show us that evil ideas and evil worldviews corrupt good morals. The Scroll says that we are to think about things that are good, and wholesome, and excellent."

He then turned to us with a look of great excitement. "The answer stares us all in the face!" he said. "If what is on the stages of the theater is good and pleasing to the Great King, then by all means feel free to go and partake. But if it is of the world, and of the Dragon, then stay far, far away."

My companions had no difficulty in following Eli's thinking, for we also knew the answer. Levi, as was his personality, wasn't able to leave Eli's original question unchallenged, so he thought of something that seemed a little more trivial.

"Excuse me," Levi began, "what about the question, *What should I cook for dinner?*"

Eli laughed, not in a way of mockery, but in enjoyment of the conversation. "That is a good one," he replied. "Well now, let's see. What does the Scroll say? What should I cook for dinner? Ha! The Scroll not only tells you what to cook, but how to cook it, and who to cook it for!"

My comrades and I all looked at each other, perplexed by Eli's words.

"The Scroll says that our body is a temple of the Great King. It also says that we are to purify ourselves from everything that corrupts our body. It also says that in everything we do, we do it with thanksgiving. Ha, ha, yes. It also says to be hospitable to your family, the beloved, and those in need. There! You have your answer! What are you to cook for dinner? Something that will nurture and bless the body which the Great King has given you. You are to cook it with thanksgiving for the Great King's provision, and you are to cook it for your family, the family of the Great King, or those in need."

He then paused, awaiting our response. I was so personally touched and amazed by the application he drew from the Scroll that I was left speechless.

"Very good," he said, enjoying the sight of our reverie. "Now I will give you a question. What does the Scroll say about modesty? How should men and women dress?"

Fortunately, I felt that we were somewhat prepared and able to answer such a question. "Well," I began, "let's see. The Scroll says that men are not to wear women's clothing, neither are women permitted to wear men's clothing. That would be the first principle: there are gender distinctions regarding clothing. This means that you should not be able to swap clothing between male and female."

I then offered to the rest of the brethren to chime in, and Daniel took up the opportunity. As this was happening, Eli's face was filled with delight.

"Your clothing should draw people's attention to your face instead of your body," Daniel pointed out. "The Scroll says that the eyes and face are the windows of the soul. To dress modestly is to create a frame for your face so that people can see your soul through your expressions. People of the world, in contrast, draw people's attention to their bodies. The Scroll encourages us to not follow such practices. It says that to have your thighs exposed is equated with nakedness. Covering such parts of your body will keep the eyes of others where they belong— on your face."

"Very good!" Eli declared.

"I also think that clothing should reflect the Great King," Justin said, thinking aloud. "For it says in the Scroll that we are to do all things in the name of the Great King. Therefore, even what we wear should reflect His character and kingdom. Our clothing should be orderly, and as Daniel said, it should bring the attention of others to our face, where our expression reflects the beauty of the Great King."

"Excellent!" Eli declared. "You see? The Scroll speaks to all things! Now, I will give you one last question. I've saved the best for last."

He then paused, apparently quite distracted, and sudden alarm came upon his face. "Our time is up," he said, seemingly able to sense something. "The enemy draws plans even now. You have a question for me. Ask it quickly."

I was frustrated at this, for Eli's words had only begun to peel back the layers of my soul and reveal my deepest needs. But I believed him and therefore obeyed him.

"Our captain, Samuel, was executed by dragon fire not long ago. His final words spoke of me traveling to my roots. Do you know what it means?"

"Go back to your roots?" Eli repeated. "Ha! Samuel. How I love him. He spoke truth, no doubt. Upon his death, the Great King gave him a vision, as is the King's custom. He opened his eyes for only a moment. He let you see what is coming."

"What is coming?" I asked.

"War," he replied. "War like never before. The battles will be fought in various places, but the war, the final war, will be fought at your roots."

"My roots?"

"Yes."

"But I have no roots," I replied. "I was born and raised for most of my childhood in Ravenhill. Will the final battle be there?"

Eli shook his head. "You think your roots begin with your birth?" he asked. "Your roots begin at the beginning of time. You are part of something larger than yourself. Aren't you glad? Doesn't that comfort you? You are confused because, like many soldiers of these latter days, you are so individualistic. When you read the Scroll, you think you are reading about the story of the Great King and *His* people."

"What do you mean?" I asked.

"Well, for example, when you read about the Great King saving his people out of slavery, three thousand years ago, and bringing them into the Pledged Land, you think that you're reading about the Great King and *His* people."

"Well, I am, aren't I?"

"No," he said firmly. "You are reading about the Great King and *your* people."

"I don't understand," I said.

"Who are those people that the Great King saved?" he asked patiently.

"The people of the Great King," I replied. "His people."

"True, but they are also your people," he said. "You belong to them and they belong to you. They are your lineage, your bloodline through faith. They are your brethren, your forefathers, your people. Therefore, their roots are your roots."

"Their roots are my roots," I repeated thoughtfully. I looked over to my companions, and they seemed to be nodding in understanding.

"What were their roots?" I then asked.

"When the Great King first made mankind," Eli replied, "He put them in a garden, correct?"

"Yes," I replied.

"Those first people were your people. Then, years later, when He rescued our people out of slavery, He brought them to that same place, remember?"

"Yes."

"And then," he continued, "in the days when the Great King returned to this planet for a short time and finished the Scroll, His chief city was in that same place."

"You mean Salem?" I asked.

"Absolutely," he replied. "It is the place of your roots, Caleb, and not just yours but all of ours. It is where all of this began, and where it will all end. It is where the

Great King will come and where He will do something mighty and amazing that hasn't yet come into anyone's mind."

"Salem?" I asked again in shock and confusion. "Are you sure? I'm supposed to take our people to Salem?"

"Without question."

"But it's such a long and difficult journey. Is there anything out there?"

"You'll just have to go and see, won't you?" he said with a smile.

"Should I take my people there now?" I asked.

"Not now," he said slowly and with much thought. "The time, however, approaches. You will know when it is time. But now, my friends, our conversation must cease. The Great King moves you on. Hurry now, for your people need you. Danger draws near."

I quickly glanced at Benjamin.

"I don't feel anything," he said.

"It is still days away," Eli said. "But then again, so are you. Go now, and may the Great King go with you."

"But how?" Daniel asked. "How shall we cross the waters again? Our sailor has perished, and the sea monsters are many."

"Behold," Eli replied. "The sun is setting, and a full moon rises. This moon sends all monsters down into deep water. Set the bow of your ship to the constellation of the archer. All depends on your safe arrival. Now go!"

We turned to leave, pleased with all we had discovered but discouraged at the sudden dismissal.

"Wait," he said quickly. "One last thing. Caleb, you are the man that this was revealed to. I have a gift for you if you are willing to take it. You are without a sword. I wonder if you would take mine?"

He unsheathed his sword and handed it to me. It was beautiful and ancient.

"This sword has been passed down from brother to brother for centuries," he said. "Use it well."

"Thank you," I said, being honored beyond what I felt I deserved.

"We will meet again," he said. "Farewell."

Chapter 25

By the counsel of Eli, we safely crossed the waters. The midnight journey encapsulated a beauty I am unable to describe. We landed and docked the boat as close to its original location as we could with our novice sea experience. We tied it to the shore and continued our journey home. Including the gift that Eli supplied me, we now had two swords for the five of us. This being the case, and by the skill of Daniel, we planned to avoid all dragons on our return trip. We spoke little during that time, I believe because of the inner contemplation each man was having over the words of Eli. They pierced us like a dagger and set our hearts ablaze.

On the fourth day of our return, we were close enough to send Daniel to our people to seek news. When we were only an hour away from the village, he returned to us, traveling faster than any beast the Great King created. "An army is coming!" he told us. "An army of men. They are coming through the forest, armed with swords and bows. They are coming for our people at the New Oasis!"

"How many are coming?" I asked.

"Hundreds!" he answered. "They are being led by Simon."

"Simon!" I exclaimed. "What is he doing in Greystone?"

"Hunting us, apparently," Daniel replied. "It seems that the villagers of Ravenhill and Greystone have joined together."

"Then let us hurry!" I ordered. "Have you informed Nathan?"

"Yes," he said. "He is ordering a retreat."

"A retreat?" I repeated. "Why doesn't he stand and fight?" I knew the answer to this question the moment I asked it and therefore motioned to Daniel that there was no need to answer.

We hurried as fast as we could and came upon our people as they were only a few minutes north of the New Oasis. I embraced my wife and children and then quickly found Nathan.

"Stop the retreat," I said. "We must return and form a perimeter. We must stand and fight! Our training is superior to theirs."

"But they are people," Nathan said. "We can't attack them."

"We aren't attacking them," I said. "We are protecting our families."

"But to stop them will likely require taking their lives," Nathan replied. "The Scroll is very clear that we should not murder."

"The Scroll is also clear that we are to protect our families," I insisted.

Nathan took a deep breath. "I will not kill people, Caleb. Not when I can run and hide my family and thus protect them. You can return if you like, and fight, but I am running and hiding. There is no dishonor in it. It keeps us in perfect alignment with the Scroll."

I knew that my brother was correct, but I didn't like it. We had worked hard to make this place our home, and I didn't feel right leaving it to others without a fight.

"Time is running out!" Nathan said. "Please, brother. We must continue the retreat."

I consented. "Do we know where we are going?" I asked.

"Yes," Nathan replied. "There is a lone mountain, about two days journey from here. It is long abandoned of dragons and should make a good temporary shelter for us."

Everyone obeyed and quickly retreated deeper within the forest, with Jedidiah, Benjamin, and Levi as the guides for our fellowship, over one hundred and thirty souls. I bid Nathan and Daniel to return with me to the northern edge of the New Oasis. He consented, and we waited hidden within the brush.

"This isn't wise," Nathan said. "They could surround us."

"I just want to see them," I said.

"You'll soon get your chance," he replied. "Did you find out the meaning of Captain Samuel's words?"

"I did," I replied. "And so much more."

Suddenly, I thought I saw something, though it was so far away that I had to strain my eyes to make it out. I thought that I saw a figure, or at least, the outlining of the face of a man, though it was masked.

"Do you see that?" I asked Nathan and Daniel.

"That's odd," Daniel said as he peered across the distance. "There is a red triangle on that man's white mask."

"Red triangle?!" Nathan exclaimed. "It is the masked man from that night. It is the murderer."

The face then disappeared back into the forest. Only a minute later, many soldiers entered the New Oasis, led by Simon.

"Have you seen enough?" Nathan asked.

"Yes," I replied softly. "Let's hurry. Daniel, run ahead with the others. We will be right behind you."

Daniel was off like lightning. Nathan and I likewise began our trek. But as we turned around we came face to face with the masked man, and not only him, but eight more just like him, and they were armed, mostly with bows and arrows which were pointed right at us.

Nathan and I quickly readied our weapons.

"Who are you?" I asked, startled by their sudden appearance.

"We are the Enlightened Ones," the man answered, his voice still hidden somewhere in the recesses of my mind. "Simon wants you because of your intolerance. Captain Jezebel and the people of Greystone want you because of your prejudice. But I want you because you interfered with my business. Not only that, but you slipped within our underground stronghold and attacked our people."

"Well," I said, "here we are. Come and take us."

"All in good time," the man said. "First, I think you should know the man who organized your death this day."

He took off his mask. It was Simon's son, Edgar, who I hadn't seen in years. The very man who had stolen the heart of Caroline and then broke it, contributing to her suicide. I could hear the men behind us, ordering the burning of our homes.

"I've been waiting for this moment for years," Edgar said. "You confused Caroline and brought her down in shame and ruin."

"I confused Caroline?" I said. "You still haven't learned, have you, Edgar? The ways of the Great King always bring life. The ways of the Great Dragon, whom you serve, always bring death."

"Death is yours now," Edgar said bitterly. "I hope you enjoy it!"

He made a motion to his men and the arrows were loosed, too many arrows for us to deflect with our shields. I held up my shield, though I anticipated the feeling of being pierced and killed. But instead, I heard the deflection of the arrows off of a hard surface, but it wasn't my shield. I looked to see eight arrows lying upon the ground in front of Nathan and me.

"What?" began Edgar, but he was silenced by the swift swing of a bow to his face. He fell to the ground while all of us looked to see my wife, Elizabeth, standing over his unconscious body. Nathan and I charged upon the other masked men who turned and scattered. I then understood what had happened. As she had done so many times before, Elizabeth had saved me through her intercession.

"What made you come back?" I asked.

"Love for you, of course," she said. "Let's hurry. The soldiers are almost upon us."

We turned and ran after the rest of our people. We soon caught up with them, for after a certain distance they had stopped to wait for us. Many of them were crying.

"It may appear that our homes are no more," I said to them. "But this isn't the case, for our home goes with us. Wherever we are, that is our home. Now let us ask the Great King to give us guidance."

Daniel and others scouted to make sure that we weren't followed. The army which had come to destroy us didn't seem to be following into the forest, though, a part of me knew that it was only a matter of time until they did. That first night we camped deep in the forest and devoted the evening to prayer. By the following sunset, we arrived at the lone mountain and were able to find temporary lodging, for there was a large overhang off of the south side of the foothill which created a large shelter from the elements.

As we made camp that evening, Judah approached me. "I just wanted to say how thankful I am for everything you've done," he said. "You've saved my life, multiple times."

"You're welcome," I said cheerfully. "But it was the Great King who saved you. I'm sure the time will come when you will repay the favor."

"I look forward to it," he said.

"I'm sorry that all of this has happened," I told him, taking in our surroundings, "but it is the way of the Great King. He doesn't promise that we will escape hardship, only that He will give us the strength to press on."

Judah nodded his head in understanding. "At least we were able to bring the chess set," he said smiling.

"I still owe you a game," I said.

"We are already playing," he said under his breath and walked away.

I then noticed Benjamin speaking with Susanna. I could tell, with her eyes, that her heart was for my son. But was she the one? "Open our eyes," I prayed to the Great King. "Show us all who is the bride of my son."

I then sought out Nathan, for we had much to discuss. "We ran from the soldiers," I said, "and it was the right thing to do. But if they seek us here, we will have no place to hide. Eventually, if they persist, we will have to stand and fight."

"But that would go against the Scroll," Nathan said.

"We will be going against the Scroll either way," I said. "For the Scroll also commands that we protect our family. Therefore, the question is, *Which commandment should we put before the other? Which commandment is of the greater priority?* I believe that the protection of our family comes first."

"I'm not sure," Nathan said, shaking his head. "Killing others is a serious offense against the Great King."

"So is abandoning your family to die at the hands of heretics," I said.

"We must pray on this," Nathan said. "As for me, if the enemy comes, I and my family will run. There is a chance that you and I will not see eye to eye on this, Caleb, and may end up leading our families in different directions."

"Regardless," I said, taking a deep breath and offering my hand to him, "nothing will take away our fellowship."

He grasped my hand. "For certain," he said. "We are brothers until the end."

I then told him about our time with Eli and all that I learned.

"Salem?" he said. "Well, I've always wanted to see that place, though, I've heard there's not much left."

"It seems like a dream," I said, "our time with Eli that is. It all happened too quickly. I hope he was correct."

"I believe he was," Nathan said confidently. "He trained Captain Enoch, years and years ago. He never led him wrong. I don't think he will lead us wrong either."

"Well," I said, "let's just pray that the timing is obvious and that the Great King provides for our needs in the meantime."

"Oh, He will definitely provide," Nathan said. "He promises to do that."

Dinner was prepared consisting of venison and wild berries. The mood of our forces was very sober, yet still thankful. We listened to the words to the Scroll and devoted ourselves to prayer. Watchmen were placed around the perimeter of the camp, for we were no longer living in an oasis but within the dense forest itself. Fortunately, by the will of Providence, the rock formation we camped under was curved, like a horseshoe, and made a barrier for us against the enemy. Only a few warriors would be able to fight off dozens of dragons if needed.

By sundown, all was still. Families were huddled around different fire rings, enjoying the goodness of the Great King. I held Elizabeth in my arms, while my three older daughters rested their heads upon us. Baby Rachel was snuggled up beside us, sound asleep. Benjamin was standing guard upon the perimeter.

I relayed to my ladies the full account of the journey to find Eli. When I spoke of the battle upon the waters and Daniel's narrow escape Violet was moved to tears. Elizabeth held her close.

"Papa?" Rose said, her precious voice breaking the silence about us.

"Yes, my dear?" I replied.

"I'm scared," she whispered.

"Don't be," I said. "You are safe here. We will protect you."

"Remember," Elizabeth said, addressing her daughters, "that the Great King is in control. Nothing can happen to us unless He allows it."

"Do you think the men will attack us here?" asked Lily.

"I'm not sure," I said. "But I hope they don't."

"What will we do if they attack us?" she questioned.

I hesitated.

"The Great King will guide us," Violet answered, having calmed down from the news of Daniel. "But don't think about such things, my beautiful sisters. Think about good things. We are together, and we love each other, and the Great King is smiling down upon us."

For many weeks, we remained isolated and in peace within the shadow of the mountain. No dragons came near us, and we were able to live well off of wild game and foraging. We continued to explore the mountain, especially Benjamin and Judah. After being there six weeks, they discovered an ancient entrance to the mountain which led to a series of tunnels that exited out the other side.

"This was a stronghold of the enemy," Nathan said, as we explored it together. "The entrance the men discovered near our home is small, likely only for young dragons. It is obvious that many of the passageways have been blocked off by the erosion of time. Nevertheless, it will make us a wonderful place of refuge, if any threat comes again."

"That is what we will call it," I said. "The Refuge. I suggest we store some of our resources and provisions within these tunnels, just in case."

This was accomplished. Our food stocks continued to grow, for some of our people found wild vegetables that we were able to harvest and plant in our new location. Peace returned to our lives, and we grew closer together as a people.

Daniel made continual scouting trips to the village, and his reports were always alarming. Things were exponentially getting worse. People were falling into deeper degrees of immorality. The very foundations of society and family were crumbling. Dragons and humans were becoming more intertwined. It was evident that the agenda of the enemy was working. Through deceptive philosophy, people were falling into the trap of the Great Dragon. Their sons' and daughters' hearts were already won by the enemy in their early childhood. Purity was non-existent, for linking was widespread. Not only that, but natural relations were abandoned for unnatural ones. My heart broke for the world, but I was thankful for my family, for by His grace, we were following the Great King.

One evening, just after I had tucked my three daughters into bed, Benjamin asked to speak with me and his mother. "Father and Mother," he said, his face reflecting a bit of excitement, "do you remember how you told me that if I ever had strong feelings for a sister, that is, if I ever thought of one as a potential bride, do you remember how you told me to come to you first?"

"Of course," I replied, eager for his next words.

"Well," he said, "there's a certain girl I want to talk to you about."

"Oh really?" I said with shared excitement, for I could feel Elizabeth squeeze my hand with anticipation. "You think this girl might be the one?"

"Yes," he replied. "I love her."

"Tell us, son," Elizabeth said calmly. "Who is she?"

Chapter 26

Benjamin smiled, and in that expression, I saw a reflection of true love and devotion.

"It is Rebekah," he said.

"Oh," replied Elizabeth, "she is such a delightful young lady." She then looked to me as to hear my opinion.

"You have chosen well," I replied with a smile. "Rebekah is an amazing woman. Come, my son. Let us pray together." We joined hands, and I led us in prayer. "Great King," I began, "You who created the earth and the sea and all that is in them. Our son has found a woman who he believes in the one. Please, Great King, give us confirmation. Guide our hearts and open our eyes. Amen."

"I have watched you and Rebekah closely," I said. "She seems like such a noble and good woman. She loves the Great King and clings to the Scroll. Your mother and I have always prayed, even since you were in your mother's womb, that the Great King would provide for you a woman of like-mindedness, who embraced her role in the Scroll—to be a devoted wife and mother, to manage her home well, and to honor and obey her husband. You have chosen well, my son, for Rebekah is in the image of her mother, Leah. Now, you must go to Nathan, Rebekah's father, as you have been taught."

"I will, Father," he replied. "Thank you."

He then excused himself to bed, after which his mother and I discussed the situation.

"I am pleased," she said. "I believe that it is a match."

"I am also," I agreed. "And I rejoice that Levi and Benjamin will now be brothers by marriage. It isn't actually a big change for them, however, for they have always been close."

"But I do, however, hurt for Susanna," Elizabeth said. "She is a good woman, and I don't want her heart to be damaged."

"She will be disappointed," I said. "But I am confident that she will be alright. Our son has treated her with honor and has protected both their hearts. She will find another in due time."

"And what of Daniel and Violet?" she asked.

"I believe it is time for that also," I replied. "It seems that much change is happening."

"That is the grace of the Great King," Elizabeth replied in wisdom. "For even though Violet will be so happy for her brother, losing him would have been hard on her. But now she will be joined to another, and her heart will be filled with joy."

"That is so true," I said. I took a deep breath, convinced in my heart of what needed to happen, and rose to my feet.

"What are you doing?" Elizabeth asked gently.

"I'm going to speak with Daniel," I said. "I know it is late, but I am confident he won't mind one bit."

The following morning, as Elizabeth and I, along with our daughters, were working in the garden, I saw Benjamin and Nathan walk together into the forest.

"It's happening," I said quietly to my wife.

"What's happening, Father?" Violet asked me.

"Your brother is going to speak with Nathan," I replied. "He's going to ask if he can have permission to marry his daughter Rebekah."

"Really?" Violet replied with excitement.

"Yes, my dear," replied Elizabeth, "but you mustn't say anything. We need to wait to see what happens."

Suddenly Daniel appeared, sword strapped to his side. He bowed low in respect.

"Good morning, Captain Caleb," he said kindly. "I wonder if I might have a word with your daughter."

"Of course," I replied.

Daniel then approached Violet, who was standing still, mesmerized by the man who had captured her heart.

"My dear sister, Violet," he began, "it is wonderful to see you this morning."

"And you," she replied with a bow.

"I wanted to tell you," he said with controlled emotion, "that I have watched you grow into a woman of the Great King. And your beauty and your heart have entirely captivated my soul. I have asked your father for your hand in marriage. He has said yes. And now I ask you. Will you marry me?"

Violet's lips began to tremble and tears came to her eyes. "Of course!" she said smiling wide. "Of course, I will marry you."

The two remained there, looking upon one another with hearts of cheer. Elizabeth and the other sisters were all in tears.

"Then it is settled," I said joyfully. "Daniel, you will soon be my son and Violet, your wife. We must make the necessary arrangements. You two must be very cautious until then, and must continue to live by the rules which you have always lived by. Never be alone. Never be physical. All of this must be protected until your wedding day." We then prayed together, and Daniel left us with joy and happiness beaming from his face like I had never before witnessed. Violet ran into her mother's arms and wept tears of joy. Only a few minutes later we saw Benjamin returning with Nathan. They were both smiling and speaking together as they neared us.

"Hello!" Nathan greeted us cheerfully.

"My brother!" I replied as we embraced.

"Well," he said, "it seems like the same children will call us grandfather. What a joy this is, the joining of our two families!"

"The Great King be praised!" I replied, and I shook my son's hand, who was beaming with pride.

We then turned to see Nathan's wife, Leah, approaching with Rebekah, clad in a gown of white.

Elizabeth and Leah embraced each other with tears of joy, and Elizabeth kissed our future daughter-in-law and blessed her.

"This has been a most joyous day!" I exclaimed to Nathan and Leah, "for my daughter Violet is also pledged to be married to Daniel."

"Your life is one truly blessed," Nathan said. "I remember when we first met. Ah, to think of all the Great King has done since that day!"

Nathan and I embraced, for truly, the grace of the Great King was manifested at that moment in a way that brought tears to both of our eyes. I realized that but by the grace of the Great King, we would have nothing at all.

Benjamin bowed to Rebekah, who blushed and could barely contain her smile. She bowed low in return, and she and her mother returned to their home.

"Come," Nathan said, "let us visit."

I accompanied my old friend deeper within the forest.

"I've been praying for this," Nathan confessed.

"As have we," I replied. "They are young, no doubt about that, but you yourself know that age isn't so much about years as it is character."

"Indeed," he replied. "They will do very well. When do you think they should marry?"

"As soon as possible," I replied. "All that Benjamin lacks is a house."

"So, maybe a fortnight?" Nathan asked.

"Perfect," I replied. "I'm sure they will be pleased."

We prayed together and fellowshipped until evening. I returned and relayed the news to my family, who was eager for the details.

"A fortnight?" repeated Benjamin. "I could have built a house in three days!"

"Well," I replied, "better safe than sorry. A fortnight isn't too long of a betrothal. Much of the community is still busy building shelters, so you will not have much help."

"Besides," Elizabeth replied, "I'm sure you men can build a cottage in three days, but will it be an adorable cottage that a woman will appreciate? I think that fourteen days will be just enough time, but only if we all work together."

Violet then asked for a private meeting with her brother. The two siblings walked for an hour in the forest, and though I don't know all that was said, I later came to understand that the exchange of that moment reflected the deep connection that these two friends had with each other. After their return, they shared that they had also spoken with their betrothed, Benjamin with Daniel and Violet with Rebekah, and they all desired to be married on the same day, at the same time, if that was acceptable to their parents. Elizabeth and I gladly permitted this desire, as did Nathan and Leah.

We began the next morning at sunrise building the homes of Benjamin and Daniel. Others helped, such as Levi, who was excited to have Benjamin as a brother, as well as Jedidiah who was so happy for his brother Daniel. By the thirteenth day, the cottages were complete and everything was made ready for the ceremony and celebration on the following day.

The next morning, at sunrise, Nathan and I stood before our people. Accompanying us were my eldest son and daughter, along with their betrothed. My son and Daniel were dressed as warriors of the Great King, and Rebekah and Violet as princesses of light.

Seeing as Daniel had no father living, and that I had become his father, I proceeded, "Listen, my children," I said to Daniel and Violet. "On this day, you will become one person; you will become husband and wife. The Scroll gives you all you need to have a good marriage. Daniel, you are the representative of the Great King in this relationship. That means that you are to treat Rebekah the way that the Great King would. You must love her, sacrifice for her, and die for her daily. Rebekah, since Benjamin is the representative of the Great King, you must treat him as such. It is as if you were married to the Great King; honor and reverence him. Serve him and obey him. And remember, both of you, that one day you will both stand before the throne of the Great King. On that day, you will answer for how you treated each other in light of the Scroll's commands. Do you understand?"

They both nodded, after which they turned to each other.

"I will love you forever," Daniel said. "I will provide for you and protect you. You are my cherished one."

"And I will honor you forever," Violet replied. "I will serve you with all of my heart. You are my chief and leader. I will stand by you and serve with you. You have captured my heart forever."

"It is finished," I said with joy. "You are one. You may now join hands."

Everyone paused to witness the first holding of hands. My joy, as a father and captain of my people was at its limit. The goodness of the Great King was paramount in my mind and heart. To see my daughter arrive at the marriage altar completely pure and undefiled was a joy beyond description. Their fingers interlocked, and their faces reflected the joy and bliss within their hearts.

Nathan then stepped forward, and motioning to his daughter, addressed me with great respect. "Today, our two families enter into covenant together. My daughter, Rebekah, is pure. She will love your son, Benjamin. She will be devoted to him and will follow him. If she fails in these responsibilities, you can hold me personally responsible."

"And I also covenant with you, my friend," I said nobly. "My son, Benjamin, is a man of purity. He will provide for your daughter and protect her. He will be faithful to her and lead her with the love of the Great King and with the direction of the Scroll. If he fails to do this, you may hold me personally responsible."

We then motioned to Benjamin, who turned and gave his words to Rebekah. "I will love you with all my heart," he said. "You are my treasure and crown."

"And I will love you," Rebekah said. "You have all of my heart, forever, unconditionally."

I declared them one, and they likewise held hands. Oh, the joy and emotion of that moment!

I then motioned to all of those present. "Rejoice!" I shouted. "Two new families have been born this day!"

All present lifted their voices in cheer.

But suddenly, and to my horror, something happened. An arrow, shot from I knew not where, lodged into Rebekah's thigh. As she cried out in pain, the bright sun was blotted out by a horde of dragons. The shouts of men and the whistling of arrows filled the air. The enemy was upon us.

Chapter 27

Rebekah screamed out in pain and agony. Benjamin scooped up his bride within his arms. "Dragons!" I shouted. "Dragons and men together! Arm yourselves!"

The words were still on my lips when another volley of arrows fell within our ranks, striking many people to the ground. What took me back, in addition to the overwhelming numbers, was the fact that both black dragons in the sky and red dragons on the ground had men upon their backs, equipped with swords and bows.

Benjamin was still holding Rebekah in his arms, her leg still pierced with an arrow.

"Get her to the Refuge!" I shouted. I then addressed everyone else. "Prepare to fight!"

Most of our company were armed and were forming a defense. Shields were raised just in time to block the dragons' fire, though some others didn't make it in time, for my friends Reuben and Esther were both devoured in a moment before our eyes. I had now counted nearly a dozen red dragons and just as many black dragons. Formations of foot soldiers from the village were also exiting from the forest around us. I recognized Simon leading them, sitting upon a red dragon's back. Jade was also mounted upon the dragon next to him. She looked at me with evil hatred.

"First battalion attack!" I shouted. "All others fall back to the Refuge!"

Our ladies released their arrows; it was a deadly volley and seemed to slow down the enemy. Justin shot forth his lightning, causing the nearest red dragon to fall dead, its human rider being cast upon the ground. I heard a familiar but not pleasant voice. It was Eric's.

"Kill the heretics!" he shouted. "Death to all traitors!"

He was upon a black dragon's back and seemed to have learned some entry level skills with a sword. An arrow sliced my neck, missing my jugular by only a fraction of an inch. I now saw Violet, fully aflame and courageously standing against the enemy. Dragon fire was poured upon her but to no avail of the enemy. She then let three arrows fly, each one of them sending dragons flying in various directions, for they each caused massive explosions.

I heard another command of the enemy, this time coming from a woman. She was upon a black dragon and had a scepter in her hand.

"Kill that girl!" she shouted, referring to Violet. "Kill her now!"

Both dragons and men came upon Violet, but she was instantly swept away by Daniel, her fire not hurting him at all.

I looked to our rear guard, most of whom were already near enough to the Refuge to make it without much danger. I knew we must act quickly.

"All men, attack now!" I commanded. "All women and children, run to the Refuge!"

The men surged forward without fear. They were men of bravery, for their beliefs made them as comfortable on the battle field as in a hammock. They knew that the Great King was in control and that His will for them would be accomplished. If this was the hour of our deaths, then we would die as men of courage, honor, and conviction. I sprinted toward the nearest dragon, Jedidiah and Levi beside me. We quickly overcame the beast, whose rider retreated in fear. Other dragons were being slain while some of our numbers were also breathing their last breath.

I then turned to find a black dragon coming down upon me. I ducked under its grasp and came back up with a deep cut to its gut. The creature flew out of sight. The lines of men were now approaching. I didn't want to kill them, though I was resolved to defend my family at all cost.

"There are too many of them!" Nathan shouted from about thirty yards away. I scanned about and noticed that there were indeed many men, likely three hundred, while more dragons were also appearing. I turned to see that most of the women and children had made it to the Refuge.

"Run!" I commanded. "Run to the Refuge!"

I didn't see this command as cowardly, for our objective was to protect our families, not defeat all who had attacked us. I had just turned, along with some other thirty men with me, when I noticed that we were being flanked. Scores of men, along with a few dragons, had come up over the mountain and were about to cut off our retreat. I knew at that time that not many of us would make it back.

"Everyone together!" I shouted. "Punch a line through the enemy!"

This was a formation and strategy that we had practiced very little, for our main tactic was to always stand our ground and fight. I could see Elizabeth and my two middle daughters, the last of the women and children, waiting at the entrance to the Refuge. I guessed that Daniel had sprinted Violet around the mountain to the side on the other entrance. Even over the distance of about eighty yards, I could see the expression on Elizabeth's face. She was gauging whether or not I would make it in time, for I was at the far end of the retreat. Dragons were now nearing the entrance, as were the men from the village. With all my heart I prayed for Elizabeth and my girls to run deeper within the tunnel. My life was nothing; theirs, everything. Suddenly, to my horror, they all exited the entrance and began running in my direction. They even had baby Rachel wrapped tightly around Rose's back.

The three female warriors ran within about thirty yards of where I was and began emptying their quivers. I heard Elizabeth say to our daughters, "Spare no arrows!" Their attack was fierce and allowed me and the few men with me to join them. As we did, my three ladies turned their attack to the enemy which had surrounded the entrance, in an attempt to give a few of the last of our brethren an opportunity to enter.

Their accuracy gave our men a few helpful seconds to dive within the entrance and continue on to safety. Unfortunately, it left my family and a few other men completely isolated within a sea of death and carnage. Besides Elizabeth, Rose, Lily, and myself, there was Justin and three others: Andrew, Lamech, and Samson. Behind us were about six red dragons and two scores of men. They had held their position during the initial battle but were now gaining momentum at the sight of our dwindling numbers.

"Why did you come out here?" I asked Elizabeth with fear and frustration.

"I felt the Great King command me to," she said, "and in doing so, we saved many of our brothers."

"Dragon fire!" Justin shouted. We barely made it together with our shields to keep anyone from getting burnt.

"What now?" Samson shouted. "We can't make it to the Refuge!"

I looked at the entrance, which was now being overrun with the men of the village. I only hoped that the women and children had followed instructions and had escaped deep within the tunnel and cavern. I knew that within the tunnels, a few of our brethren could hold off over one hundred men from the village.

"We must make for the forest!" I shouted above the carnage. "We have a chance if we move now!"

This, however, wasn't good enough for Justin. As he saw the men of the village pouring into the entrance, and as he considered his beloved wife and family within, something came over him. Without any word or warning he bolted toward the entrance, sword in hand and a shout upon his lips. It was such a quick move that none of us were prepared to follow. Some men saw his advance and ran out to meet him but were quickly taken off guard by what happened next.

Lightning, the size and power of which I had never seen, shot from Justin's sword. It created an explosion within the entrance of the Refuge that sent earth and men flinging within the air. The doorway collapsed with tons of earth on top of it, either killing or trapping about two dozen of the village warriors who had entered. No sooner did this all happen then did a huge black dragon swoop down upon Justin, bite down upon his body, and carry him off into the distance.

The event created a distraction for us, and we began to run for the forest to the west side of the battle, where there was an opening in the enemy's ranks. A volley of arrows followed us, piercing both Samson and Andrew. Another volley was shot and Lamech was killed. We were now within the trees, though dragons and men were on our heels. Elizabeth and the girls shot at one of the nearest dragons while I engaged another. I then saw Captain Asa running toward us with men around him.

"We have them!" he shouted.

I began to accept that this was the end. We were overwhelmed and had no place to escape. I had killed the dragon across from me but was now defending myself against two swordsmen. They were not nearly as skilled as I was, so I had no difficultly disarming and wounding them. I didn't kill them, though a part of me definitely wanted to. Three more dragons were approaching, in addition to Captain Asa and the men with him. They would all be upon us in only a few seconds.

"I'm sorry," I said to my wife and daughters. "I don't think we will make it out of here alive."

"Then we will die fighting together!" Elizabeth said with resolution in her voice, and the girls shouted in approval.

Chapter 28

I looked at my daughters and they nodded in understanding. This was our final stand, and we would die in honor and glory.

I then heard the voice of someone behind me. It was Judah.

"Hurry!" he shouted. "Follow me! There is a way of escape!"

I looked at him in a second of disbelief and then quickly obeyed, motioning for my girls to do the same. Arrows whizzed past our ears. We followed Judah to a series of giant boulders which formed a narrow path that shielded us on both sides. I could hear dragons overhead, but the thick foliage above us concealed our location. After a series of turns, Judah pointed to a small opening that led straight down into the ground.

"Quick!" he said.

I motioned for my girls to enter.

"It goes straight down," Rose said.

"You won't get hurt," Judah assured her. "But you must hurry. They are coming."

My daughters all entered and then my wife.

"Your turn," I said to Judah.

"No," he replied. "I must cover the hole, and then enter another way that is easier to conceal. It is further up the path. You must hurry."

We could both hear the voices of the men coming up behind us.

"You are unarmed," I observed. "Here. Take my sword."

"Very well," he replied. "Go!"

I quickly dove within the hole, after which Judah covered it. The downward tunnel was like that of a slide, and yet it was pitch black. After about ten seconds of rapid descent, I landed upon the bottom. It was a rough landing but didn't cause any real damage. My wife and daughters embraced me, as best they could in the darkness. They were all safe and without injury, including sweet Rachel, who was fast asleep upon Rose's back. We could hear nothing of the men or dragons above. All was silent.

"I can't see a thing," Elizabeth said.

"I have my tinder kit," I replied, "but the flame will only last a few seconds."

"I can see," Lily said. "We are in a large room."

I hadn't considered my youngest daughter's ability.

"Well done!" I said to her. "Is there any danger?"

"No," she replied. "It is beautiful and peaceful."

"Do you see anything we could use?" I gently asked.

"Yes," she replied. "There is a torch on the wall."

"A torch!" I exclaimed, so pleased at the goodness of the Great King. "Lead me to it."

We soon had the torch lit and could take in the surroundings. The first thing I noticed was that we were within a fairly large cavern which had been formed by either dragon or man, for the room was surrounded by earthen stone, but it was flat on the sides and dimensional, clearly the work of someone or something.

"This must be part of the passage that Benjamin found," I said "though it has somehow been separated from the Refuge."

178

"Do you think we can make it to our brethren?" Elizabeth asked.

"I hope so," I replied. "All that matters now is that we are together."

"Praise the Great King," Elizabeth said. Her face then grew grave. "Dear Justin...," she said.

"It was a good death," I said with a deep sigh, thinking about my oldest friend in the faith. My eyes swelled up with tears. Justin was a special brother to me, for he had rescued me from doubt and then I rescued him from man's religion. "He undoubtedly saved the lives of many today," I said. "Though he leaves behind a wife and children."

"We will be a family to them," Elizabeth said, her eyes full of tears. "We will provide for them and teach them the ways of the Scroll."

"Daddy!" Rose exclaimed. "Your neck is bleeding!"

I then remembered the arrow that had cut my neck. It wasn't too severe, but it was still bleeding slowly. To my astonishment and joy, Rose reached up and touched my neck, and the wound soon vanished, leaving my neck perfectly healthy.

"Oh, Rose!" Elizabeth exclaimed. "You have found your ability! You can heal!"

Rose smiled with pleasure of her dream coming true.

"What wonderful warriors my children are," I said with joy. I then thought of Benjamin and Violet. Elizabeth seemed to be able to read my thoughts.

"I saw Daniel take Violet deep into the forest, in obedience to your instructions," she said. "Benjamin and Rebekah immediately entered the Refuge and should be safe. They are all in the Great King's hands."

We now entered a hallway that was sloped downward, entering a smaller room that had a sunken floor. The room only had the ramp as an entrance or exit and the ceiling was extremely high. There was a fitting upon the wall for the torch, which I used, allowing me to leave it there as we examined the room.

"What is this place?" Lily asked.

"It was a den for dragons, long ago," I said. "I'm not sure what the purpose of this room was back then, but I fear that it wasn't pleasant. It has the feeling of death in it."

"I do hope that Judah is safe," Elizabeth said. "He should have joined us by now."

"I hope so too," I replied. "I want to thank him for saving our lives."

At that very moment, something happened that none of us expected. A cage, which had been harnessed high above us and out of our sight, fell down. It was the size of half the room and came right in between me and my family, them within the cage and me outside of the cage. A loud clang from the fall echoed throughout the long-forgotten halls. Then silence returned.

"Is everyone alright?" I asked, panicked by the unexpected entrapment.

My women were breathing heavy, and little Rachel was crying. Fortunately, no one was injured.

I reached through the beams of the cage and held Elizabeth's hand, while my girls also reached through and took hold of me.

"Don't be afraid," I said. "It's an old trap, and nothing of danger is here to harm you. By the grace of the Great King, Judah will join us any moment now. He has my sword, which can easily cut through these bars."

"What if he doesn't return?" Rose asked fearfully.

"Don't worry," Elizabeth said to her girls. "If need be, your father will go and fetch the tools he requires to get us free. We have provision enough upon us for two days, which will be more than enough time."

"Your mother is correct," I said in an affirming voice. "There's no one here to hurt you. This is a safe place."

The girls took in a sigh of relief, and I squeezed my wife's hand. "We will wait a little longer," I said. "Judah will come."

An unknown noise then echoed around us. It was soft and first but grew continuously louder.

"What is that?" Lily asked.

"It sounds like it's coming from within the walls," I said.

Then, to our horror, we noticed multiple holes in the walls of the room. Water suddenly began gushing out of them.

"Caleb!" Elizabeth shouted.

I then understood the purpose of this room. It was sunken down so that it could hold water, like a giant tub. The cage was around seven feet in height, and the sunken floor was over ten feet in depth. The room was an execution chamber, and the method was drowning.

Elizabeth and the girls were screaming frantically, for the water had already risen a foot off the ground in only a moment. I tried to lift the cage but it was too heavy.

"My sword!" I said. "Great King, please, give me my sword!"

I then noticed something upon a ledge about fifteen feet above us that I hadn't seen prior. It was Judah!

"Judah!" I shouted. "My sword! Hurry! Give me my sword!"

Judah stood there looking down upon me and my family. He was unmoving.

"Judah!" I screamed in anger. "Help us! What's wrong with you?!"

Judah then knelt down and continued his gaze. A cruel and wicked smile formed upon his lips, and his eyes were filled with evil.

"Checkmate," he said.

Chapter 29

I was in a nightmare beyond anything I could imagine. My wife and my three daughters were trapped within a cage of torment, and there was nothing I could do. The cure was my sword, strapped upon the hip of a young man who I had brought into my home as one of my own but was a man different from who I thought he was. I looked up at him again.

"Judah," I said firmly. "If you don't help me then they will die."

Judah's face remained posed in evil delight. "What goes around comes around," he said.

"What does that mean?!" I shouted above the roars of the water.

Judah didn't reply. He simply stood to his feet, gazed into my eyes with a look of hatred, and walked away into some hidden passage I hadn't yet discovered. I looked back, and Elizabeth and my daughters were screaming hysterically and fearfully beyond anything I had ever before witnessed.

"Daddy!" Rose cried. "Help us! Please!"

"Caleb!" Elizabeth shouted, her eyes full of a fear that she had never demonstrated before. "Do something! Please!"

"I don't know what to do!" I shouted. We were all frantic and out of control. The water was now up to our waist, causing Rose to pick up Lily.

"Here!" Elizabeth shouted, taking Rachel from her back. "Take the baby!"

She handed me Rachel's body, but her head wouldn't fit through the bars. Baby Rachel screamed and cried from the pain at our attempt to pass her through from death to life, but it was impossible. The water was now approaching Elizabeth's shoulders, and the girls were climbing up to the ceiling of the cage to prolong the inevitable.

I couldn't believe what was happening. It seemed impossible. Where was the Great King? Surely, He wouldn't allow this to happen. I had no options; no way of saving my family. I simply began to weep and cry aloud, "I'm sorry!"

Then something happened. Elizabeth, who had been frantic and scared this entire time, now had a look upon her face of utter calmness and tranquility. She smiled, and reaching through the cage, pulled me to her. "Don't be afraid," she said. "It is all as it should be."

The water was now up to her neck and the girls were crowded around her. Rose was holding Rachel as high as the cage would allow. All of my daughters were crying uncontrollably.

"Elizabeth," I said, not sure of what to say, though my eyes were filled with sorrow and regret.

"It's alright," she said. "I love you so much." She then addressed the girls. "Girls, say goodbye to your father. We are going home now. It will all be fine. Don't be afraid."

Rose and Lily, whose faces were all pressed as high as the cage would allow, all began shouting. "Goodbye, Father! We love you, Daddy!" Their arms were reaching through the bars and grabbing hold of me. There was so much I wanted to say. So much I wanted to tell them. But our time was finished. At the last moment, just before the water rose above the cage, Elizabeth called out to me one last time. "Don't give up, my love! Fight till the end!" She then took her last breath and pulled my face to hers and kissed me. I stayed under the water as long as I could. But my tears and sobs didn't allow me to remain long, and I shot back out of the water screaming.

I was now kneeling upon the top of the cage, the water having risen a foot above it. I could see my wife and daughters all looking up at me, their eyes fixed upon me. At that very second, the water level reached the torch I had hung on the wall. Within a flash the light was extinguished, leaving me in utter darkness with the knowledge that my wife and daughters were right there, only a foot away, and now dead.

I don't remember how long I screamed and cried out in anger. The water eventually stopped filling the room, but it wasn't draining. I knew that my wife and daughters were dead, but I still waited for the water to leave the room so that they could rest on the floor. I then felt that I would die in that place. There was no way I would abandon them there, in pitch darkness, in a watery grave. I sat atop the cage, still able to feel their hair with my hands. All was silent. I could feel my heart pounding. And to sit there, knowing that their hearts had stopped beating was unbearable. I began to shiver from the chill of the water. A part of me wished I could enter the cage and die with them.

"Great King, let me die!" I shouted, my voice echoing into the distant reaches of that place. "I've done all I can! I've nothing left to live for!"

I then remembered a verse from the Scroll which read, If we live, we live to the Great King. And if we die, we die to the Great King. So whether we live or die, we belong to Him.

I pictured Rose, my little girl, with her sweet freckles and precious smile that would warm my heart. I thought of Lily, oh, precious child! I would not see her married and pregnant with children. Why? Baby Rachel, who was entrusted to me by her own mother, was now dead with no chance to enjoy the sweet things of life. And my dear Elizabeth. Life without her was as death to me.

I knew that I was to live for the Great King, that I was to continue on. But I didn't see how I could. Not without my Elizabeth. Not without my Rose, Lily, and Rachel. I then thought of my unborn baby within my wife's womb. It was also dead. Elizabeth had guessed it to be a boy. Oh, my son! Had he suffered? I began to weep again. I knew what it was to lose a child. I had lost Isaiah years earlier. But that was different. This was so many loved ones at the same time.

Deep within me I heard a voice. *Benjamin and Violet still need a father.* I still had two children living. And they would be crushed at the news of their mother and sisters' deaths. It took everything within me to move away from that place. Slowly, and struggling for every movement, I inched away from my loved ones. I found the ramp and began to crawl out of the room. For nearly half an hour, all I did was crawl. I then rose to my feet, and feeling the walls with my hands, tried to find a way out. Multiple times I fell to the ground and either cried or slept. I didn't know how long I was asleep. I soon lost all track of time. I could have been in that place for a few hours or a few days. Severe thirst began to plague me, and I imagined that I would die in that horrid hole, all alone in the dark.

Then, when I thought all hope was lost, I thought I saw light. It was so faint, and yet, in such darkness so bright. I was soon exiting out of a small hole into the full light of day. It took me a few minutes to adjust my eyesight. By all I could guess, it was midday. I wasn't sure if one day had passed since the battle or many. I guessed that I was on the opposite side of the mountain, having passed through, and was therefore not too far away from my brethren, if they had yet exited the mountain. I then heard footsteps approaching. It sounded like many men coming, so I mustered just enough strength to hide behind a boulder. I was able to make out about twenty masked men walking together, all armed. They wore the same white masks from the night I was taken by the dragon as a recruit. I wasn't sure if they were looking for someone or if they were simply traveling to a certain destination. I stood up to follow them and made it only a few steps before I was knocked over the head.

When I awoke, it seemed to be nighttime, for I could hear the cicadas, and I was in a place scarcely lit. I could also tell that I had been given water to drink in my unconscious state, for my thirst was quenched. I could see out the barred windows the faint twilight of the starlit evening. I was in a prison cell, which was inside a larger room. I wondered, for a moment, if the water and drownings were all just a dream. I considered, with desperate hope, that maybe it was all just a nightmare, and I would soon see my wife and daughters again, that I would hold them and laugh with them.

Outside of the cell was a table with candles upon it, giving just enough light for me to take in my surroundings. Next to the table was a chair with a man sitting in it. Within the dim light, I could see his eyes, fixed upon me. Those eyes seared my soul like a hot iron. Hatred, rage, and malice, that of which I had never felt before, began to grow within me. The man was Judah.

"How did it feel?" he asked. "How did it feel to watch them die?"

Chapter 30

If I had my way, in that moment, I would have broken through the cell walls and killed that man, slowly and inflicting as much pain as possible. But even amongst my rage and sadness, I knew that to do such a thing would be wrong and that it would dishonor the memory of my wife and daughters. They were now with the Great King, and no amount of anger or rage would bring them back. I didn't know if it was real, but I liked to think, in that moment and following, that they were watching and cheering me on. I suddenly felt a sense of peace that I thought would be impossible in such circumstances. My heart was still grieved and broken beyond description, but I also possessed a peace that transcended all understanding. Despite everything I had been through, I still felt the presence of the Great King. And even though I didn't understand why He allowed my wife and three daughters to die such a cruel death, I still trusted Him.

I was now left with the perplexing question of why Judah had betrayed my family. What did I ever do to him to deserve such treachery?

"It was a splendid game," he said with a smile. "I honestly didn't think I had it in me, but I proved to be strong."

The fact that he referred to all of this as a game made me furious. I stayed focused though. I couldn't let my flesh get in the way.

"I lured in your queen," he continued. "And was able to take her down along with many of your pawns. I still have two of your knights to take care of, however. As for you, only a few more minutes and you'll be removed from the board."

"Why did you do all of this?" I asked, my lips trembling.

"Why?" he repeated, his face growing angry. "You should know the answer to that. You were there." His eyes travelled back in time, and tears welled up within them. "It was the most beautiful dragon I had ever bred," he said. "I kept it warm, nursed it, and loved it. Then, suddenly, it lay bleeding and dying in my arms."

"I don't understand," I said.

"Your wife murdered my dragon!" he shouted as loud as he could, standing to his feet. He then paused and sat back down. "As my friends rejoiced around the fire at my precious dragon, she killed him."

I then understood. Nearly twenty years earlier, before I had joined Elizabeth and her people, I found myself hunched outside of a fire circle. There were five figures around that fire that evening. Three of them I knew: Caroline, Edgar, and Captain David's son, Joseph. But there was another named Judah, whose face I didn't see. I remembered how he cried out in anger and vengeance when the baby dragon was slain.

"You are Judas," I said soberly.

"I am," he replied, with pride in his voice.

"You would kill innocent people because of a dragon?" I asked with shock and disgust.

"They weren't innocent!" he replied. "They were murderers and intolerant bigots. I seriously didn't think I could go through with it," he continued, smiling with evil conceit. "But Captain Asa assured me that I could."

"Captain Asa?" I repeated, shocked at the mention of the name.

"Oh yes," he replied, excited at my horror. "Captain Asa was also around the fire that night. He has discipled me in secret all of these years. It was his idea that I should carry out my revenge."

I was beside myself. The fact that Captain Asa was a captain of a castle, and the fact that he was around the fire that evening, made me want to shout aloud. I knew that there were a few people in that Castle that sincerely wanted the truth. Even Captain David, before he disappeared, wanted the truth, deep down. But Captain Asa was deliberately going against it.

"It's actually been enlightening," Judah said. "During my time with you, I've learned much. The Castle will benefit extremely from the intel I will relate to them."

"But how?" I asked again, still perplexed at Judah's conscience. "How could you murder women and little children?"

"Because they were nothing but accidents that pollute society," he replied.

"Accidents?" I repeated. "They were human beings, created in the image of the Great King."

"Ha," he laughed. "That narrative makes you so weak! The Great King isn't real. We all came to exist by time and chance. Your wife and daughters were nothing but accidents. That's what we all are. Like I said, at first, the thought of taking their lives was difficult, but the more I focused on the truth, the easier it became. When you realize that humans have no true value, killing them is as easy as swatting a fly."

I remained still and quiet, recognizing the wicked doctrine which I had first heard within the pits of the enemy. This was the ultimate result of such heresy: death of the innocent. It made me wonder how many more innocent people would die because of such philosophies.

"And what of your beloved dragon?" I asked. "Was his existence just an accident?"

"No!" he replied. "It was beautiful."

"Your thinking is filled with inconsistences," I said. "I pity you. You have made yourself an enemy of the Great King, and He will judge you."

"Ha!" he said. "You are wrong. I won't be judged. It is *you* who will be judged. It is nearly midnight, and your executioner draws near. Soon a masked man, likely accompanied by others, will enter this room. He will aim an arrow at your chest, and it will pierce your heart until you die. I wanted the privilege to do so, but there is an old friend that desires it more."

"Who?" I asked.

"Edgar," he replied. "Just as your wife took away my dragon, you took away Edgar's beloved Caroline."

"That's nonsense," I replied. "Caroline took her own life, due to the sin and regret in her heart, for she knew that she had betrayed the Great King."

"It was the foolish teaching of the Scroll that killed that girl!" Judah bellowed. "She couldn't settle in her conscience the expectation of you and her parents, and so she finally took her life."

"It was Edgar that broke her heart and drove her to her death," I said, "not the Great King."

"How could he love a girl that wouldn't embrace his passions?" Judah asked.

I shook my head. "You speak of love, passion, and conscience. Those don't sound like things that exist in a world made by random chance. You're a fool. We took you in. We loved you and gave you a hope and a future, and you threw it all away because of the lies of the enemy. When you die, you will be all alone. And you will die in the knowledge that your dearest friends, the dragons, have betrayed you. On that day, with your final breath, you will realize that the Scroll was true. You will realize that you came so close to the truth, only to throw it away. You will want to come back and do it all over again. You will want to choose the correct path, but it will be too late. It will be beyond your reach."

A flicker of doubt flashed in Judah's eyes, and an unknown fear seemed to penetrate his heart, though he tried to hide it. I could tell he was weighing the options in his mind. If he was right, then he would enjoy the favor of the dragons until he died and existed no more. But if I was right, then he was doomed to eternal damnation and destruction. He finally looked at me, and his gaze of evil resolution had returned.

"You're wrong," he said. "*If* the Great King is real, and that's a big *if*, then the Great Dragon is stronger and wiser. He always has a trick or two up his sleeve. There are other scrolls besides just the one you have. I have read them, special scrolls that can only be read in secret places. They are older than yours, and they contain truths—truths that you don't know of. Would you read them? If you did, you would discover that you've been deceived."

"I have never read them, and I will never read them," I said. "Scrolls that have been penned by the Great Dragon or his followers are not worthy to be read. They are false and evil. You've chosen the wrong scroll."

Judah then looked upward, like he was listening for something. He smiled. "We will see who is right and who is wrong," he said. "You will be the first to undergo the great experiment of death, for I can hear your doom coming. Edgar and his companions are here."

The door soon opened, and four masked men entered. They all had white masks on and were dressed in white. The lead one had a bow in hand. Judah stood and made his way beside them.

"You will now die," he said. "I wish you could tell me how the adventure goes. You will find out first, I suppose, which of us is right and who is wrong. Any last words?"

I stood to my feet, resolved to honor my wife and daughters with a courageous death. "I have only this to say," I began. "First, the Great King is Lord of the heavens and the earth. And second, I forgive you, Judah. And I pray that you repent before the end."

The man with the arrow notched it to the bow, pulled it back, and aimed it right at me. To my surprise, the masked figure switched targets as fast as lightning and let the arrow fly. It sank deep within the chest of Judah.

Chapter 31

I stood in shock, unsure of what to do.

Judah fell to the ground clutching the arrow. "Why?" he cried out. "Why?"

The archer removed his mask.

"Benjamin!" I shouted, running to the bars and grasping them in both joy and disappointment mixed together. The others removed their masks as well; they were fellow warriors.

Benjamin didn't look at me or answer me but instead continued to gaze upon Judah. "You want to know why?" he repeated. "It's simple. You took from me my mother and my sisters and my unborn sibling. This is your just penalty."

My son's face was empty, void of all emotion and life. It hurt me to think of the lamentation that he had suffered during the previous twenty-four hours. Judah continued to cry out in pain as his life slowly ebbed away.

"Benjamin, my son," I said softly, "this isn't the way. Bitterness and hatred will only bring destruction to you and your future family." A tear began to travel down his cheek; his face was still fixed upon Judah. "You must forgive him, my son," I continued. "You must love him. It doesn't mean that he doesn't deserve justice; justice will find him. But it won't be from your hand."

Benjamin's face softened a bit then hardened once again. "I hate him," he said. "The coward. He ate at our table. He pretended to be my friend! He deserves to die."

"He does deserve death," I agreed. "Death would be fitting for him. But what about us? Before the Great King forgave us and welcomed us into His family, death was a fitting end for us as well. The Great Dragon desires for you to do what you're doing, for it will make you his slave. Listen to me, my son. The only way to freedom and victory for you and your family is to love your enemies and leave vengeance to the Great King."

I could tell that Benjamin's heart was softening. I then noticed Angela, who was waiting outside, peering in through the window. I motioned her to come inside

"Look," I said to Benjamin. "Angela is here. She might be able to heal Judah, and in doing so, save you from the guilt of murder."

"This is no murder," he replied. "It's an execution."

"If you go through with this," I said gently, "it will not bring back your mother or sisters. Neither will it heal your heart. It will only bring damage and danger to you and your family. Think of Rebekah. Victory and honor are in the forgiveness of one's enemy. Be brave, my son. Be courageous. Be a man."

Angela stepped forward. "I can heal him," she said to Benjamin. "But only if you will it to happen."

Benjamin hesitated. For nearly a minute he stood still, his eyes fixed on the dying man who murdered those dearest to him. Then at last he spoke. "Very well," he said. "Heal him if you can."

Angela quickly approached Judah, and without hesitation, ripped the arrow from his chest. He cried out in pain, his shirt soaked in blood. Angela pressed her hand upon the wound, and within only a short time, it was made whole.

Judah blinked in disbelief and sat up. "What happened?" he asked. "What did you do to me?"

Benjamin took a step toward him. "You've been healed by the power of the Great King," he said. "Justice, however, will find you. If you want life, you must repent and turn to the Great King. I forgive you, Judah. I forgive you for your deceit and treachery to my family. If, however, you choose to come upon my family again, it will not be vengeance but the protection of my family that will guide my hand. You will see my sword, and you will feel it. And it will hurt more than an arrow."

Finding the keys, they released me while locking Judah in the prison. He just lay on the floor, silent and thoughtful. My sword along with my shield were there where Judah had sat previously, and my friends and I escaped together into the night.

After we were a few minutes away from that place, Benjamin and I stopped and simply wept together for about half an hour. We embraced and took turns comforting each other. It was the beginning in a process of grieving that would likely last until our deaths. We then continued on, leaning on each other emotionally for support.

"Is your wife safe?" I asked my son.

"Rebekah is safe," he said, "and is recovering well from her wounds."

"And what of Violet?" I asked. "Is she alright?"

"Both she and Daniel are safe and sound," he replied.

"The Great King be praised," I said, relieved. "What about our people? Where are they?"

"Our people exited out the backside of the mountain and are hidden in the forest, awaiting your arrival. We lost over thirty souls in the attack."

"What a sacrifice," I said in reflection. "Was it mainly men?"

"Yes," he replied. "We lost two women in the battle itself. All the rest were men."

"How did you learn of your mother and sisters?" I asked.

"You know my ability," he replied. "I could sense their danger as death drew around them. It was deafening to my soul. I quickly went toward their pain, which was fleeting and only lasted a moment. There were masked men exploring the mountain close to where we were. I knocked one out and disguised myself with his mask and cloak. I then infiltrated their camp and overheard everything; Judah's plan of revenge, how it was carried out, and where you were and what was planned for you. The amount of self-control required for me to not compromise my cover was from the Great King Himself."

"I'm proud of you, my son," I said. "How you saved your wife, what you did in finding me, and how you forgave Judah; this was, without a doubt, your greatest rite of passage."

"How were you able to contain your grief?" he asked. "When we found you in the cell, you seemed to be doing remarkably well."

"My hope of seeing you and your sister is what kept me going," I said. "Otherwise, I think I'm still in shock. The Great King has brought healing to me, but I'm still in need for more."

"Well," he said, "I didn't think it possible, but what happened in there—me forgiving Judah—lifted a weight of burden from my heart."

A large moon now filled the night with a blueish glow, and as we followed the trail and entered a grove, we came face-to-face with five masked figures. I could tell by the red triangle on the mask that the middle figure was Edgar. He had a bow and quiver upon his back. For a split second, we just stood there, shocked at the sudden appearance of the other.

"You've come too late, Edgar," I said. "There will be no executions tonight."

"We will see about that," he replied as he and his companions drew their weapons. We were quicker on the draw and were armed first.

"You won't win this battle," I said with sword and shield ready. "We are far better trained."

He hesitated. "I should have simply ordered Judah to kill you himself."

"That would have worked better," I said smiling, for this enemy was little threat to us. "We bid you to go on your way and let us pass in peace."

Edgar removed his mask and tossed it upon the ground. "I've been waiting too long for this opportunity to let it slip away again."

"Edgar," I said with a voice of caution, "if you attack us, we will defend ourselves. You and your friends will likely die. We desire to live in peace."

"Peace?" he repeated. "No. You desire to make havoc. In memory of Caroline, I'm going to kill you now."

"That wasn't my doing," I said plainly. "I tried to lead her to the truth. It was you that crept in to our ranks, pretending to be sincere about the Great King. You won her heart and then broke it. You led her away from her Creator and King. The only person you should blame for her fate is yourself. You chose to go against the Scroll, and therefore, death and sadness were your inheritance."

Edgar notched the arrow upon the bowstring.

"This is your last warning," I said. "If you attack, we will fight."

"So be it," he said.

What happened then was tragic. Edgar and his companions attacked us. They were poorly trained and easily overcome. Fortunately, all of them were spared death and were only wounded. Edgar, however, received a blow to his wrist that severed his right hand. I looked upon this man, now bleeding severely and crying aloud. He was the same boy who I was asked to help so many years before. I remember him being a source of thanksgiving and joy when he supposedly chose to follow the Great King. Now he was crippled, both physically and spiritually.

"You'll never get away with this," he said. "My father will find you and kill you for this."

"My life and my fate are in the hands of the Great King," I replied. "Whatever He desires to happen will come to pass. But listen to me, Edgar. Your physical state now mirrors your spiritual condition. You have been crippled spiritually your entire life. Repent, and turn to the Great King and you will be healed."

Angela helped Edgar as best she could. His bleeding eventually stopped, and we left him with his companions who were also battered and torn.

"How far are we from our people?" I asked Benjamin.

"Only two more hours," he replied.

"I wonder what we should do now?" Angela said. "Find another place to bunker down and survive?"

"We have received instructions," I said. "And I believe it's time to follow them."

Benjamin looked at me. "Are you saying it's time to leave?" he asked.

"Without a doubt," I replied.

"Where are we going?" Angela asked.

"To the city of the Great King," Benjamin replied soberly. "We're going to Salem."

Chapter 32

I was rejoined to my people, and immediately sought out Violet. We embraced and wept for what seemed like hours upon hours. As I held her, however, I praised the Great King that I still had one daughter to hold. Our people were broken, for we had never suffered such a loss. Together we wept and rejoiced for the fallen. Justin's wife and children were all safe. Many of the fathers had sacrificed themselves for their families. Never before had we left our dead unburied, but the enemy was overrunning the forest. We had a day of honor for our fallen. Few words were spoken that day; tears were shed and prayers uttered in silence.

The vision of Salem was still something that was a mystery to me. I believed that the Great King spoke through Eli but doubt still gnawed at my mind. Without Elizabeth, I felt crippled and incomplete. The morale of my people was at rock bottom. Everyone was looking for my assurance that the vision of Salem was correct and that I wasn't acting in desperation, but I felt that I was unable to hear the Great King. His presence seemed to be far from me. With resolution and fear mixed together, we set out for Salem.

We departed at nighttime and, under the cover of darkness, left the forest and began our trek along the plains. Our destination was far within the vast deserts to the east. We knew that we were unprepared for the journey, but we had to trust that the Great King would provide for us in the wilderness, just as He had done so for His people in ancient years long ago.

Our number was a little more than one hundred. We were beaten and weary, and yet we tried to sing and pray as we walked along. My mind was continually on Elizabeth, Rose, Lily, and Rachel. I thought of how wonderful it would be to have their company, to just walk with them and be together. I still didn't understand why the Great King allowed them to die, and I was trying to trust in His providence, but it was proving more and more difficult.

As the days continued, I noticed both Violet and Benjamin's joy return, if only a little, mainly due to the comfort and love of their spouses. To have such loss upon your first day of marriage was something I couldn't imagine, and yet, it seemed to me that they were able to endure it. Their faith in the Great King allowed them to do so. They weren't simply young people in love; they were kingdom warriors.

About three weeks into our journey, we came upon the border of the vast desert. We were concerned of what it would hold for us, but we believed we were doing the will of the Great King. After another week in the desert, we found only sand and dry creek beds. Our food and water were nearly spent, and our faith in the vision of Salem was fleeting as well.

That night we rested under a small clump of palm trees. No one spoke. We were too exhausted. I fell asleep with a heart full of fear and sorrow. "Please," I prayed as I drifted to slumber, "please bring us to Your city."

The next morning, we began again. And as we came over a rise in the sand, there it was. It was the city of the Great King. It was like nothing I had ever seen before. There were buildings stretching up to the heavens. A lush river flowed down the middle of the city and trees grew on both sides of it, bearing fruit.

"Where is everyone?" Benjamin asked as he and his wife walked beside me.

"I'm not sure," I replied. "But let's eat and drink!"

Our people ran toward the river. We had heard correctly! We were free from danger and persecution! Then, without warning, an enormous dragon burst forth from the earth. It wasn't a random sentinel dragon; it was the Great Dragon! His arms shot forward and picked up Violet in one hand and Benjamin in another. I cried out in fear and dismay. Without hesitation, the Great Dragon bit both of them in half. I fell to the ground and put my head down between my knees and covered my ears. Fear, like I had never felt, mixed with a feeling of worthlessness and failure, pierced my soul.

Then I woke up. The stars were overhead. I was still under the palm trees. I put my hand on my chest in relief and heard a voice within me. *You mustn't fear, My brother. You must believe. You must find My joy.*

The sun eventually rose in the east, and we trudged along. I meditated on the dream. It seemed that the Great King was revealing to me the true condition of my heart: fear.

Nathan walked beside me. "What do you think will be waiting for us at Salem?" he asked.

"I'm not sure," I replied. "Last night I had a dream. It wasn't good."

"I think we will find the Great King," he said. "I believe that He will be there, waiting for us."

"I hope you're correct," I said. "I only wish He would give us a sign of His love and presence. How long is it until we reach the city?"

"At this pace," he replied, "another week at least."

I sighed. "We are virtually out of food and only have two days left of water. You realize what that means, don't you?"

"What's that?" he asked.

"It means that we can't go back," I explained. "The closest water supply behind us is eight days away. It means, Nathan, that we will likely all die out here of thirst and starvation."

"I don't care," Nathan said, his voice full of exhaustion and pain. "If we die, we will go to be with the Great King. If I'm going to die, I'm going to die doing what I think the Great King wants me to do."

We suddenly stood still. Something was happening ahead of us; dust was raising to the heavens above.

"What is that?" I asked. "A dust storm?"

Someone else shouted, "It's an army!"

"No," said Nathan. "It moves too fast to be an army."

"Horses," I said. "It's scores of horses."

"In the desert?" Benjamin asked. "What does it mean?"

"I think it means that the Great King hasn't abandoned us," I said timidly.

The horses came upon our number as old friends, tame and loving. They were magnificent animals and seemed to be inviting us to ride them.

"This is our chance!" someone said. "With these horses, we can return to the water source and then return home. These horses have been sent by the Great King to save us!"

"But what about the prophecy?" another asked. "What about the Great City?"

Every eye was upon me.

"You must choose," Nathan said to me. "We either return home, or we continue on."

I had already mounted and sat upon my horse, and looking out over the vast desert. There was nothing to be seen ahead of us except for dust and sun. I thought of the forest, its beauty and abundant provision. Despite my severe thirst, hunger, and sadness, I couldn't stop looking ahead of me in the direction of Salem. Something within me said, *Caleb. Everything that has happened in your life has led you up to this moment. What you choose now will be the defining moment of your life.*

I circled around to my brethren. "Come, my friends," I said. "We ride for the Great City."

There were no cheers or affirmation. Only a sense of resolute determination to finish the quest. We rode long into the night and again on the next day. Upon the third day, our provisions—both for man and animal—were spent. We noticed something ahead.

We pressed forward and found it to be nothing but rubble. It was a series of ruins, mostly made of dried mudbricks. Some walls remained half-standing. Only one or two rooms still had half-roofs over them. The well was dry and there wasn't even a single tree. It was obvious that no one had been there for centuries.

"What is this place?" I asked.

Uriah, our navigator, looked at his maps.

"This is it," he said. "This is Salem."

"This?" I asked. "This is the city of the Great King?"

"It seems so," he replied.

I looked around me at the desolation and waste.

What are we doing here? I thought to myself. This was a mistake.

Chapter 33

For nearly ten minutes, we all just stood there, some people looking about them while others sat down and put their heads in their hands and wept.

Nathan approached me. "Caleb, we have no water. The horses are laying themselves down, likely to die, and we will soon follow them. What are your instructions?"

I hesitated. A part of me felt like crying, another like shouting aloud to the sky in anger and frustration. Yet, something within me was kindled. It awoke. Since the drowning of my wife, unborn child, and three youngest daughters, something within me seemed dead, and suddenly, in this place, it was now risen. It was hope. I decided then that I was done acting like a child and walking in self-pity. I was a captain in the armies of the Great King. If we died the horrific death of dehydration, we would do so with our heads held high and with the praises of the Great King upon our lips.

I had suffered much in the last few weeks. Most of my family, along with various dwellings, had been taken from me. I had possibly led my people to their doom. But I knew that all had been done with the desire to follow the Great King. I was tired of being afraid. I had to trust in the sovereignty of the Great King and that His purpose would stand forever. If we were to die in that place, then I would lead my people to a death of praise and worship of the Great King.

"Hear me!" I said, raising my voice. "The Great King told us to be here, and we have obeyed. Now we must remain. Do not be afraid. If the Great King wants us to be here and to live, then He will provide nourishment to sustain His people. However, His provision isn't always easy. So let us strive to find it and do so with a joyful heart. Come, my beloved brethren. We must dig. Water is to be found below. Use your swords and shields for spades. Divide into small teams and dig. And pray as you do so."

"We are with you!" Nathan said, as was his way. "Come, everyone! Let's search for the nourishment of our King!"

It was about mid-day, and the sun was beating upon us. Our throats were parched and our heads spinning. As the sun sank low in the west, we had still not found water and many were unable to continue. They lay upon the ground, heads aching, not able to stir. Just as the stars started to appear in the east, a cry went up. It was Angela.

"Water!" she cried. "We have water! Hurry!"

Those who were able ran to her. The teams she was working with had dug a hole about fifteen feet deep. At the bottom, the earth was moist and if you put a cup down low in the earth, it would trickle full of dirty water in about five minutes. We made a filter out of cloth, and in this way were able to give everyone a sip of water within two hours. Meanwhile, revived by the little bit of water received, we kept digging. By the early morning hours, all had been refreshed, and the well was now over twenty feet deep, providing a good supply of cool, clean water. Everyone slept most of the following morning, rehydrating as they could, finding shade amongst the ruins of that ancient city. Our horses were also watered and refreshed, and we lost none of them.

There was now the matter of food to consider. It came to many of our minds to slaughter one of the horses for meat, but this was an unattractive option, seeing as we were convinced that the Great King had gifted them to us. There wasn't, however, any food at all to be found in that place. Not a leaf of a tree or bush, not a bird or rabbit or snake. There was only dirt.

As the night came on, our hunger was overwhelming.

"We must begin to eat horses," Jedidiah said. "They did their job in getting us here. Besides, they will soon starve as well, for there is no grass here."

"Perhaps we should consider returning to our home," someone said. "We could likely make it, seeing as we could butcher a few horses as we travel along."

"But the Great King told us to come here," Nathan replied. "Eli has the gift of prophecy and foresight, much like Captain Benjamin did. I don't think that he got it wrong. Remember also, it was our very own Captain Samuel, with his dying words, who told us to travel. Something is going to happen, and the Great King wants us to be here."

"Then I pray it happens soon," Daniel said. "Otherwise, we will perish."

"It will," Nathan said. "Or else the Great King will provide ways for us to prolong our time here. His will is going to happen. We must be faithful. What do you say, Caleb?"

I was unsure of what to do. The Great King gave us water, but without food, we couldn't sustain ourselves. And He had put us in the middle of a desert.

"He's trying to teach us something," I said. "We must be learners. We are committed now to this place. Our destiny remains here. We must be resolute."

All was quiet. Each man wrestled to take hold of the truth and courage he needed to go on. Suddenly, Rebekah cried out and pointed to the south. "Look!" she said. "There are lights over there!"

We looked, and what we saw was an extraordinary, yet troubling, sight.

There were lights, hundreds of them, coming our way.

"Look," I said to Daniel, "and tell us what you see!"

Daniel peered out into the night, his eyes squinted. "They are men," he said. "Men with torches in one hand and swords in the other."

"The men from the village and Castle," I said. "They've tracked us. I can't believe it. They won't stop until we are all dead."

"We must run!" a man said.

"No!" replied another. "We must stand and fight! Let's ride out to them and at least have the honor of attacking instead of always defending!"

My heart sank down within me. The evil of these attackers was relentless.

"To death and glory!" a man said. "Let's die fighting!"

I raised my sword to order formations.

"Wait!" Daniel said, still squinting his eyes and peering. "I also see woman and children."

"Woman and children?" I said.

"And provisions," he continued. "They are dressed modestly and honorably.

"They are our people!" Benjamin exclaimed. "Come!"

He jumped upon his steed and began to ride out to them.

"Benjamin, wait!" I shouted, but it was too late. He was off like lightning.

I motioned to a few of the men, and we followed him. By the time we reached him, we were only two hundred yards away from the newcomers.

"Stand your ground!" I ordered my men. "We don't want them to mistake us for the enemy. We are already in range of their archers."

Soon the approaching company paused. They stretched nearly a quarter of a mile wide. I guessed that they had seen us, for even at night, upon the white changeless sands, we stood out like a lone clump of trees upon the prairie.

A few of their riders began to approach us. As they neared, I raised my hands as a token of peace. They returned the token and came up to where we were, five men, all of them appearing as men of integrity and truth.

"Greetings," I said. "My name is Caleb. We are from the village of Ravenhill."

"Greetings," one of them said. "I am Thomas. We are looking for the ancient city of Salem."

"You have found it," I said soberly. "But who are you? And why are you looking for it?"

"We are followers of the Great King," Thomas replied. "And I'm guessing that you are too."

"We are indeed," I said. "But I don't understand."

"The Great King told us to seek out His city," he explained.

"How many of you are there?" Nathan asked.

"We number nearly six hundred," Thomas replied.

"An army of six hundred!" Nathan exclaimed.

"We didn't all set out together," Thomas explained. "We are actually made up of over a dozen armies of the Great King with independent captains. We met upon the road."

"You mean that the Great King is telling multiple armies of His to come here?" I asked.

"Absolutely," Thomas said with a laugh. "It's incredible. I believe that He is calling all of His people. Each of us was greeted by horses along the way. I'm not sure what He's doing, but the Great King is up to something big."

"Well then," I said, overwhelmed at the work of the Great King. "Welcome. We are around a hundred in number. We have water, though we will likely need to dig more wells. We are out of food, however."

"Do not be afraid, my brother," Thomas said. "The Great King provides. We have an abundance of food for both people and horses."

"Excellent!" I said. "This is a miracle for us. Come, my friends! Come into the Great City!"

"There's one more thing," Thomas said. "Am I right to assume that you are the lead captain of these people?"

"We have no lead captain," I replied, "but I am one of our captains."

"He is indeed the lead captain," Nathan said. "He is the lead captain by his example."

"Then you, Caleb, are special to the Great King," Thomas said. "All of us who have arrived here tonight were all told to come here. But we were also told that there would be one army here before us. And that the captain of that army would be our captain as well. We look to you, Captain Caleb. We look to you to lead us until the end."

Chapter 34

Everyone was welcomed within the city, and we feasted together late into the evening. The food provisions that our brethren provided revived us immensely. I found myself around a campfire with nearly a dozen men, most of whom were captains from other fellowships.

"Well," Thomas said, "here we are. There are more coming, for our scouts have seen them from afar. We have been longing for this city ever since we heard the Great King calling us, though I must confess," he looked around a bit, "this isn't quite what I expected."

"It was difficult for us as well," I testified. "Though it is just as the Scroll tells us: *Man looks at the physical; the Great King deals with the heart.*"

"Yes, exactly," Thomas said with a smile. "It shouldn't surprise us. It is actually, I think, very much like the Great King to bring us to such a place. He is ever-teaching us, ever-growing us."

He then looked around the circle. "Seven of the fellowships that I arrived with are represented here," he said. "There are other captains who are still helping their people find lodging."

He then went around and introduced the other captains. Most of them were from villages I had never heard of and had travelled months to arrive.

"So," Thomas continued, "tell us your story, Caleb. Was the persecution in your area severe?"

"It was," I replied. "Some were captured and executed. Others killed in assaults and invasion."

"This is the story everywhere," he said. "In my own village, our children were lured away from us and taken. We fought to retrieve them and were only able to save a little over half of them before they were executed."

"How dreadful!" I exclaimed.

"The pain we experienced in losing our children is one that words cannot adequately describe," Thomas said.

Another man spoke up. His name was Jethro. He was from a village by the sea, far away. "In our village, they made it where we were unable to buy or sell in the market place. We were driven within the mountains, and many of our children either froze to death or died of starvation."

"In my village," said a captain named Andrew, "they burned our Castle to the ground."

"Your Castle?" I asked. "You mean, an actual building?"

"Yes," he replied.

"Well," I said, "it sure is assuring to know that there are still true followers of the Great King meeting in Castles. I'm sorry to hear that it was burned."

"It ended up bringing us even closer together," Andrew testified.

"That's the reality of the enemy's efforts to thwart us," Thomas said. "It is difficult. But it ends up making us stronger and bringing the Great King more glory."

We said *amen* to his words.

Another captain named Stephen then spoke up. "The greatest confrontation in our village wasn't the persecution; it was the ideals that were being introduced to our society. This new teaching that is known as *progression*. It has won the minds of the citizens of our land. They accepted an alternate history of our world, as well as an alternate definition on things as elementary as marriage and gender."

"They are connected," another captain explained. "When the people accept a false history that doesn't include a Creator, then it is only a matter of time until things like marriage and gender are bent and tarnished."

"In our village," spoke another, "they even justified the killing of infants, saying that they weren't human until they were able to think for themselves."

"They did the same in our village," another testified.

"In short," I said, getting all of their attention, "in short, the entire world has progressed, or I suppose digressed would be a better word; they have digressed to an immeasurable evil. And in doing so, the light of the Scroll is too bright for them to be willing to tolerate. Our very presence exposes their wicked deeds to the light of the Scroll, and they want to live without guilt or conviction."

"What do you think is their plan now?" Jethro asked.

"I believe they mean to find us here and exterminate every single one of us," I said plainly. "I don't believe they will stop until we are all dead."

"Are you speaking of the dragons or the men?" Thomas asked.

"Both," I replied, "though the dragons are the ultimate leaders between the two of them. I've been deep within their ranks, and I've seen more dragon eggs than I could count. Tens of thousands of them. They should have hatched by now. An army will soon be released upon this world."

Some men shuttered while others shook their heads.

"My father speaks the truth," Benjamin said. "I have also been amongst them, and I've heard their scheming. The enemy doesn't want to be left alone; they want to be alone. The thought of us, even on a remote part of the planet, won't satisfy them. The Great Dragon, who is ultimately behind their thinking, hates us too much."

"We need information," Jethro said. "Let's send out our fastest scout."

"But we are weeks away from civilization," I said. "Even our fastest scouts won't be able to get there and back for days upon days."

"You speak the truth," Thomas said. "But have you ever seen what happens when two scouts travel together? Their speed is like the wind."

A man named Jeremiah came to us. I then called to Daniel and addressed the two men. "Go at all speed back to the dwellings of men and see what is happening. Get an idea of what may be before us."

Violet approached and grasped tightly to her man. They exchanged a gentle kiss.

The two men then bowed in submission and were away at a speed that is hard to describe. It was as if lightning was in their feet.

"Well," Thomas said, "if it's a war they want, then it's a war they'll get. We may be fewer in numbers, but we are trained and gifted. And most importantly, we have the Great King on our side."

"I have set my sight on this city with resolution," I said. "This is our final stand. We will either win, or we will all die. I'm fine with whichever because I believe in the sovereignty of the Great King."

We spent an hour in earnest prayer but were overcome with weariness, for it was nearly morning. A man named Titus, who was with us around the fire, spoke with me afterwards. "I have greatly enjoyed this fellowship and prayer," he said. "Being around so many captains at once is such a privilege."

"I'm glad you enjoyed it," I said. "We are glad to have you. How far away is your village?"

"Over two month's journey away," he said. "Very far indeed."

"And where are your captains?" I asked.

"We have only one," he replied. "But he is better than ten. I wish so badly that he would have heard this conversation. He would have had much to contribute."

"I'm sorry we missed him," I said. "Where is he?"

"He has been tending to some of our elderly tonight, for they are weary from the long travel."

"I know it is late," I said, "but if he is still awake, I'd love to at least shake his hand."

"Yes, of course," replied Titus. "He is right over here."

He then led me to where most of his fellowship was resting. There, spreading a blanket over an elderly man, was Titus' captain. Our eyes met, and I froze still. His deep blue eyes pierced me like an iron, yet his smile refreshed me like a cool brook.

"Captain Caleb," he said warmly, "I've missed your face."

I wanted to reply but was unable. I wanted to return the compliment but was too shocked. All I could do was utter his name.

"Captain David," I said gently.

Chapter 35

He was clad as a captain of the Great King. His face had aged in the decade since I had seen him; it carried many stories upon it, yet it was gentle and at peace. This man who I had once esteemed, who I had prayed for and loved but also had seen shackled by the invisible chains of religion and the fear of man, this man was now free! I approached him and we embraced.

"Look at you," he said smiling. "You're a captain. I'm not surprised."

"I have so much to say," I replied. "Some of the things I said to you many years ago were not said as they should have been. Sometimes I spoke the truth, but I did not always speak it with love. It has been a burden upon my heart all these years."

"A burden needlessly carried," he replied gently. "I never bore you any animosity. You helped me, Caleb. Your words, even years after you spoke them, continue to minister me. Most of all, your example has helped me."

I took in a deep breath. "I am relieved," I said. I then motioned for us to sit down. The stars continued to twinkle in the sky, and a cool night breeze brought us comfort. "What happened to you?" I asked. "You suddenly disappeared, and no one knew of your whereabouts. I finally concluded that you had died."

"I did," he said, "in a way. I died to myself and the expectations of others. But it was a difficult and grueling process." He then looked up to the sky thoughtfully and then returned his gaze to me. "My wife grew ill, around twelve years ago. It was a cancer of some kind, and it took her quickly. No one really knew my wife, at least, not the way I did. She was quiet. She didn't fit the mold of a captain's wife in the Castle, so she simply stayed in the background of my ministry. Looking back, the Castle was more a wife of mine than she was. We grew further and further apart.

"During that time, I'm ashamed to confess, I was envious of something I saw in my wife. She had a relationship with the Great King that was beyond what I had. It was frustrating. I realized that what I saw in the Scroll, the victory and the freedom we are supposed to have in the Great King, was void in my life, and not only in my life, but the life of the Castle as well. I wasn't able to obtain it. Neither was I able to give it to others. I went to the Great Castles for help, but they weren't able to answer my questions. Don't misunderstand me; they gave me techniques that would get more people in my Castle, but I was still unable to train my flock to kill dragons. The Great Castles taught me how to build bigger buildings and how to get people excited about being there, but what I saw in the Scroll was still, by and large, absent.

"On my wife's death bed, with her last words she said this: *Stop the deceit. Give up this madness. Start over.* I asked her what she meant, tears flowing down my cheeks. She said to me, *You must start again, not with a Castle, but with you. Just you, the Great King, and the Scroll.* I told her I was sorry for the husband and father I had been, but it was too late. She was gone. I sat there, my son and daughter with me, and we wept."

As I listened to Captain David recount his tale, I wept as well, tears of sadness but also tears of thankfulness for the goodness of the Great King. "Well," he continued, "my wife's final words haunted me. I knew they were from the Great King, but they scared me. Meanwhile, the Castle was growing in numbers but not in maturity, character, or skill. I was beginning to see everything differently. My eyes were continually opened. The more I looked in the Scroll, the more I saw the error of the Castle: the Youngling Guild, the gender confusion regarding roles and weaponry, as well as the fact that we weren't fighting dragons. I couldn't believe that we had actually allowed dragons to enter the Castle. It seemed like everything was beyond repair.

"I tried to open up people's eyes to what I was learning, but it wasn't working. I then remembered the words of my wife and realized my only hope was to start with me. It wasn't enough for me to simply see the issues; I had to grow in maturity. I had to become an example of the solution. I remember my final day at the Castle. It was King's Day. The service had ended, and I was walking through the crowds of people asking myself, *What did today's ceremony really accomplish?* The Great King seemed to fully open my eyes. People were smiling and fellowshipping and acting like everything was well in their lives; yet I knew them. Their marriages were falling apart, and their children were extremely worldly. Multiple people came up to me, telling me how excited they were about the Castle, but none of them seemed to truly be following the Great King. They were, like myself, barely scratching the surface of Kingdom living. Eric then came up to me and got everyone's attention. *Listen to me!* he said to the crowds. *Look at all this Castle has accomplished! Look at this army! We are well over a thousand soldiers! All of this is due to the diligence of our greatest warrior and leader, Captain David!* Everyone cheered. I looked around at them, not able to even smile. *What have I done?* I thought to myself. *What have I accomplished?*

"Don't misunderstand me. There were some true followers of the Great King in that Castle, but I had failed to bring them to maturity. They were on the right team, but they weren't efficient warriors. That day, as I left the Castle, I quickly found my son and daughter. I told them I was leaving and that I wanted them to come with me. A few tears were shed, mainly by my daughter, but in the end, they declined. They were already young adults by then, and my daughter had given her heart to another man, out of wedlock unfortunately. My son, as I had known for years, was a dragon breeder and was just playing the Castle game. I believe it was my hypocrisy that drove them away, for I was a different man at home than at the Castle. I lost their hearts, and so they pulled away from the Great King.

"Leaving them was the hardest thing I ever did, though I knew it was necessary. I had to follow the last words of my wife. I had to find the Great King for myself. For many weeks, I roamed the countryside. I asked the Great King to lead me to where I was supposed to be. I ended up coming upon a small village named Stonewall. I attended their Castle and found the same thing there that I had left: wonderful people, doing seemingly wonderful things, but in the end, not accomplishing much of what the Scroll commanded. I would simply sit in the service and ask, *What are we accomplishing here?* The answer was crystal clear.

"I then spent many days simply sitting in the market and observing. I felt very strongly that the Great King desired me to stay in that village. And I felt that He wanted me to find true followers of the Scroll. I became, in that time, a studier of people. I examined how they treated their spouses and children and also how the children treated their parents. I looked at how they carried themselves and how they spent their money. The market was a perfect place for this, and I began to be pulled to a few families. My soul gravitated to them; it was remarkable. There was something about them that attracted me, and I believed it was the Great King in them. After some time, I approached one of them and asked if they were followers of the Great King. They said yes, and I became friends with them. After earning their trust, they invited me to their fellowship, which met various times throughout the week. Immediately, I knew that this was what I was searching for. I could see the Scroll lived out in them. They reminded me of my wife, and I put myself under their teaching and training. Eventually, after a few years, and through many circumstances and adventures, I became their captain. I believe it was the first time for me that I had truly been a captain, for I was actually able to help them obtain the freedom and victory in the Scroll. There is much more to my story, but that will suffice for now."

As I listened to David's story, I was overcome with a love for him, and I gave the Great King praise for what He had done in David's life. The first glow of morning was now rising in the east.

"It's a beautiful story," I told him. "And I am happy beyond belief at how the Great King has rescued you from the deceit of this world. You were willing to be mistreated with the remnant rather than enjoying the praises of men. You have done well, brother."

I was going to say more but something happened. I sensed it, more than ever before. I sprang to my feet and looked to the north.

"What's wrong?" Captain David said, coming to my side.

"Dragons," I said. "They're coming. I've never felt anything like it."

"Our numbers here are over seven hundred," he replied confidently. "How many dragons are there?"

"It is beyond count," I replied.

"Beyond count?" he said to himself.

"There's something else," I said. "I've never felt it before but I think I know what it is."

"What is it?" he asked.

"It's the Great Dragon," I replied.

Chapter 36

I raised my voice for all to hear. "Dragons!" I yelled. "Dragons are coming!" People jumped to their feet and grabbed their weapons. Captain Thomas was quickly at my side. "Where do they come from?" he asked.

"From the north," I replied. "Their number is beyond measure."

Captain Thomas turned around and called aloud for a woman named Esther. She quickly came before us and raised her hands to the north.

"How many?" he asked gently.

"A little more than twelve thousand," she replied. "They will be upon us in ten minutes."

"Look!" Nathan said. "Our scouts return!"

Jeremiah and Daniel were quickly coming across the desert toward our camp, the dust flying high behind them. They came up to us.

"Dragons!" they said. "Dragons are on our heels!"

"We know," I replied. "And what of the humans? Are they riding the dragons?"

"There are no people," Jeremiah reported, his eyes filled with lament.

"You mean they remain back in the villages?" I asked.

"No," Daniel explained. "All of the villages are destroyed and not one human remains alive. The dragons turned on them and devoured them all."

"But what about those who were aligned with the dragons?" Nathan asked. "What about Edgar, Captain Asa, and Judah? What happened to them?"

"All gone," Daniel testified. "I saw Edgar's death. He cried out that he was a worthy servant. He was swallowed without pity."

I stood there processing what I was hearing. After a few seconds of consideration, it didn't surprise me. The dragons never intended to join with the humans, only to use them, as the useful fools they were, until they didn't need them anymore. I pitied them though. It would have been a cruel end.

The scouts continued their report. "Judah, however, wasn't eaten," Daniel said. "He was burnt alive by the Castle before the dragons came."

"Burnt alive?" I repeated. "That doesn't make sense. Only followers of the King are burnt alive by the Castle."

"And what about our other brethren?" Thomas asked. "Is anyone else coming?"

"No," Daniel replied. "No one else made it. This is all of our people that are left."

"Then it will surely be enough," Captain David said. "Caleb, what are your orders?"

I looked to the north. There, on the horizon, we could see them coming. A line of red upon the ground and a cloud of black within the sky. I then looked to my son, Benjamin. He nodded with both understanding and consent. I then looked to Violet, who shared her thoughts by her body becoming engulfed in flame. I drew my sword and addressed our people.

"If this is our final battle," I said aloud for all to hear. "If we are indeed the last of humanity upon this planet, then we will not wait for the enemy. We will ride out and meet them." I then raised my voice. "All captains, ready your people! We ride upon them as one unit!" Within only a few minutes, we were upon our steeds and ready. The dragons were only a mile from us now and closing in. I looked over to

Nathan. "Fight well, my brother." I then addressed my people. "Ride!" I shouted with my sword pointed toward the enemy.

"For the Great King!" Everyone shouted, and we burst forth.

Benjamin, Violet, and their spouses were upon my right; Nathan and his family upon my left. My only wish, within the passion of that moment, was that Elizabeth and the rest of my family would've been with me. The wall of dragons that were approaching were beyond anything I could have imagined. The depth and breadth of their line was overwhelming.

"Archers ready!" I shouted as we rode. The wives and daughters readied their bows with grace and elegance as only daughters of the Great King were capable of.

"Fire!" I shouted. The command went down the line, and the arrows were loosed. Many of the arrows were flamed, and many of them splintered into dozens of arrows. Some exploded on impact, sending multiply dragons falling to the ground. The dragons now breathed their fire upon us. Our shields went up, as well as many invisible shields. The heat in that moment was as the sun falling upon us. A battering of armies then took place. Arrows, fire, swords, and blood clashed together.

Rebekah quickly loosed seven arrows, each of them hitting their marks, mainly the eyes of dragons. Violet had left her mount and was standing firm, the ground around her burned by the dragon fire that was continually falling upon her. She didn't even blink, but let her arrows loose even through the oncoming fire. All dragons that crossed her fell dead.

I came upon multiple red dragons. They were young and inexperienced but as rampant and deadly as a tornado. Benjamin and I defeated them, and eight more took their place. Captain Thomas then rose before us and slashing his sword in the air, something like light shot from it, severing all eight dragons in half. I then beheld Captain David leading his people. They were in a circle, back-to-back, with dragons encircling them.

"Never quit!" he was calling to them. "Don't be afraid! Fight to the end!"

He then raised up his sword and came at the dragons on every side. He was a like a whirlwind of furry. His people followed him, and together they were unstoppable.

We were killing dragons, but for every one we killed, it seemed like five replaced it. I looked over my shoulder and saw Captain Jethro in a dragon's mouth being devoured. Screams of death filled the air, and as more of our people were slain, we began to be overrun.

"We must pull back!" Nathan shouted to me amidst the carnage.

"But how?" I shouted. "There are too many of them!"

Nathan hesitated. "Tell my family to fight to the end," he said. "Tell them I love them."

He then turned his horse and rode toward the main line of the enemy. Putting out his hands as he rode, he seemed to push back the enemy with his ability, rolling them up as he moved, though his horse was slowing under the pressure.

"What is he doing?" Captain Thomas asked.

"Trying to give us time to retreat back to the city," I answered with tears in my eyes.

Captain Thomas smiled and laughed. "He will need help! Hurry, Captain Caleb. Sound the retreat and lead our people until the end. We will try to give you all at least a few minutes to rest and pray."

The captain then spurred his horse and rode after Nathan, who had pushed back nearly all of the line of dragons but was about to be overcome. Just in time, Captain Thomas came to his aid, riding past him slashing his sword in the air, the light from his blade cutting through the enemy, allowing Nathan to drive them back further. For a moment, I was unable to withdraw, for I was so moved by the bravery of my two brothers. I finally came back to myself and ordered the retreat. Only a few dragons were between us and the city, and we cut them down as we retreated. The sun was darkened by the dust of battle, during which I never beheld the Great Dragon, though I was certain that I sensed him.

We returned to the city and took the afforded moment to rest and dress our wounds. We had killed over a thousand dragons, but our numbers were reduced to only a hundred and twenty. Daniel stood next to me, battered and bruised, as he gazed into the distant line of dragons. A tear rolled down his cheek.

"What do you see?" I asked.

"The death of Nathan and Thomas," he answered. "By their skill, the enemy has been pushed back a few miles, though they seem to be reforming their lines. We have only a few minutes."

Rebekah stepped forward and shouted toward the battle line. "Father!" she cried with eyes full of tears. "I will join you soon!" Violet embraced her sister-in-law to comfort her.

"First, Justin and now, Nathan," I said, my heart unable to weep because of the depths of despair within me. "One led me to the Great King; the other to the truth of the Scroll. Oh, Nathan. You were my dearest friend and brother. Be at peace. A good death found you."

I lowered myself off of my horse and sat upon the ground.

"They're too many," Benjamin said, falling beside me, his body suffering from minor burns and cuts. "What are we to do?"

Captain David drew near to us, his sword stained with the blood of dragons. "Now is the time," he said, "for one last charge. Now is the time to die well."

I looked up at him. I remembered when I first saw Captain David, years before upon the stage of the Castle, how much I esteemed him back then. At that time, I wanted to be just like him, though I later discovered that his righteousness and bravery were only skin deep. Now, looking at the same man, the feeling returned: the feeling of love, wonder, and admiration—except this time, he was that man. He was fearless, and the Scroll was written upon his heart.

"I need your help, Captain David," I said. "I feel that I can't even stand or speak. Please, help me."

He smiled. "I will help you, dearest of all my brothers. And as I help you, your strength will return."

He then drew the attention of our fellowship. "Rally to me!" he called out. "Rally to me!" Everyone gathered to him, their faces sober with conviction and perseverance.

"Look!" he said, pointing to the dragons who were already making their way toward us. "The dragons return. They are innumerable, and we are only a few score. Any other group of people, if they were in our circumstance, would cower and run and hide. But not us! We are warriors of the Great King! Others would run out with a white flag and try to make peace with the enemy. But not us! We have a cause that is worth dying for. Soon, my friends, we will be in the presence of the Great King. Let us give Him glory by fighting with hearts courageous. Come! Make ready to charge! Fight to the death! And whoever of us is the last on the battlefield, let them exclaim a shout of praise at their death, that they may have the honor of being the last soldier of the Great King to glorify Him in this world!"

As Captain David spoke, my heart was moved. His words lit a fire under me that penetrated to the depths of my soul. I stood to my feet and mounted my horse. Captain David came upon my right, and Benjamin upon my left. I drew my sword and pointed it toward the enemy.

"To the death!" I shouted, and all shouted it with me. We could hear the dragons roar in response. I was just about to spur my horse when a sound filled the air. It was crisp and clear, and its note seemed to wash away the death and horror of that day.

"That's a horn," Benjamin said.

"Not just any horn," Captain David said smiling. "It's a shofar."

"What does it mean?" I asked.

"It's from the Scroll," he replied. "The shofar will sound, and the Glorious One will come with His glorious ones."

I hesitated for a moment. "The Great King?" I asked.

"Without a doubt," Captain David said, his eyes burning with a holy fire. "The Great King has come."

Chapter 37

The dragons heard the shofar as well, for they stopped in their tracks and put their claws over their ears.

"Look!" Violet said, pointing to the east. Under the rising sun, a wide cloud of dust clung to the ground. She quickly called out to Daniel, who ran up beside her and peered out across the endless desert.

"It is a great number of men and women," he said.

"A great number?" I repeated. "Hundreds? Thousands?"

"Tens of thousands," he said with a smile.

"And who leads them?" I asked with immense anticipation. Daniel continued to scan, then his eyes remained fixed, and his face shown in wonder.

"It's Him," he said. "It's the Great King!"

I turned to David. "Should we wait here, or ride out to Him?" I asked.

"I would ride out to Him," he answered, "for with Him is the best place to be."

"Come!" I called out. "Hurry! Ride to your King!"

Everyone cheered, and we rode as fast as we could. The dragons were still clutching their ears, for the shofar continued to sound over the land.

We were as a tiny ant riding out to meet a huge island. As we neared them, we could hear His voice, for it echoed over the land like a canon. "Behold more of My children," He said. "Welcome, brethren!"

The tens of thousands with Him shouted a cry that must have been heard around the planet. We came up to the Great King and stopped only a few yards before Him. To describe what it was like to behold His face for the first time is difficult. It seemed impossible to pull my eyes off of Him, not because He was handsome in the world's way of thinking but for the simple reason that to look at Him was to look at Someone who encapsulated all wisdom, knowledge, and everything you held dear. He was the fullness of all that was joyous and good. When I looked into His bright brown eyes, I felt like I was looking through a window into eternity, and not just that, but also into the eyes of my Father, Creator, and greatest Guide. He was limitless in His attributes and knowledge. I felt that I could study His face for an eternity and still understand only a fraction of Him. Yet at the same time, I felt that all of who He was had been given to me. For a moment, He just looked upon us and smiled. He then spoke. I believe, that if He hadn't spoken, I would have sat there looking at Him until I died of thirst or sleep deprivation.

"Well done," He said smiling. "You have fought bravely and you have overcome. Now there is stored up for you the crown of righteousness, which I will soon place upon your brow ere the day is over."

I then, for the first time since His arrival, looked to the side at the company which arrived with Him. To His left, and nearest to Him, was a man who I had never seen before, but I knew who he was immediately. I could see it in his eyes. He was Petros, one of the earliest followers of the Great King, from years long gone by. He sat upon his horse like a pillar, confident and true and without fear of what lay ahead. I then heard Violet's breath tremble as she was mounted beside me, and looking to the right of the Great King, my breath was also taken away and my heart moved more than I thought possible.

There, upon the front line of the host of the Great King, was my dearest and closest friend. Her blue eyes were fixed upon me as her red hair waved in the gentle breeze. Elizabeth. Her smile was like a warm fire to one trapped in a blizzard. Her grace, beauty, and form like a spring rain, which is able to gently wash away the grime and worry of the day. Next to her, I beheld my three younger daughters, Rose, Lily, and Rachel. They were fully grown and mature women. They also had their eyes fixed upon me and smiled with a love that knew no limits. Their bows were in their hands with their quivers upon their sides. Their eyes shown like stars whose brightness can even shine during the full light of day.

My gaze returned to my wife, who had followed my eyes and was rejoicing in all I was seeing. And as I saw them, my ladies, my heart gave praise to Him who rules over all. And I realized that all of His ways are good and that He never does wrong. I was just about to turn my attention back to the Great King when I saw my wife nod ever so slightly to one side, and following her movement, I noticed a man beside her. He was tall and strong, and his beard was full and his eyes clear. At the sight of him, my eyes swelled up with tears, for he was Isaiah, my son, whom I had lost nearly five years earlier. He looked at me and nodded with a smile. The meaning and depth contained in that smile would take days to describe. Benjamin, who was next to me, stretched out his hand to his brother and greatest friend, as did Violet.

My eyes then went on down the line, and next to Isaiah was another man, and though I had never seen him before, I knew who he was. My son, unborn last I knew him, sat there upon his steed, a man of the Great King. I wondered at his name, and yet it didn't matter. There we were, reunited with all that we held dear, in the presence of the Great King, about to fight the greatest of all battles.

The Great King, knowing all that I was thinking, spoke. "There will be plenty of time to gather with those long missed," He said with pleasure in His voice. "But now, we must fight. Grip your bow and sword well, for this will be the last day you use them. Look!" he said. "The Great Dragon is having to rally his hoard, for they are scared of My army."

We looked across the way and saw the largest dragon ever imagined, more than four times the size of any black dragon. He was speaking to his army. I couldn't understand his words, for they were spoken in some ancient tongue."

"Come!" the Great King said. "We ride to victory! Don't worry about the Great Dragon. He's all mine."

Benjamin and I came alongside our family and joined the charge. We laughed and sang as we rode forth. The dragons were now charging as well, though the Great Dragon couldn't be seen.

"Fight well!" I said to my children. Elizabeth, who was beside me, looked over as we were just about to enter the fray. She smiled. "We fight together again," she said, "one last time."

As we neared the enemy, we noticed foes that we had never before seen. Great scorpions, as large as dragons. Their deadly tails high in the air and the pinchers open and ready to strike.

"Scorpions!" Violet cried aloud. She then seemed to gather her courage. "No matter!" she called out, readying her bow. "They can also be pierced!"

I was at that moment reminded of the words of the Scroll which said, *You will trample the serpent and the scorpion under your feet.*

"Archers!" the Great King called out, His voice echoing throughout the desert. "Loose your arrows!"

A stream of arrows flew over our heads so thick that it seemed to blot out the sun. Much of the enemy was wounded but their lines continued.

"Charge!" the Great King cried aloud.

We broke into the line of the enemy, whose strategy seemed to be to sacrifice their pawns, for the front row of red dragons simply poured into us, not heeding the value of their lives. This immediately drove a wedge between myself and my family, as well as knocking me from my horse. I landed hard upon the ground and was nearly trampled by my own brethren. Soon, however, I regained my footing and stood to face the enemy. Multiple red dragons were around me.

I spun around holding my sword outward. The first sprung at me. I quickly darted to one side and came down with the point of my sword upon its head, pinning it to the ground. Other warriors joined in on the attack, just in time for me to notice a black dragon swooping down upon me. He grasped my shield and tried to wrench it from my hands. I countered by leaping upward, and using the momentum from the dragon's pull, I imbedded my sword deep into the beast's gut, causing it to release its grip and try to escape. A bolt of lightning past over my head, casting the dragon dead upon the ground. I turned around to see Justin and his family riding together, though he didn't see me. They were cutting or shooting down everything that came upon them.

My eyes scanned for my family as I now spun around, though there were literally thousands of dragons and brethren battling. The carnage, dust, and tightness of the combat nearly blocked out the sun. I found a stray horse and, hopping upon its back, continued to engage the enemy. I was galloping upon the field when I noticed another rider beside me. It was Judah.

"Hello, my brother!" he shouted over the chaos.

"Judah!" I said with surprise and joy in my heart. "Look at you!" It was both pleasing and amazing to me that my initial reaction to this man who had betrayed me and done the worst atrocities imaginable was complete love and fellowship. I saw in him a dear brother and friend. And I could see, in that split moment as we rode together, that his eyes were free of all guilt and bondage.

"You are a warrior of the Great King!" I exclaimed.

"Thanks to the example of your family!" he shouted back. "I'm forever in your debt!"

We then noticed an opening in the ranks before us where there was no ally, only the enemy. Countless dragons and scorpions were advancing directly before us. Judah quickly began to swing his sword over his head in a circle, and as he did so, something resembling a tornado formed above him. Then, just before the enemy was upon us, he swung his sword forward, which seemed to throw the tornado into the oncoming hoard. The many dragons and scorpions, who were about to trample us, were sent whirling backwards, rolling upon the ground and suffering immensely. I was just about to commend my brother when a black dragon came and clutched Judah so quickly that I couldn't react. He was carried off into another part of the battle.

I now came upon a sight that stirred all the courage and manliness within me. Captain David, my son Benjamin, and Nathan were all circled tightly, backs together, upon a hill of dead dragon carcasses. Numerous black dragons surrounded them, their claws and fire trying to break the circle. I rode my steed up on the hill, and coming upon the nearest black beast, I leapt from my horse and drove my sword into its back. Using the momentum, I leaped down upon the mound, just beside my three comrades.

"Shields!" Captain David said as I rose to my feet, and only too soon, for I came next to him and lifted my shield just in time to block the dragon's fire.

"Caleb!" Nathan shouted as he struck down a dragon across from him.

"Did you miss me?" I shouted back.

"Very much so!" he replied. "You make our number four. That should be enough to hold this position."

"I don't know!" Benjamin shouted, gazing before him. "Look!"

Nearly two score of black dragons, clustered together for invincibility, were coming straight for us.

"Form a wall and get ready!" Captain David ordered. "Benjamin! You form the rear guard!"

"Stand strong!" Benjamin replied as we obeyed orders. "Help comes!"

Just then, Elizabeth and my daughters ran up beside us.

"Girls!" Elizabeth shouted. "Break those dragons apart!"

Violet, who was engulfed in flames, shot her arrow, which flew straight and true directly into the middle of the oncoming hoard. An explosion, like that of a volcano erupted within them, sending dragons in every direction, many falling dead to the earth below. Lily then aimed and shot. Her arrow, as it went forth, split into nearly twenty arrows, each finding its mark and diminishing the enemy. Now Rachel and Rose drew their bows together. "Now!" Rachel shouted. Their arrows shot forward, and something like nets of light spread out from them, entangling the enemy and casting many to their doom.

Ten black dragons remained and were now upon us. They inhaled deeply and their fire followed. In response, Elizabeth stepped forward and raised her palms. The fire encircled us at a distance, for the intervention of my wife was strong. She didn't stop at just blocking the fire, however, but raising her voice ever louder, and bringing her arms slowly inward, she suddenly shot her palms outward with a shout. The result was that the ten dragons were flung so far from us and at such a speed that I doubt they survived the impact.

"Well," Nathan said calmly, "thank you, ladies. That helped."

"Where is Isaiah?" I asked Elizabeth.

"There!" she pointed.

Below I could see Isaiah and three others fighting together. They were like a whirlwind. Everything that came upon them was cut down quickly. Isaiah was the greatest swordsman I had ever beheld.

"Who are those three men with him?" I asked, for they were quite distant.

"Don't you recognize them, Father," Violet replied. "They are Captain Samuel, Captain Enoch, and our baby brother."

"Samuel and Enoch?" I said in amazement. "With our son?"

233

"Of course," Elizabeth replied gently. "Who do you think has been training our sons Isaiah and Benaiah?"

"Benaiah," I said to myself. "I love the name."

"I thought you would," she said.

She then whistled for her horse, which within a second sprinted to us. She jumped on the mount and rode to the side of our sons. Leaping from her horse, she released nearly twenty arrows in half as many seconds, every single arrow hitting its mark. We all followed her off of the mound and stayed together as one force. As I came upon Captain Samuel and Captain Enoch, I was delighted to be near them. They looked young but with still as much wisdom written upon their faces as before. As we continued to fight, another pack of dragons surrounded us. Benaiah spoke the name of the Great King, and it seemed to cause many of the dragons to fall to the ground and cover their ears. Isaiah then lifted his sword in the air and brought it down with great force into the earth. The result was an ever-growing ball of light, which passed harmlessly around us, expanding and taking the dragons with it, casting them to the ground lifeless.

Daniel and Levi had now joined us, their swords black with dragon's blood. Daniel's skin was burnt by dragon's fire quite severely. Rose touched him and within seconds his skin was made whole.

"Look out!" he shouted, as a scorpion as large as a black dragon quickly came upon us. We ducked attacks from both of its pinchers, which were exceptionally quick. All of our ladies shot their arrows, but to no avail, for its hide was thick and strong.

"How do we beat this thing?" I shouted.

"Let me show you!" another answered. I knew the man's voice, but couldn't believe it was actually him. The hooded figure came out of nowhere, and just in time, for the enemy's tail had come upon me as quick as lightning. The man cut off the giant stinger, and in two more quick strikes with his sword, removed the enemy's pinchers as well.

"Eli!" Levi and Benjamin exclaimed together. The old man smiled as he leapt high into the air and came down upon the scorpion with his sword penetrating directly into the beast's head.

"Eli!" I shouted. "You can see now!"

"See?" the old man said as he looked in my direction. "I don't quite know what you mean." And with those words he charged into the fray of the enemy which was still on all sides.

At last the enemy's numbers began to thin, and I felt that the battle was nearly over. I noticed, however, on the fringe of the combat, a woman fighting a black dragon all alone. I immediately recognized them both. The dragon was missing an eye, due to my blade from over a decade earlier. The girl was Sarah, the biological mother of Rachel, who had been slain by the same dragon within the pits of the enemy.

"Hurry!" I said to those near me. We began to run towards them. I could tell that Sarah was weakening, and I could hear the dragon cursing at her.

"How dare you betray me!" it bellowed. We were within bow range, and my ladies hit the creature with everything they had, which knocked the dragon down and gave Sarah a chance to rest. I cried aloud, "Remember me, Gadreel? I will take your other eye if you'd like! Now I am the one luring you to *your* doom!"

The dragon turned its attention to me and Elizabeth, for it recognized both of us and began charging towards us. I was thankful for this opportunity, for this was the same dragon that lured my true love and I deeper within the forest as children. It had set our village on fire and had kidnapped Elizabeth. To have the privilege to see it fall was a gift from the Great King. My three sons and I, along with Captain David, Nathan, Levi, Daniel, Samuel, and Enoch were charging to meet the dragon.

"Finally!" the dragon said as it neared. "I will finally kill you!"

"I will get his right eye," I said to my companions as we ran. "Each of you pick a different part."

They each named their target, and we jumped into the air to meet it. There was the sound of several sword strokes, followed by the dragon falling upon the ground, blind and with multiple limbs severed from its body. Sarah then stepped forward, and pulling back her bow, finished the dragon off with a shot to the heart. Sarah then looked at us and smiled. Rachel ran into her arms, and the two embraced.

"My first mother," Rachel said proudly, speaking to us of Sarah. "She didn't abandon me when most would have. She gave me life so that I might know the Great King."

Our celebration was cut short by a roar that nearly made us fall to the ground. All of the dragons were now dead, except one. Turning around, we saw the Great Dragon standing in the middle of the field of battle, with the Great King walking toward him.

"The time has come," the Great King announced, and even though His voice was gentle, it still echoed throughout the land.

"Yes," replied the Great Dragon, in a voice that seemed to shake the earth. "The time for your own destruction."

Chapter 38

The Great Dragon seemed to grow as it strode toward the Great King. It was so large and formable that despite the fact that we were with our King, we were still terrified at its presence.

"Before I destroy you," the Great King said, "I will rid the land of your cursed offspring." He then tapped the ground with His sword, and the earth seemed to swallow the countless dragon and scorpion carcasses which surrounded us. Our people had formed a semi-circle around our King, on the opposing side of the Great Dragon, and were ready to watch the destruction of His chief adversary. As I stood there, I tried to take in the moment. *I am here!* I thought to myself. *I am going to witness the final and chief battle of all history!*

The Great King gripped His sword and shield. "You've seen this day coming," He said. "It is inevitable. You chose this path for yourself, long ago, when you betrayed the love that I showed you. I gave you life and freedom and joy, and it wasn't enough. You wanted the one thing you couldn't have: the worship that was due to Me alone. Now you stand guilty and condemned. The atrocities that you have committed and the damage that you have done is nigh limitless. And so, Dragon, face up to the full measure of the wrath that awaits you! You are undone. Your army is defeated, and you are all alone."

The Dragon laughed. "Ha! You are mistaken about much. You did not give me joy but rather slavery. Neither did You give me love, for You cruelly made me too wise and beautiful. If I had been dumb and naive, like all of those here, I would have seen You as great and perfect in all Your majesty. But instead, because of my intellect and creativity, I saw You for what You really were: Someone with power but not with wisdom. Someone who makes an empire and puts creatures of dirt to govern it. As far as they are concerned, I suppose You are worthy of their worship. But You were never worthy of mine. I looked for such a person to esteem but could find none. Only then did I realize what was truly inevitable. That I was the one to whom all should bow and worship, for I understood how to truly govern and rule and create. I will soon start afresh, and all the Universe will see and judge between us, and they will see that I am the better."

"We shall see," the Great King replied.

"You are also mistaken about the following," the Dragon continued. "I am not alone. I have numerous eggs within me; eggs that I will hatch as soon as You are destroyed, for none of Your followers, not even altogether, can defeat me. Do You think I have been idle in my seclusion and silent scheming? I have discovered the secrets of the hidden power; the power that You, in Your selfishness, will not share with anyone else. Long ago, You prepared a place for me and my followers, both human and dragon alike, a place of fire and sulfur that knows no limits."

The Great King remained silent.

"Behold," the Great Dragon continued, "I have bred within me that same fire, a fire that you cannot withstand. You will melt before it like wax. I have also hardened my scales beyond the sharpness of your blade. Ha! You think my army is gone. You are wrong. All these people who surround you will become my army, for once You are destroyed, they will bow to me, for I am the one who wields the power now."

"Your language is that of lies and deceit," the Great King replied. "How can any of your words be trusted?"

"Grip Your shield tightly," the Dragon hissed, "that shield which You formed from the Tree of Life that was within the Garden. Ha! It cannot resist this fire. Why do You tremble, oh Great One? Is it because fear has entered Your heart? Is it because You have come against one that knows too much? And now, what was said to have never been possible will happen. You will die."

"Enough talk," the Great King said at last, stopping the Dragon. "I have much to do this day and you are but a trifle. Let's fight!"

The Great Dragon roared and shook the ground with the stomp of its limbs. He then breathed his fire, and the results were concerning. The flame, which we all expected to be red, was white, pure white. The blast came down upon the Great King, but He dove to one side, dodging it. The heat of that fire was so hot that it literally melted the earth where it touched. The very place where the Great King had been, only seconds after He leapt to the side, was now white lava, and it was so hot that it sank down into the earth leaving a giant hole in the ground.

The Dragon didn't allow the Great King to counter and breathed again. This time the Great King dodged by rolling toward the Dragon, and springing to His feet, He struck His sword upon the breast of the Dragon. Then something happened. The King's sword shattered into a thousand pieces. He looked at the broken hilt in His hand only long enough to feel the dragon strike Him, sending Him flying through the air and landing hard upon the sandy desert ground.

The Dragon now inhaled again and shot out his white flame. The Great King jumped to His feet and held out His shield proudly. What happened next made me nearly drop to the ground in disbelief. The dragon's fire quickly melted the shield. The King remained standing in the same position of defense, and within another second, His arm was melted. The Great King cried out in pain, a cry that seemed to be heard in every corner of the earth. Within another second, His flesh and bones were exposed. The ground then opened underneath Him, from which fire and sulfur bellowed forth. Then, to my horror, I saw the remains of the Great King fall into the pit and the hole close around Him.

Chapter 39

It is hard to describe the feeling that I felt in that moment. Whereas only a few seconds before, my King was standing boldly against the Great Dragon, He was now dead and wiped off the face of the earth. Whereas I was looking upon the all-powerful Creator, now I was looking upon nothing. All that remained in that place was tens of thousands of warriors of a dead king, and the Great Dragon, who was pure evil. No one moved. We all just stood there, looking upon the unbelievable scene. The only sounds were the slight breeze of the day and the breathing of the Dragon. Not even weeping could be heard because of the immense shock of the moment. No one believed what they had seen.

Finally, the Dragon broke the silence. "Look at you all," he said mockingly. "I stand here, justified and alive while your phony king is dead. Ha! You all thought that nothing could defeat you. You were wrong. You all thought that the Scroll could not be disproved. You were wrong! Here, before you, you have seen the truth. And this is the truth: There's no hope. You will now all be my slaves for eternity. You are all nothing; you are worthless. You are just dirt--unintelligent, weak, feeble dirt. Come forth now, those who will serve me. The first ones to volunteer will be given the highest positions of honor. Come! You have nothing to fear as long as you please me. Come! This invitation is before you. Who will be the first?"

There was utter silence. No one moved. Not one single person, within the tens of thousands, moved a muscle. We didn't speak or move. We simply remained still.

The Dragon grew frustrated. "Don't be fools!" he roared. "You've seen the truth. The Scroll is nothing. You thought it was a rock for you; it wasn't. The Scroll is worthless. Why can't you see the truth? The Scroll has been broken."

A stray voice then pierced the silence. "You are wrong," the voice said. It was Petros, standing tall before his brethren. "The Scroll has not been broken. It has been fulfilled."

The Dragon laughed slowly in morbid pleasure. "Petros," he said. "I will enjoy killing you a second time, just as I did when you walked this earth. Why in the world He chose you, I'll never know. You were a coward and a fool back then so why should I expect anything different now? The Scroll has indeed been broken, seeing as your king is dead and buried."

"We shall see," Petros said. He then held up a Scroll in his right hand. "This is the Scroll, the original Scroll, penned down by the very hand of the Great King some six thousand years ago." He then opened the Scroll. "Here," he continued, "in the book of prophecy, it reads thus: *The chief servant of humanity will taste death so that everyone in Him might live. He will suffer and die, but He will then rise to victory.*"

"A meaningless prophecy," the Great Dragon said. "It was a symbolic poem to try to give people inner strength in hard times."

Petros smiled. "You are mistaken. It isn't symbolic. It is fact. We haven't been worthy soldiers and followers. All of us, because we have sinned deserve the fires of the pit below, the pit made for you and your offspring. We all, like you, deserve to be cast out from the presence of such a majestic and awesome King. But now, because of what has happened here, we don't have to go to that fire."

The Dragon became uneasy, and doubt and fear shown upon his face.

"The Great King bore our suffering for us," Petros continued. "He was burnt to death with the fire and sulfur so that we wouldn't have to be. You tried to destroy Him; you have instead venerated Him. You tried to thwart His plans; you have instead only played your part in carrying them out. You foolish serpent. Don't you know that there is only one Great King? Don't you know that His ways are perfect?"

Just after Petros finished speaking the ground began to tremble. All of us looked around in fear and uncertainty. Then there was an explosion. The ground, right where the Great King had been, burst forth, leaving a wide opening. We all looked on, nearly holding our breaths in anticipation. A strong hand immerged from the pit, grabbing hold of the ground. It was the Great King!

No longer was His army silent, for at the first sight of Him, we put out a shout of cheer and praise that likely deafened the Dragon. The Great King then took a few steps toward Petros and held out His right hand. Petros handed Him the Scroll, which then morphed into a brilliant sword. The Great Dragon was furious and without warning, inhaled a deep breath of its white fire. The Great King, without a shield, took His stand. The Dragon then came down upon the Great King with the mightiest blast of white fire thus given. The Great King simply stuck out His chest and took the full brunt of the force. All of us cheered as our King received the enemy's attack, unharmed and unmoved. The Dragon then stepped back, full of terror.

"Be free of your guise," the Great King commanded. "Return to your first form." The Dragon began to shrink. It transformed down into something resembling a man dressed in black, armored with sword and shield. The fallen angel then began to attack the King but his skill was lacking.

"No longer will you deceive the nations with your lies," the Great King said, and swinging His sword, He cut the tongue from His enemy's mouth.

"No longer will you abuse and mistreat my people." The Great King then severed both of His opponent's hands.

"No longer will you look upon my people," the Great King declared, and within a second, both eyes were gouged from the face of the deceiver of the world.

"Now begins your eternal torment," the Great King said, and He drove His sword clear through the heart of His enemy. The chief rival of mankind then fell into the hole that the Great King had climbed out of. The ground remained open, and something seemed to draw all of us to it.

Slowly we made our way, and as we did so the hole increased in its dimension, allowing each of us to peer within. What we saw, far below was the torment of both dragon and human. The fire burned them, but they didn't die. I felt a sensation in that moment that was at the time unexplainable. There I saw the eternal destruction of people, some of them loved ones I had known. But for some reason, I wasn't sad. It's not that my compassion was taken away, but instead that when I looked down within that lake of fire, I saw the justice of the Great King at work. What was happening in that place was right and good. Then, all of a sudden, the giant chasm closed, and all that remained was us and the Great King.

Chapter 40

For a moment all was still. The Great King stood upright, His sword covered in the Dragon's blood. He motioned to Petros who came forward and poured water over the blade, washing it clean. The Great King then sheathed His sword and looking at us, He raised His hands high in our direction. A strong wind then blew upon us, and I wondered if it wasn't coming from His own mouth. The effects were instant. It felt as if my body and soul were transformed. It was as if the old me was blowing away and a new me remained. The pain in my body from the battle, along with the cuts, bruises, and blood stains had vanished. There were no aches or discomfort. Not only that, but I felt that all remained within my soul was goodwill and love. I mentally poked around for some bit of hate or bitterness or impurity; they were gone.

"My friends," the Great King said peacefully, "it is done! There will be no more death, or fighting, or pain. The old things have passed away. Behold all things are new."

At the very moment when He spoke the word *new*, green grass sprouted up all around us and underneath our feet. The breeze went from warm to cool, and a river formed in the midst of us.

"My fellow brothers," He said, His face beaming with joy, "hold up your swords one last time."

We all did so.

"You have fought and led well. You have kept My words and have not turned away. Well done! Now, drive your sword into the ground before you."

We obeyed, and immediately after our swords entered the soil, roots shot from them and they grew to be enormous trees, reaching high within the sky. We could no longer see the Great King, for what was only a minute before a desolate desert was now the most beautiful forest I had ever seen.

"This is the Forest of Remembrance," the Great King announced, His voice echoing throughout. "Here we will always remember the battles that we fought and the honor that was ours. Now, my sisters, release your remaining arrows into the sky."

The ladies obeyed their King, and as their arrows filled the air, they were transformed into different birds. In only a moment there were thousands of the most beautiful and colorful birds throughout the forest. Their songs were like nothing I had ever heard in the old world.

The Great King invited us to come to the edge of the forest. There we found Him standing before the ruins of the Salem, which was still old and falling apart. He raised His sword high.

"Behold," He shouted, "the city that I have prepared for those who love me!" And sinking His sword into the ground, a city that spanned beyond the distance of my vision burst forth. Buildings and structures that I could have never imagined raised up into the clouds. The final appearance was that of a colossal wall which surrounded the city. Before us was an open gate.

"Come!" He said. "It is time for us to feast together!"

An eruption of praise and gratitude came from the army of the King, and we entered His gates with thanksgiving in our hearts. For hours we walked down that great street, within which flowed the river which we beheld in the forest. We didn't tire and our legs or feet didn't ache. Elizabeth and I and our children just gazed and marveled at the city. We talked and sang songs, hand-in-hand and arm-in-arm, as we walked together. There was no joy lacking, and there was no joy that could have been added. We then came to a giant banqueting table. It was shaped as a circle, yet it was woven and linked in a way that words cannot describe. Everyone had a seat. No one was left out. At the head of the table, upon a throne of gold, sat the Great King, and a crown of emeralds, rubies, and sapphires was placed upon His head.

Children dressed in white with olive wreaths upon their heads served us. The food and drink were better than any we had ever tasted or even imagined. We ate and sang and laughed. Words of praise were offered to the Great King and many stories were told throughout the banqueting table, for our number was tens of thousands.

After the meal, the Great King stood and raised His cup. "Today," He said, "begins the rest of your lives. We will never be parted. Nothing but joy and happiness and glory awaits you. This city has much for you, for each of you has your own habitation here. But the world also offers you a home, for it is a new earth. None of what was in the former world remains. Explore, discover, and live. Build homes and plow your fields and be merry. Work with your hands, share with your brethren, and enjoy the fruit of your labor. There is no more time to be lost or gained; all time is yours. I am yours, and you are Mine. Together, we will reign in peace and harmony for ever and ever!"

We all applauded and offered praise to our King. For many days, we remained near to that table, for our fellowship was sweet. As I ate with my family, I felt a tap on my shoulder, and turning I saw a face that filled my heart with joy. "William!" I cried aloud. My dear brother laughed, and we embraced.

"Well," he said cheerfully, "it looks like we both got wise before the end, for here we are."

"You were as a father to me," I said with thanksgiving. "I would not have been the man I was without you."

"I can say the same about you," he replied. "The Great King used you to revive my love for life. Now, here, we can enjoy all the life that eternity holds. Speaking of fathers," he continued. "I met a man and woman that you know, though, you've never seen them before."

William then brought before me a man and woman who looked familiar to me even though we had never met.

"You did well," the man said to me, his face beaming with pleasure. "You made me and your grandmother proud. The ambition we had, in the beginning, to fight dragons was manifested through you."

I then understood. These were my grandparents who Captain Samuel had tried to train in his youth, who ended up dying at the hands of dragons. My grandparents embraced me. Then my grandmother, looking at my children, laughed with delight. "We have much to talk about," she said, "and all the time necessary to do so."

For weeks we explored the city, always having food and rest and fellowship. There were libraries, gardens, and museums. Many theatres were there, and the white-robed children performed for us. Some of their stories were epic tales of the old world; others were delightful fiction. There were orchards, vineyards, and parks, all planted and built for the glory of the King. One day, as I was sitting with my family and friends, I felt a hand upon my shoulder. I knew the second I felt it who it was. I quickly turned and fell to my knees before my King.

"Rise," He said gently. "Come with Me." Together, hand-in-hand, my King and I walked down a street of gold.

"You have done so well, My son," He said to me.

"Only because of Your grace," I replied. He smiled.

"I have much for you to do," He said. "About a month's journey by foot south of here is a luscious land, where the soil is black and the grass green. Soon a village will be built there, and I want you to be a governor to our people there, to serve them and love them."

"It would be my honor and pleasure," I replied.

"There is a lake there," He continued. "I believe it would make a perfect location for a home." He then turned to me and embraced me. "I love you, Caleb. I love you with all that I have and all that I am."

We walked together for what seemed like days, talking about Creation and much of the ancient world and also about what the future held.

"Caleb," He said as we traveled along, "I have a favor to ask of you."

"Anything," I replied, excited to serve my King.

"I want you to write your story," He replied. "The story of your life. Specifically, the beginning of your story, from childhood until your marriage to Elizabeth. And then the end of your story, how you led your people to victory."

"My story?" I asked. "Of course, I can do that for You, my King. But who is it for?"

"It is for a people of another time and another place," He replied kindly.

"I don't understand," I said.

The Great King smiled. "There are still mysteries, my brother, and there always will be. But rest assured: All that lies in your future is glorious and perfect. We have before us days unending. Days of love and peace and sweet fellowship."

And so, I, Caleb, have done what He asked and have written a brief telling of my story. I do not know if it will ever be read, but if you are reading it now, I want you to know the following: that I love you, whoever you are, with the strongest love possible. And that the Great King, or whatever name He's revealed to you, loves you even more. He is good, and His Kingdom is eternal. He does as He pleases, and no one can thwart His plans. Seek Him, my friend. Seek Him while He may be found.

If He has given you a Scroll, cherish it above all else. It is the Scroll that shows you the King. It is the Scroll that shows you the truth. Follow it! The world will laugh at you and the religious will mock you. Don't let that bother you. Their praises are empty while His praises are eternal. They either deny the Scroll or adjust it to fit their culture. But you must be different. You must hold unswervingly to the eternal principles and culture of the Scroll. If you follow the Scroll, you will often feel all alone. Nothing could be further from the truth. Though you may be alone in the context of the world, you are surrounded by tens of thousands who have gone before you. You are in good company.

Love your family and make them your greatest priority. Be aware of the strategies of the enemy, for they are many. Deceit and sin will pull at you. You must resist. Stand firm. Be different than the world. Cling to the Scroll. Pray at all times. Resist the evil that is so prevalent. Seize every day for your King.

My last words to you are this: The Great King is like no other. Know Him and fear Him. He is perfect and good and the only true life. No one who lives for Him regrets it. Praise be to the Great King! He is with you, beloved! Amen and AMEN!

Author's Note: I appreciate you taking the time to read this and hope you enjoyed it. I also thank you for showing grace to me for some of the liberties taken in this allegory. You may wonder, for example, why the redemptive work of the Great King is achieved at the very end of the story instead of where it belongs. This was an attempt, on my part, to show a few things. First, no plan of the Great King can ultimately be thwarted. Secondly, it was through His death and resurrection that the Great King achieved our eternal life. Above all else, it was my desire that this story bring about a greater love for the Scroll. Always consult the Scroll. Many blessings!

– Jared

The adventure began in:

The Castle and the Scroll

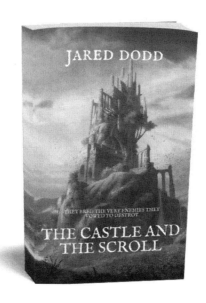

Jareddodd.com

Also Available on Amazon.com

Discipleship Streamable 10-week Bible Study

Discipleship Book & Kindle editions

Discipleship MP3 Audio

Discipleship DVD set

Jareddodd.com

Also Available on Amazon.com

Bible Studies

Immersion Streamable 10-week Bible Study

Immersion Book & Kindle editions

Immersion MP3 Audio

Jareddodd.com

Also Available on Amazon.com

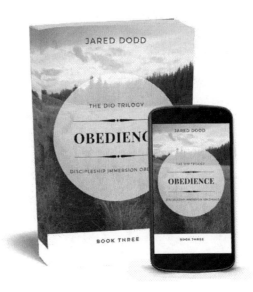

Obedience Book & Kindle Editions

Coming Spring of 2019!

Obedience Streamable 20-week Bible Study

Obedience MP3 Audio

Jareddodd.com

Also Available on Amazon.com

Biblical Fiction

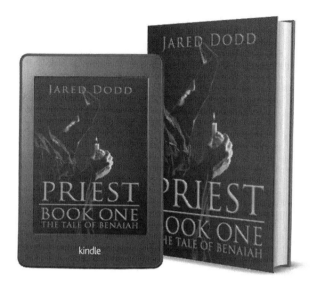

Priest: The Tale of Benaiah

Book & Kindle Editions

Jareddodd.com

Also Available on Amazon.com

Science: A Literature Approach

Pre k- 1st grade

More guides coming in the future!

Jareddodd.com

Also Available on Amazon.com